Let That Be
the Reason

Let That Be the Reason

A NOVEL

Vickie M. Stringer

ATRIA PAPERBACK

New York London Toronto Sydney

ATRIA PAPERBACK
A Division of Simon & Schuster, Inc.
1230 Avenue of the Americas
New York, NY 10020

Copyright © 2009 by Vickie M. Stringer

First Atria Paperback edition March 2009

ATRIA PAPERBACK and colophon are trademarks of Simon & Schuster, Inc.

For information about special discounts for bulk purchases, please contact Simon & Schuster Special Sales at 1-800-456-6789 or business@simonandschuster.com.

Designed by Nancy Singer

Manufactured in the United States of America

10 9 8 7 6 5 4 3 2 1

Library of Congress Control Number: 2008922287

ISBN-13: 978-1-4165-7048-6
ISBN-10:   1-4165-7048-9

For Valen-Mychal Stringer,
my reason why

Let That Be
the Reason

One

"Hello, may I help you?"

Click.

Ring . . . ring.

"Hello! May I help you?"

"You got any girls that speak Greek?"

"*No!*"

Click.

What did he mean by that?

It was my first day answering the phones—my phones. I could not believe I had actually started my very own escort service.

I was living in a very expensive two-bedroom apartment with my only child, my beautiful son. He was seven months old at the time. My stacks of bills were getting taller and taller by the day, but there was no help from his father or his father's family. It was rough. I refused to ask for help from my own family because I had too much pride. When I was forced to go on welfare, it broke my spirit, but my son needed medical care. So I did what I had to. I was struggling to maintain the lifestyle I'd had with his father, Chino. Which led me right to tricking and the escort service.

Chino was a self-made millionaire. Okay, maybe not a millionaire, but he was *paid*. He was a big-time drug dealer, so we had plenty of material things and a ghetto-fabulous lifestyle. That came to a harsh end, and now he has a new wife and a new life.

Chino and I had been owners of an exclusive, full-service hair salon that we built from our vision . . . our dreams. The space we rented was in an up-and-coming shopping plaza on Columbus's east side. It started as dry-walls and cement floors. I can remember the excitement we felt as we watched the salon take shape and evolve into the vision we shared. On a daily basis, I walked the square footage of the salon planning, dreaming and envisioning what it would become. By night I browsed magazine layouts with the desire to duplicate the sleek images on the pages. With passion and complete faith, I communicated my particulars to the contracting team.

After months of hard work, our salon was finished—its black-and-white color scheme blended with state-of-the-art salon equipment to form our stylish yet practical enterprise. We included everything a salon should have: European-style shampoo bowls with padded recliners, marble countertops and inlays to hold hair products, silver cage towel holders and brass magazine racks placed within reach of the clients seated at the dryers. We installed individual oversized dryers with see-through hoods, which lined the west wall of the salon. In the reception area sat an oversized black lacquer desk with a fresh-cut flower bouquet. To show our clients that we appreciated them, we placed a counter stocked with complimentary snacks by the entrance.

Our salon was fit for the pages of a trendsetting magazine. It was the first of its kind in Columbus, Ohio, something the city had never seen. And we did this together. One could not have succeeded without the other. We were a team, and L-O-Quent Hair Salon was our dream. A dream that came true.

One of my numerous opening duties included wiping the fingerprints and smudges off the windows from the faces pressed against the glass the previous night of people peering inside to behold the transformation of the salon. We put over $50,000 into that place. Well, he did, because after all, it was *his* money. But it was my sweat and stress that pulled it all together.

I can remember Chino and me in the salon, when we had it all finished. We were alone, holding hands and walking around feeling the rush. Chino said, "Look, Pooh, we did it!"

Breathlessly I said, "I know, it is so beautiful. Thank you. Are you proud?" I always needed his approval. His opinion was everything to me.

"Pooh, I am so proud of you. It looks great. Let's put on some music." He turned on the Sony surround-sound system and jazz floated through the air.

After turning off the lights, he took me in his safe and reassuring arms, and we danced on the shiny checkerboard floor. I tingled from his touch and felt as if I were floating. At that moment, success was already ours and I knew there were even more remarkable things to come. The business partnership was only one facet of our commitment to each other. We knew that together, the sky was the limit. Chino and I even hoped to open an all-inclusive day spa if L-O-Quent was successful.

I became accustomed to the financial and emotional stability he offered, and to top it off, we had been discussing marriage. I was on cloud nine and ready to seal the deal. Pammy and Chino together forever. Whoever said that forever meant for life was a damn fool because my "forever" ended sooner than later.

I began noticing a change in Chino. He began to distance himself from me and what we had created together. I figured he was under a lot of stress and hoped that what he was going through was only temporary. After all, I was his Pooh.

Three years later, my whole life came crashing down. I sold my dream salon for only $20,000. A small fraction of what it was worth, but I was thankful for even that price since I had no money left. During our breakup, I allowed the salon to fall apart. Everything was jeopardized; the phone, lights, water—all threatened to be turned off. But the staff kept working, anticipating my return to work. I refused to go in and was unwilling to take phone calls from the stylists seeking answers. I had none. Unable to face them and deal with my situation, I walked away.

The breakup was humiliating. I escaped to my mother's home for solitude, and I let go. I recklessly sped through money like everything was a bad dream and wasn't real. I wanted to believe that my Chino wouldn't do this to me.

Not to me! We had everything, or I should say, he had everything. I was just the temporary beneficiary. After Chino left, to add more fuel to the fire, he refused to give me any support at all. Bastard! Alone for the first time in many years, I needed to learn to budget and to pick up other commonsense skills I had not developed under Chino's controlling rules.

How could he be so cruel? I have asked myself this many times. How could he be unwilling to lend support to his son? Whatever the circumstances surrounding our breakup, he should not have allowed our child to suffer. That was not the man that I had fallen deeply in love with. This Chino was a stranger to me. His cold indifference toward my situation made me feel like I never meant anything to him, and that the child we shared was nothing more than an inconsequential result of a night's passion. He was obviously punishing me by withholding support, but why?

"Chino, I can't deal with this shit! Bitches callin' the shop looking for you. What's up with that?"

"What are you talking about? I'm right here, right now, with you. I can't even walk in the door without you stressin'."

"Darling, it's three motherfuckin' a.m. What am I supposed to say, 'How was your day?'" As easily as he had come into our home, he snatched up his coat and car keys to leave. Not wanting him to go but to stay and discuss how we had come to this, I asked the obvious: *"Where are you going?"*

"Out!"

As much as I was overwhelmed by feelings of vulnerability, I was even more compelled by maternal instinct. The survival of my child was what mattered most. Flat broke, I was unable to provide for him. My family had given me enough "I told ya so's," so I couldn't go to them. I needed money, and fast. I got a Sunday newspaper and began a diligent job search.

I was qualified for a little of everything because of my work at the salon: public relations, decision making, accounting, problem solving, and so on. Problem was, I had no "paper" to substantiate that fact. The importance of a college degree became apparent, and I immediately regretted not continuing my college education. I became a college dropout the day I met Chino. How could I trade in college so easily for a life of uncertainty? Only someone who has never met Chino would ask this question. He could persuade you that the sky was green when you knew it was blue. The gift of gab was what this man possessed, and eventually, he possessed me, too. It's called selling a dream, or in my case, purchasing one.

Blinded by my first love, I bought into his ideas about how our life should be. At age seventeen, his words filled my heart and I abandoned my courses for his vision for the family—his family—the Triple Crown Posse.

I went on several interviews at fast-food joints and for secretary gigs, but no one called back. I couldn't fully understand why. I had run a very successful salon. I had won hair show competitions and was even on TV because of it.

I'd had a full staff of outstanding stylists and two reception-ists. I'd sold hair products, clothes, makeup and more. *Why am I not qualified?*

In my desperation and embarrassment, I returned to the cosmetology industry. It was difficult for me to work in someone else's salon since I had been a successful owner of my own business. But I had to feed my son, so I did it. Every day, customers wouldn't allow me to forget that I was a has-been.

"Didn't you own L-O-Quent?" a snobby woman with a mud mask inquired.

"What?" I replied with obvious contempt for the question.

"Did he take it from you?" someone else would ask.

"Did Chino take your salon from you?" The questions seemed endless.

They cut close to home because they all seemed true. Basically, I lost my salon over a piece of ass and a nervous breakdown. I discovered Chino was having an affair while I wore an engagement ring that I thought symbolized our bond. Chino wanted to betray me, and I wanted to escape the pain. Ultimately, he let go of me, and I simply let go of everything.

On the outside, I acted indifferent about it, but inside, it tore me into tiny little pieces that are still not together and may never be. But I had to go on, and I pray that one day I can let go of the pain for good and move on for the sake of my son.

I did well in this other person's salon, and my confidence

grew. After a few months, I could walk into work and not feel badly about myself. I was healing.

It wasn't long before the salon owner began to demand longer hours from me. She was a very insensitive boss. I'd been a boss once and I knew the difference between reasonable and unreasonable demands. I had an infant and his day care closed at 5:30 p.m. I had no sitter for him; my mom lived in Michigan, the next state over. I had put all my trust in Chino and got burned, so I was reluctant to set myself up for another letdown by trusting other people to take care of my son. I quit working at the salon and began to do nails at home. The hours worked better, but I wasn't earning enough money. For a normal lifestyle, it was enough, but what was normal for me? In my former life, the word "budget" was not in my vocabulary. I wasn't used to worrying about rent, utilities, clothing and car maintenance. Welfare covered the food, but eating bologna when you're used to eating prime rib is a big adjustment. Life with Chino was like "Whatever my Pooh wants, she can have." Chino gave me the luxury cars, the expensive jewelry, and he kept a roof over my head. He took me on spur-of-the-moment vacations to Vegas and Mexico and on romantic getaways when he thought he hadn't been paying enough attention to me. He would have paid someone to wipe my ass if that's what I wanted. Going from being the center of his world to being shit on wasn't something I thought would happen in my wildest nightmares.

With the demands of single motherhood and day-to-day living, I began sinking further into debt, all the while trying to live the lifestyle to which I was accustomed, hoping Chino would come back. I began to pawn things to get back on track. I even sold my son's bedroom set to a children's resale store. *Yes!* It was like that. So I returned to the newspaper with the hopes of finding something . . . anything that would help me live outside my definition of poverty. With tears in my eyes and a weight on my heart, I read: HELP WANTED. START TODAY. ESCORT. GREAT MONEY. I thought, *Can I "date" someone for sex?* It repulsed me, but desperate times call for desperate measures, so I called.

A man named Tony answered the phone and was so convincing. Tony was a smooth talker. When I informed him of what I already knew about escort services, he didn't deny or confirm anything. Instead he dangled the carrot of unlimited income in my face. He told me that most of the girls made a minimum of a grand a day. That did it. I took the bait and he reeled me in. I went to the address Tony provided and was disappointed that I did not find a building like in the movies, all glamorous and glittery. Instead, I found a house in the ghetto off Cleveland Avenue, and here I was in my nicest suit.

Tony had the look of a retired playboy, with a body that seemed like it used to be in shape. He had a few cuts on his arms that were visible as he took drags on his cigarette. He had handsome, light hazel eyes, but some facial scars like he had gotten his ass whipped a time or two. He had a way with words, using them to get his way. I knew it was a game. Chino had taught me a lot about smooth talkers.

Not enough to outsmart him, but enough for me to spot a con. He'd say, "Pooh, game recognize game." But I was desperate; the perfect *mark*, so I went for it.

Tony said, "You can make two hundred in fifteen minutes."

That's $800 an hour, I calculated quickly.

We talked while the phones rang like crazy. As I sat there, he described me to a caller.

The money got me moving. I went to what is called an outcall. An outcall is when the girl goes to the guy, known as a "john." The address was a hot tub rental place, and when I pulled up in front of the building, my heart sank to the pit of my stomach. Feelings of shame swarmed over me until goose pimples surfaced on my arms. Dirty, filthy, tramp-like visions played tricks on my mind.

Please, I don't want to do this, God, help me. Chino, where are you? I am about to sell my pussy. Having sex for money— something I vowed I would never do. Now look at me, I am a whore. I am a prostitute.

I thought about my mother. What would she think? What would she say if she saw her youngest child, Pamela, doing this? I was raised to be better than this. Educated in the Catholic parochial school system, college-bound and geared for success. Small tears began to roll down my face, and I wiped them away, careful not to smudge my makeup.

The client peered out the window, noticing me in my Jeep. I took a deep breath and then another one. I closed my eyes and formed a vision in my mind to focus on. I saw my son with new clothes on. I saw the stack of bills on my kitchen counter getting smaller. I saw the eviction notice torn into small pieces as I wrote a check for my rent. Then I saw me smiling. I knew what I had to do.

I opened the car door, plastering a fake smile on my face, and walked toward this old, stinky, fat white man. He had requested a hand job for $150 or a blow job for $250. I went for the hand job. Stinky flopped down in the chair behind a cluttered desk. He asked me to model for him. Turning around in a slow circle, I felt his eyes on my backside. They felt stuck on my ass. Rolling my eyes out of his view, I then turned toward him with a Chester Cheetah–like smile on my face. I kneeled between his legs, looking up at him and thinking that his exposed dick looked like a piece of raw bacon. He began to rub his dick, stroking it up and down. Then he reached out to touch the side of my face with the same hand he had used to caress his two-inch hard-on. I instantly wondered, *How can I sterilize my face?*

He said, "Blow on my cock, baby, make me cum." I blew on his dick and caressed it with one hand as I fondled his pink hairy balls with my other hand. He came, squirting on my shirt, below my chin and all over my fingers. I continued to stroke him up and down as he moaned, head tilted back and eyes closed. He continued to reach for my face as I did a slow boxerlike bob-and-weave routine to avoid being touched by him again. Three minutes of work. I was so ashamed. I felt dirty and so low. I've never had any desire to be touched by a white man, but there I was, touching him, giving him pleasure.

This deepened my hatred for Chino. I resented him

because I felt he drove me to this. I just needed a little help from him. I would have been thankful for $100 a month. He was off flashing, wining and dining while his son and I were taking a real live beatin'. It had my head all messed up. But for my son, I'd do anything—even turn tricks.

I blocked out my feelings and focused on a come-up to help my son and me. I went on seven more outcalls that day: a well-to-do white businessman, a sixtyish black man in a wheelchair, another who was blind and only wanted to eat me out, a couple who wanted me to watch as they had sex, a diabetic with both legs amputated who asked me to climb into his bed and ride 'im like I was a cowgirl and an elderly white man who wanted to be called "massah." I opted to call him "mister," and he just flipped up my skirt and got on top of me, fucking me, calling me "Kizzy." That sicko tipped me $100. My last call was a young white doctor who had been poppin' pills and drinkin' vodka. All he wanted to do was have me model and discuss all the dates I had. I made up sordid details as he jacked off. The first date was the hardest, but I just rolled with the flow from there on out. In four hours, I made $1,200. I paid my late rent, electric bill, got my VCR out of pawn, went to the grocery store and finally had food in the refrigerator and freezer at the same time. I took a shower to clean off the filth of those johns. I prepared a nutritious meal, picked up my son from day care and was back home by 4:45 p.m. We ate, and then I gave him a fun bubble bath.

The following morning, I took the baby to day care. Around 9:00 a.m., I called Tony, and it was on again. With more confidence, I requested more tips. I made $1,600 in about four hours. I paid my phone bill in full, ordered cable TV and got other backed-up expenses in order. I purchased some much needed clothes for my son. It felt so good to be able to *do* something. I even got a free car wash when I filled up the gas tank.

On the third day of this new career, I learned about in-calls. The escort rents a hotel room and waits for the client to come to her. Not quite familiar with this aspect of the business, I was nervous.

To save money, I shared a hotel room with a girl named Beverly. She also worked for Tony. She was a white girl who made more than two grand a day. Beverly had the typical white girl look—dyed blonde hair with a perm that she spent endless hours scrunching with hair spray. Her eyes were a beautiful green, and she constantly sprayed her body with that instant tan stuff in a can. Beverly was on the short side with very large breasts. Luckily, we clicked as friends immediately.

It's true that prostitution is the world's oldest profession. Sex sells—fat sex, skinny sex, black sex, white sex, male-on-male sex and yellow sex—it all sells. This was only my third day of work, but I was an entrepreneur. No one could pay me better than I could pay myself. I wanted my own. I told Beverly I wanted to open my own service. She looked me straight in the face, took a drag on her cigarette and said, "Hell, go for it! Send me some calls. I'll work for ya." Bet! One employee down.

I took the money I made that day, went to CellularOne

and bought a pager. Then I went to *The Columbus Dispatch* and placed a help-wanted ad in the adult section, listing my pager number.

Later, I picked my son up from day care and headed home to make a voice message for my pager. In my most professional voice, I recorded, "Hi, are you looking to make lots of money with a safe, reliable and stable service? Well, you've called the right place. I am hiring models for full-service sessions. Please leave your physical description, measurements and number, and I'll contact you for an interview. Please, no drug users. Thank you. Bye."

Requesting no drug users was naive; I quickly learned that the majority of women working for escort services have habits. They work to support their habit, their families, their man and *his* habit. There are a variety of reasons, yet the goal is the same: *money.*

At 8:00 the next morning, the vibration of my pager woke me up. The message read: FULL. *Wow!* I told myself, *Go for it! This is my come-up.* Chino had always said to be for self because self-preservation was the nature of man, and I intended to survive. I returned the calls and selected a variety of applicants. I set up interviews with twelve candidates at the Knight's Inn hotel.

I was surprised by the high turnout, and they were surprised that I was a woman since most services are run by men. They also liked my professionalism: I was dressed in a sleek pantsuit and offered coffee and doughnuts. The response was great. I held only one open, informal interview session for all the girls. While running my salon, I had acquired very good managerial skills, so I communicated well. I explained my rules, emphasizing that there was to be no stealing. In this profession, it's easy to lie about what you make, but because I was business savvy, they knew they couldn't get away with that at my service. I kept it all very simple. After all, we were there to make money, not friends.

I scanned the room with the mind and eye of a man. What would make me turn my head? What would make me spend money to be with them? I knew I needed a variety of girls. I chose nine of the twelve girls. And if I hadn't been so pressed to get paid, I would have taken my chances with the dogs, too, just to see who in the hell would fuck them. But I chose the best looking and began to qualify them for my purpose. I hired these ladies because they were curvaceous, sensuous, childlike, seemingly innocent, well groomed, and easy listeners. Some were experienced. Some were first-timers. Only two had their own transportation. One very attractive young lady who was new to the business had her own transportation, no children and no habit. I wondered why she was in this line of work. But I hired her and continued on. I wrote down all the girls' information and gave them working names.

The half-black, half-Chinese girl, I named China. She was absolutely beautiful, with olive-toned skin, an oval face, slanted, coal black eyes and silky, curly hair. She had a lot of street in her. Every word out of her mouth was fly. She had an hourglass figure and an aggressive attitude, which I liked right away. I knew she could talk a john out of some money. Problem was, she had a crack habit that was out of this world—a $1,000-a-day habit. China was upfront and open about her habit and everything else about her. She said, "Stay out of my business, and I'll stay out of yours. I work twenty-four-seven, so let that be the reason you send me all the calls you want." I really took a liking to this girl, so I bent my "no drugs" rule. China was worth this violation.

Then there was Gabrielle. She was a young, caramel tender with 44 DDs. The men would love her. Also among the array of tempting treats whom I chose were: Renaye, Spice, Sheela, Toy, Shy, Chrissy, Sugar, Cinnamon and Pie. Pie was petite and very flat-chested. She looked like she was twelve years old. The men would love her, too. Perverts!

When Gabrielle asked for my name, I rolled "Carmen" off my tongue. It came from nowhere. From that day on, I became Carmen, my alter ego, a totally different person from Pamela. Carmen was strong, emotionless and untrusting. Pammy, well, she was the opposite: weak, emotional and trusting.

I told them they must report in by phone with their locations by 10:00 a.m. or pay a $25 fine. When they reported in, they were to give me their locations—hotel and room number for incalls—and availability for outcalls. I informed them that the phones were off at my house by 4:30 p.m. so I could devote my time to my son. This disappointed them because they wanted more hours and more flexibility. Some even asked about working for other services. I informed them that it was no problem as long as it did not conflict with my "calls." Chino had taught me so much. I knew the way you went into something was the way that you came out of it. Thus, I went in hard. I always kept in mind all the things that I had learned from him, lessons of the streets. Rule number one: get paid; rule number two: don't trust anybody, not even yourself; rule number three: stay free.

It was time to accept the fact that he had raised me as far as the streets were concerned, but now it was time to raise myself.

Once the ground rules were established, we dispersed, and I went to the newspaper to place my ads for the following week. I placed one exclusively for African-American girls. It read: CARMEN'S BLACK MODELS. One for SUGAR & SPICE—my bisexual white girls who did one-on-ones and threesomes. And one for the petite Cinnamon that read: A TASTE OF HONEY.

All the ads were listed with my pager number. I went home and changed the message on the voice mail. With jazz playing in the background, the new message was: "Hello and thank you for calling Carmen's. We offer full-service sessions—$200 an hour, $150 for a half hour. We cater to your every need and all of your wants. We want you to call 555-9402, come 555-9402, enjoy 555-9402. We are waiting." The number was to the extra phone line I'd had installed in my home so that they could call and I could arrange the dates. It was important that during the day the phone was answered, dates were arranged, and calls were made to prepare the awaiting lady. I knew they would not leave a number for a return phone call. The wife or girlfriend might answer or something.

The next morning the phone was ringing off the hook and so was the pager. Under normal circumstances, all the ringing would have gotten on my last nerve, but today, it was music to my ears.

Each tone of the ringer filled me with excitement and a compelling desire to dance. But instead I got the baby dressed and off to day care in a hurry.

I returned home and prepared myself for a day of answering the phone. Seven of the girls called in and gave me their locations. I had read up on the sex business and all the desires of men. Golden showers, balls in the butt, anal sex, titty fuckin', peep shows, you name it. Freaky desires. Normalcy was for the wives of my callers. Erotica was for the girls, and men with vivid imaginations. If the wives only knew how vivid. If they only knew. So I began my first day on the job, my first day owning my new business, Carmen's Escort Service. I do believe it had a nice ring to it.

Two

"Hello, may I help you?"

"Good morning," a masculine voice chimed.

"Good morning, may I help you?"

"I'm Dave. What do you have, say, around eleven a.m. in the north end?"

"Dave, I'm Carmen. I have black girls and white girls. What's your pleasure today?"

"I'd like a blonde."

"Okay, I have a petite blonde. She's five-three, 115 pounds. Her measurements are 38–24–36. Her name is Sugar, and she's very sweet. We have a special on *doubles* today," I offered enthusiastically.

"No. I'll take Sugar at eleven a.m."

"Okay, please call me from the pay phone in the rear parking lot next to the tree near the Continental Plaza. I'll instruct you from there." The clients provided the pay phone number so I could determine their proximity to the hotel. If they were at the right pay phone, it meant that they hadn't backed out and that they were only minutes away from the hotel.

"Bye."

"Thanks!"

"Hello, may I help you?" I said to the next caller in my most professional voice as if I were working for a large corporation and this were just another day at the office.

Click! The caller must have thought he had the wrong number, or maybe he lost his nerve, because my question was answered with a dial tone.

Ring . . . ring.

"Hello, may I help you?"

Click.

Getting hung up on didn't faze me. Someone else would call in a minute. The phone was ringing, my business was booming and I was excited. I was making a come-up, and it felt good.

Ring . . . ring.

"Hello, may I help you?"

"Are golden showers in the forecast today?" a deep voice thick with lust queried.

"They sure are, from light rain to a thunderstorm. What's your pleasure?"

"I like it when it's a light drizzle," Deep Voice replied.

"On the east end of the city, your experience awaits. Gabrielle is waiting off Hamilton, near the Eastland Mall. Contact me from there, okay?"

"Thanks," he whispered.

How someone gets off on getting pissed on is beyond me. But for $300, some of the girls would do it. Spinning a pencil around the notepad in my lap, I answered my next phone call.

"Hello, may I help you?"

"Your line stays busy. I've got jungle fever. I like them plump and juicy."

"Great, big guy, I have something special for you on the north end, close to Colerain. Call me from a pay phone at Northland Mall. Bye."

My pager was buzzing. I've always been told what a nice phone voice I have, so I added a hint of seduction to it. I figured, always put your best foot forward, so I gave the service my all. I thought of an idea for a tantalizing business card. The card was neon pink with a silhouette of a curvaceous female figure. This way the girls and I could pass them out, and the clients could keep my number with them. I also decided to place them on cars in parking lots wherever I went, just like I had done with my salon business cards. Hell, I even thought about placing one in one of those fish bowls at a restaurant to try to get a company lunch or something. I was doing well, but I was at the lower end of the escort business. There were services out there charging double my price. But I'd do better when I could.

"Hello, may I help you?" I answered.

"Do you offer male to male?"

"*No!*" I snapped, taken off guard, then I quickly regained my composure. "Um . . . no," I said hesitantly, "but . . ."

Click.

Hmmmm . . . an idea.

Ring . . . ring.

"Hello, may I help you?"

"Who has the best head on her shoulders?" the caller asked, and I confidently responded, "Renaye. With her full lips, she definitely has the best head on her shoulders."

"Okay. I'm ready. Where?" I directed him to a pay phone in a business-and-residential area on the north side of Columbus known as the 161 area.

"What is your name?"

"Steve."

"Great, Steve. Please call soon."

As the day continued, I thought about all the new services I could offer, even male on male. I also rethought my location. I was stuck in the apartment and I needed mobility. In between calls, I contacted CellularOne and gave them bogus information to set up my other means of communication. They wanted a $500 deposit and I didn't have a credit card. I would have to go into one of their stores, but I didn't have the money. "Damn!" I said to myself. "Phone, don't fail me now. Keep ringin'. I need some loot!"

Ring . . . ring.

"Hello, may I help you?"

"Hi, it's Dave. I'm on 161."

"Great! May I have the number to the pay phone?"

"It's 555-7787."

"Okay, I'll call back." Quickly I learned that some guys called just for the pleasure of calling an escort service, desiring the forbidden, the unknown, the fantasy of unknown pussy with no strings attached; however, those were the ones who bitched up at the last minute. That's why I never called the girls until the customer called from the location I told them. Immediately, I dialed the number to the hotel where one of my girls was waiting.

"Cross Country Inn," the receptionist answered.

"Room 112, please."

"Hello," a voice whispered. Coincidentally, Sugar, the name I had given her, was both her work name and the name that she went by outside of work. It was an odd choice considering how she got it. She said that her father had given her that name when he started climbing into her bed at night not long after her thirteenth birthday. She had the customers call her the same—she clearly had some daddy issues. Her father died of cancer, but she missed him greatly, despite the fact he took her virginity. Just hearing a man call her Sugar reminded her of the same feeling of love she had gotten when her father stroked her hair and called her that as he held her head tightly between his legs while she gave him oral sex.

When I met her and gave her this name, I had no idea she had gone by that name before and didn't know the story behind it. I just called her Sugar because she had such a sweet personality.

"Sugar?"

"Yeah."

"Dave is on his way over. He's an hour."

"Thanks, Carmen."

Ring . . . ring.

"Hello, may I help you?"

"Carmen, it's Sugar. Dave is here. I'll call again."

"Be safe," I instructed.

"I will," she assured me. I marked $75 in my ledger for my commission from Sugar.

Ring . . . ring.

"Hello, may I help you?" Listening to China's voice, I twirled the phone cord around my finger as she began to talk.

"C, it's China. I have a problem."

"What's wrong? You okay?"

"Yeah, I'm okay, but my client doesn't want to see me."

"Why?"

"Guess."

"I don't have time for games, China."

"Let's just say our mothers are sisters."

"Huh? I'm not getting it. Just spit it out."

"I don't have a problem seeing him, but he has a problem seeing me."

"Ask him if he wants someone else."

"C, he's embarrassed."

"Why?"

"Because he's my cousin."

"Damn! Girl, we never know who will use our service, huh? That's so funny."

"Yeah, I know, and my family talks about me being on the streets, and here he goes getting some ass behind his wife's back. Imagine that."

"China, keep ya head up, girl. I'll mark off that call and get you another one. Okay?"

"Thanks, C."

"Bye."

Ring . . . ring.

"Hello, may I help you? . . . Yes, sir, I have a China doll. She's beautiful . . . Your name is Peter? Okay, Peter, I'll call you back." I made the call back and then called China.

Ring . . . ring.

"Yeah?"

"Hi, China, it's Carmen."

"Hey, girl, I need some calls."

"Well, one's on his way. His name is Peter."

"Let that be the reason. Bye."

Ring . . . ring.

"Hello, may I help you?"

"Carmen, he's here."

"Be safe!"

"Let that be the reason." *Click!*

I marked China for $75. I kept immaculate records. Already that day, I had made over $1,000 in commissions. This had my head all swole. I was envisioning loot stacked to the ceiling, and I liked what I saw.

Around 4:30 p.m. I headed to all the hotels to pick up my money from the girls. At every opportunity, I made improvements. I encouraged the girls to stay at the same hotels and perhaps share rooms to split costs. When one had a session, the other excused herself. My interest and professionalism were really appreciated by the girls.

I was shocked to find how open Columbus was to the sex market. The newspaper is vital in the sex trade, and I had no trouble placing ads. The prices were even reasonable. There was little doubt that the adult entertainment section was a big moneymaker.

Time flies when you're making money. Especially fast money. Even though I was making more and more money, I just wanted to save enough so that my son and I could leave Ohio. I only remained in Columbus after the breakup with the hope of returning to college and establishing some form of relationship between my son and his biological father. I soon realized it wouldn't happen. So I just hoped for another plan. I figured I'd keep the service until something else worked out.

Many wonder how a person becomes a criminal. We learn rules from our childhood years and our family. Then, as we get older, society becomes our family. We tend to adopt its views and perceptions of law and order.

When a person sees that rules can be bent so easily, it's encouraging. Newspapers fully supported me and enabled me an outlet to conduct an illegal profession, legally.

The hotels were accommodating, to say the least. There were very few obstacles to running my service, though I can't say that if I weren't allowed to place ads or rent hotels, I wouldn't have pursued this. As we all know, challenges can be used as motivation and I was a person who loved challenges.

I had professional men as clients. The majority of them were white. Granted, our society is racist; however, in the sex game, inhibitions fade away. It's true that the white girls made more money, perhaps because there were more white callers. But in fantasy, the forbidden is the desire.

Many white men desired the dark meat just as many black men wanted the white meat. This was about fantasy, and I was determined not to be outdone.

On Tuesday, I hired a driver, a young Ohio State University student, for weekends. He drove the girls to outcalls and delivered my commissions. I paid him $20 a call to ensure the girls' safety. He was happy because it beat pizza delivery. Instead of delivering pizza, he delivered pussy.

I hired a new girl who could have been Mariah Carey's twin. I named her Ashley. She was a half-black, half-Italian young lady who was totally confused. She wanted to be accepted as Italian, but was often referred to as a dago. In the black community, the women hated her because of her beauty, and the men wanted her because of it. Feeling rejected and used, she turned to drugs.

Her chiseled figure began with a 44 DD bustline, and included a bangin' backside, big brown eyes, ringlet curls of light brown and full lips revealing a perfect smile. She was a big moneymaker. Men love breasts of any size, but bigger breasts were more popular, especially if they were real. Clients loved her. She easily had twenty calls a day. I extended my hours to accommodate the calls, the girls, and my pockets. In the hustlin' game, I'd soon learn that more was never enough.

I placed China and Ashley in the same room, which was a mistake. I didn't know Ashley was an addict, but later found out she had a full-blown heroin addiction. So I had one girl, China, who adored crack, and another who couldn't get enough of smack. Two addicts. They became inseparable. This was a lethal combination, but I decided to play it cool. Separating them would have been a mistake. Their common interest in getting high was stronger than any rule I could try to enforce.

Due to their earning potential, they became my high-stakes gamble, and they were worth the risk. Neither of them had a home. Their families turned their backs on them. Or they turned their backs on their families. Depends on who is telling the story. They had misused their families so much that the ties were broken.

My girls and I enjoyed the companionship that we shared, and in essence, we became sisters. I was like the big sister.

On Saturday mornings I'd take the girls and my son to breakfast. We all began to form bonds and started to lean on one another. After Chino left me, I isolated myself and shut out the world. It was just my son and me. As I grew closer to the girls, I got closer to other aspects of their lifestyles, and that is when my life really began to change.

I received a lot of calls for private parties. The businessmen would call for bachelor parties, and I'd send Ashley and China. Soon they started turning the clients on to drugs. Ashley and China had the same dope dealer, G-Money. They'd page him, and he'd bring them their love.

One time I called the room, and he was there hanging out. I'd heard so much about him from Ashley—how he had it goin' on and how he was fun to hang out with. G-Money also sold them hot items like clothing and jewelry. This particular day, he asked to speak to me.

Reluctantly I agreed and heard a soft baritone voice come through the phone.

"What's up, Carmen?"

"Hi."

The phone fell silent for a moment and then he continued, "When am I gonna meet you?"

"You know that's not possible. I don't do dates, and I don't spend." I played him short 'cause I didn't know him. Why was this nigga trying to get to know me?

"How about lunch?"

"No."

"How about dinner?"

"Nope." I began to smile. Dude was persistent.

"Okay, Ashley told me you like clothes. I want to show you some."

Damn, one of my weaknesses. You can always break a woman down with the enticement of clothes.

"Tell me more."

"You got some good game, Carmen. I just want to talk to you."

"You are talking to me."

"Damn, why you so . . . you know what . . ." He began to sound irritated. "I'm just going to leave some things with Ashley. Tell me how you like them."

"Why are you doing this?"

"I'd do anything for you, Carmen."

I could do nothing but laugh. "You know game recognize game, but seriously though, what do you want?"

"Nothing but lunch."

He got another smile out of me.

"Okay, I'll check out what you left and see how bad you want lunch." I hung up the phone and began to think of my next move.

The following day, I went by to collect. G-Money had left me some very beautiful clothes worth more than three grand. I was impressed as I checked the labels, which revealed designer names. As my hands felt the soft fabric of the linens and silks, it brought back memories of Chino's gifts. After his road trips, my bed would hold piles of leather outfits, purses, shoes and pantsuits he had purchased for me.

Driving down Livingston Avenue, I got a page from Spice. I pulled into the Brothers Carryout, ordered a perch sandwich, a bag of Grippo Chips and a Tahitian Treat soda, then called Spice.

"What's up, Spice? It's Carmen."

She replied in a pissed-off tone, deepening her voice and speaking loudly. "Carmen, I don't think we should do all the fuckin' and you collect all the money. I think—"

I immediately cut her off. "Hold up. Wait a fucking minute."

She continued to try to talk. "No, I won't wait. I—"

"Look, Spice, I said slow your roll, boo, hold on." I placed my cell phone in my lap in case she continued to talk 'cause I was not trying to hear it. I swallowed the bite of food I had in my mouth and sipped my drink as I began to think of how to handle this.

Let's see, she feelin' herself 'cause she's made about two thousand today, and off that two grand, I'm getting eight hundred, and she has a problem, I thought. So what are the choices? I can tell her to fuck off, or I can try to silk it, 'cause she makes money for me. Do I want to miss out on my cut of what she makes? No. At this point she's valuable. But this disrespect shit gots to go. So I gotta flip on her.

"Spice, okay, I understand you don't feel it's a fair cut. So, check this, leave me what you want me to have and then go work for someone else."

"Now, Carmen, I am not saying that. All I am saying is that I think you should get less because you ain't the one fuckin'."

"Spice, you can have an opinion, but you came to me for a job and for clients. If you think you can do better on your own, so be it. If you don't like how you getting treated, so be it. I hate to see ya go, but my fee is the same for all of you, and it ain't negotiable. You pay for my clients, and you pay to be hooked up. If you don't like my program, boo, stop ringing my phone for dates. Now I gotta go. Take care." *Click!* I reversed that shit.

I decided not to go get the money or send her any calls for a while. She'd think about what I had said. I'm sure she was thinking, Can I get the same amount of dates without Carmen? Can I make two grand a day, almost every day, without Carmen? And if Carmen can afford to let go of eight hundred, then she getting money, and plenty of it. I decided she would still want to be down, or I had just lost eight hundred bills. I wasn't trying to lose no money. I figured in a matter of time, she would call me, and when I went to collect, I'd check that bitch again about callin' my phone trying to front on me about how I run my shit.

The following week, Ashley called me.

"Carmen, G wants to talk to you."

"Put him on the phone."

"Hello, beautiful," he whispered into the receiver.

"What's up, G?"

"You like your clothes?"

"Yes, they were nice. Hey, look, can you get me some Victoria's Secret panties for the girls? I need a lot of them. At least two hundred."

"Damn! Why so many?"

"It's for a promotional sale."

"You a real businesswoman. I like that in you. Yeah, I'll get some for you."

"If you do this, I'll meet you for lunch," I said teasingly.

"Promise?" G asked desperately. I had him. He was open.

"I promise," I said, wondering what good the promise of a complete stranger was to him.

The next day, I had over three hundred pairs of panties, including thongs, G-strings and lace, many with matching bras and camisoles. This package reflected the entire Victoria's Secret line and then some. I gave them as gifts to the girls to show my appreciation. And I told them of my new promotional idea. We would sell worn panties to our customers for $20. The girls would keep $10, and I'd get the other $10. I sold out of the scented panties in one day. Men are like dogs—they are drawn to scents, especially to the scent of a woman's undies. Now I was really brainstorming and stacking dollars.

I met G in the Radian Hotel lobby for lunch. He was in his midthirties, had a brown complexion and was sportin' a Polo outfit with fresh sneakers. He wasn't bad looking, but not handsome either; I'd say he was average. Cautiously, I approached him with a nod of my head and said, "Finally, I meet G-Money."

Looking me up and down, he replied, "Carmen, ooh, this is the day I have dreamed of."

"Playa, you are full of shit."

"That's right, I am. I wanted to talk with you about your escort service."

"Oh, is that right? What you want to talk about?"

"I want to talk about you and get to know you. You said that you don't date, but you own a service. I know you date or have dated. I mean, how else would you know about a service?" He asked the question like he was a psychiatrist and I was his client.

"Well, whether I did or didn't is none-ya. Feel me? So tell me about what you do."

"I want to open an escort service or buy into yours. I think it's a moneymaker, because men will always purchase sex."

We continued to make small talk as we enjoyed sandwiches on the patio of the hotel. I strung him along and said that I would consider going into business with him. To show his sincerity, he offered me $3,000 and promised

$2,000 more. We talked about a sex spa as an incall location that fronts as a massage parlor, but gives much more. That was an excellent idea, but I didn't let him know I thought so. I was still trying to feel him out. The thought of not having to rent rooms for the girls was enticing considering how much I paid per month, having a place of my own could certainly cut down on my expenses.

"I also work as a fence, Carmen. I purchase stolen items and resell them." I leaned in closer. I saw an opportunity there, and I never refuse a chance to make money.

"G, I want in," I demanded. Chino introduced me to the hustle when we first met, and here it was, in my face, and I wasn't about to let it pass me by.

"Certainly. We can work something out, Carmen."

And that was my introduction to the next level of crime: receiving and selling stolen property.

Three

$\mathcal{M}$ost people who fence usually buy any stolen item from the kitchen sink to a car's spare tire. I, of course, wanted to be selective in the merchandise I purchased. But the name of this game is supply and demand. A fence will purchase items at a third or fourth of the store's ticketed price. They will then resell them at any cost, based on supply and demand. I usually tried to offer half the price of the ticket, but whatever brought a profit was cool with me. The one line I never crossed was items stolen from someone's home. I only wanted store merchandise. I did try to hang on to *some* morals. Purchasing stolen items from another's home would do two things: one, support break-ins, which could lead to potential violence; and two, be an act of bad karma and result in *my* home being burglarized. G-Money purchased anything and everything. You could bring him a used baby's pacifier and he'd not only resell it but ask for more of them.

I had built a nice savings off the escort service. With that money I purchased my fenced items. I normally purchased clothes and perfume. The sheer volume of stolen merchandise available really amazed me. I came to realize that most of these boosters were drug addicts who had mad skills when it came to stealing. I was purchasing, on average, three garbage bags of clothes a day, and I had no problem reselling the clothes in a matter of days. I sold to my girls, and I'd campaign right out of the trunk of my car at local bars, hair salons and nightclubs. I was gettin' my hustle on out there, makin' ends. Once you gain a rep for having things, people find you. You've become a resource of cheap goods for the people who buy the merchandise and that equaled success to me. Like me, G tried to be a professional with his venture.

Every afternoon I'd have my driver pick up the clothes. I gave the girls first pick of the items. It was apparent that the boosters favored Victoria's Secret, Neiman Marcus, Caché, Saks and Henri Bendel. I wondered how badly the stores were hurt. Were these boosters *that* talented or were they aided by staff at the stores? How could they remove so many items and not be detected?

I was constantly looking out for pitfalls. I watched out for the vice squad because of the service, and now I had to be careful not to sell to the wrong person and catch a selling or receiving stolen property case.

Chino had financed his drug hustle with proceeds from selling stolen clothes. He also taught Young Mike this hustle. I saw it a lot, and oftentimes you learn best by observing.

Chino's best booster was Young Mike, a shorty he found on the streets and added to the posse. He was excellent with smash-and-grabs on small businesses. He'd drive a car into a freestanding jewelry store, smashing the front door and the cases. Then he'd grab anything of value in sight.

He executed all this in seconds. Then there were times when Young Mike would just grab. He would walk into an upscale department store and simply grab a rack of clothes or empty a sweater case, like of Versace, and run out of the store to an awaiting vehicle. Smash-and-grabs are after-hours moves, but on a humbug or if it was "sweet," Mike would do it during store hours.

I missed Young Mike. True, he was in the streets pulling capers, but there was more to him than stealing. I remember him at my kitchen table studying for his GED, trying to get an education that he didn't get a chance to pursue as a teenager. I knew him as someone trying to take care of his mother and crippled younger brother.

Unfortunately for Mike, he was busted for a petty case and went to prison for two years. Upon being released from prison he returned to society completely broken. Mike got involved with another crew from down south who were up north getting money, and after only two months, he found himself as a codefendant in their federal drug case. He got indicted, implicated on some he-said, she-said, they-said shit, placed on house arrest, and was shortly thereafter found dead. At age twenty-three, Young Mike took his life when living became too much for him. The coroner removed a nine-millimeter bullet from his dome. He was a tall, handsome young man who could have been anything in this world, but when the streets get you, there is no getting out. Young Mike took himself out. May he rest in peace.

China loved the fact that she never had to leave her hotel room—or her crack pipe. She had it all delivered to her doorstep. Going to China's room was like visiting a crack house. I was never comfortable in a place where drugs were plentiful. I was worried that at anytime the Feds would kick the damn door in.

I asked China if she shared my concern, and all she would say was, "Carmen, I wish any motherfucker would run up in my shit. They'd take me down handcuffed, getting my last drag off my pipe. Besides, I don't keep enough dope around. I smoke it too fast. The worst I am looking at is a drug abuse case. I can lie down for a weekend while I beat that shit. Sleep right through it if I have to."

Other times, she would call me and say, "Yo, C! Bring me some food."

I'd say, "Is Chinese okay?"

She would then say, "Let that be the reason." Eating Chinese food was the only aspect of her Chinese heritage she held on to. I'd take food to her, and we would sit and talk. Once, over a plate of sweet and sour pork, I confronted her about her choice in hair weave. I hated it and wished she would get rid of it. It was blond. The whitest blond I had ever seen.

"China, I hate your hair, girl. It's flamin'."

"Don't worry, I keeps me a hooker helmet nearby," she squealed, smacking her lips.

"A hooker helmet?" I inquired, devouring my egg roll.

"Yes, Ms. Carmen! A wig. I have a black one. Check it

out." She began waving an object pulled from underneath the bed.

"I like it."

"I don't care if you tell the callers I'm blond or brunette. Just get me some calls."

"And you know I will."

She showed me all the items she purchased with her new money. I told her, "China, please take care of your things. You purchased some nice stuff."

As I glanced around the hotel room, I saw a photo of a beautiful little girl who looked just like China. She had the same eyes.

"China, she's adorable. How old is this princess?"

"Four."

"Girl, let that be the reason you stop smoking," I said sympathetically.

"My grandmother keeps her. My old girl is still mad at me for stealing her checks and for giving birth to my daughter in a crack house. I took a hit and was like, '*Damn, this dope is da bomb!*' Then I felt like I had to go take a shit. The next thing I knew, I was on the toilet and out came my daughter. She looked like a wet rat. She was so tiny and so pretty. I was terrified. I called my old girl, and she took us to the emergency room. I left the hospital to go get my friend, starts with a *c* and ends with a *k*. My old girl picked up the baby, and we've been at odds ever since."

"China, she really is precious, and I think she should be the reason you turn your life around."

"Look, C, don't make me check you, 'cause I respect you and all, but we live in this real world, and you out there just like me, chasing the dollar, just like I chase my highs that I'll never catch. I may be a crackhead, but I am far from asleep. You think I wanted this for my life? You think I didn't try the traditional route? Shit didn't work for me, so I got down for mine. Was dating someone I thought was special, and he enjoyed the fact that I got freaky in the bedroom. So much so, he bragged to his friends and told them everything we did. One day his friend stepped to me and offered me a C-note to sleep with him. I was so mad that my special friend told our bedroom business, I took the nigga up on his offer with the hopes that he would go and tell the guy I was dating. Sort of a punishment for telling our business.

"Dude had a lil' paper in his pocket and didn't mind spending. I sucked his dick like a lollipop and even gave him some back-door action. Had him sayin' my name and whose it is. Hmmm, instead of him telling and me getting revenge on my dude, he kept it to himself and kept coming back. I kept fuckin' both of them. I would suck the one's dick, swallow his cum and then later that day, go kiss the other on the mouth. And they had the nerve to call me nasty? Shit, I was making them fuck each other on the down low. Eventually, the nigga fell in love with me, the neighborhood freak.

"That's when I began to see that niggas are tricks for some pussy, and then other shit happened in my life, experimenting with alcohol, drugs, and I just got caught in the streets. My motto is 'bitch gotta get paid!'"

"I live the smoker's life. Our nights are our days, and the daytime is our night. We smoke all night for several days at a time. Carmen, I have been awake for three days. I'm gonna eat this food, go into a crack coma, sleep for about twelve hours and hopefully be awakened by the ringing of my phone—a call from you with a date for me. Take a hit, pop in the shower and make my money by what I do best, flat backin'. Carmen, I see you stackin' that cheese. So what's your excuse?"

China's question brought me back to reality and Pammy was about to take over. I wasn't trying to feel . . . I didn't want to feel.

"I'll do anything for my son . . ." I stopped abruptly and got a grip on myself. Carmen took over again.

"Carmen, your son is so handsome," China continued.

"Thanks, China, and I hear ya. Do ya hear me?" We both smiled and hugged each other. China and I, for some reason, saw a lot of things eye to eye. I looked over at her and said, "All right, girl, you've checked me. Now I got work to do. No time to sit around and complain. I'm about to go campaigning and get you some calls."

"Now, that's what I'm trying to hear. I'll be sittin' right here in this room waiting on my men."

I left and drove off in silence. I just kept telling Pammy to stop thinking and Carmen to stay in control. Besides, I had to meet G for more clothes, which meant more money. I turned the music up loud and sang along to Tupac's "Keep Ya Head Up."

At six in the morning, someone was knocking on my front door. It was my boys from New York, T-Love and his brother, Abdullah. I met these money-getting hustlers through my good friend Erik. Erik and I met at Ohio State University as freshmen. He was from New York, and I was from Detroit. We both became curious about each other due to the reps both of our cities had. New Yorkers were known for being trendsetters, and the men were known for their jewelry, gold fronts, clothing, accents and money. Detroit women were known for their dressin', hairdos, game and taste in automobiles. We searched each other out to see if the stereotypes were true. Hangin' out after class, he introduced me to his crew, two of whom were T-Love and Abdullah.

"What's up, man?" T-Love said to Erik as he walked up on us in the student center. "This you?" he questioned, looking at me.

Erik began to speak but I interrupted. "Nah, this ain't him. It's me. My name is Pamela and hello to you, too." I extended my hand for a handshake, but instead he put his arm around my shoulders.

"I like this. She's feisty. Where you find her at?"

"You must be from New York," I said, becoming agitated.

"Harlem, baby, how you know?"

I smiled and so did Erik. In this case, the stereotype was true. T-Love had a big gold T emblem hanging on a fat gold chain around his neck. Both of which could be used as weapons if necessary. I also had the urge to pull up his pants, which obviously were masked by a shirt that was about three times too large for him. I'd only seen it on videos, particularly of the East Coast rappers, but if the trend of wearing pants hanging off the ass and oversized shirts was the next thing to come, I prayed that not everyone would embrace it.

"In that case, I can forgive you," I said, removing his arm from around my shoulders.

"What you talking about?"

"For disrespecting me."

"When I do that?"

"Just now. I don't know what women are like in New York but, baby, Detroit women don't go for that. If you have a question, you can ask me. I don't bite." With that, I gave him a wide smile.

Ever since then, we were a team.

They ran through Columbus every couple of months for a week at a time. Anytime they were in Columbus, they would drop by to see me. They were *ballers* in every sense of the word. They hustled by any means necessary. I think of a baller as a person who views life from a sink-or-swim perspective. In the streets, there is a philosophy that says: Everyone gets a chance. What will you do with yours? Sometimes there's that thirsty person, and they take their chance and try to take the next person's chance. Then they get out there and run full-court with their opportunity, whatever that may be, to the best of their ability.

I sold T and Abdullah clothes for their girls, wives or baby mamas. I always got a little jealous watching them fuss over the clothes, selecting the perfect outfits. Here I was, somebody's baby's mother, and no one cared. Here I was in the streets, scramblin' for me and mine while their baby mamas were home safe. But every time Pammy went soft, Carmen came out hard. *Fuck it, just tax any muthafucka.* So that's what I did. Carmen used every opportunity and created new ones. One of my escort service clients, Peter, had a BMW M3 for sale. Peter said, "For you, Carmen, $15,000 cash."

So I stepped to T-Love about it. "Yo, T, I know where you can get a nice BMW. Cash, no questions and in whatever name you want."

T-Love was like, "No doubt! I want it."

"He wants $18,000 for it, plus give me $500 to do the title and tag registration." I knew someone who worked at the DMV, so taking care of this would be a cinch. Life on the hustle is all about who you know.

I set up the deal with my client, whom I soon learned worked at the car dealer auction. He was able to get the car for a bargain. This was another valuable connection, and I was determined to make good on this sale so I wouldn't lose him. I wanted to buy my mom and myself new cars one day. A shiny motherfucker rollin' right off the showroom floor.

T-Love had me eighteen Gs by nightfall. I spoke with my client and proudly told him, "I got $12,000 today. All cash."

"It's a deal!" Peter screamed.

I made a $6,500 profit. Whoever said the middleman gets the worst deal? It was automatically assumed that it would be safe with me because I never went anywhere, or so they thought. I flossed that bitch for a week and didn't have a problem doing it.

I'd learned long ago that ballers always look for the easiest, hassle-free way out. T and Abdullah used my house to hustle everything from dope to women. After three months, I'd had enough of being compromised. I played hostess twice a month with nothing in return, but that was going to change.

I began to resent the blatant disregard the guys had for me. See, at first you try to be a trooper and do all you can for the team, doing your part, going that extra mile, but then you realize that it's not appreciated.

They just assumed I'd be there and always be available. I guess I had a major attitude. Carmen was not having it.

I'd read that someone could be so traumatized, an alternate personality takes over to protect them. I had been traumatized in my own way.

Betrayal is a very big pill to swallow. Two very important things in my life were gone: my Chino and my salon. I felt like I had no control. I am learning now that you always have control of your life by doing the best you can with what you have. I'm a firm believer that everything happens for a reason and when God says, "Be," that's just how it is. The only way I can explain Carmen is that she appeared and saved me from what I couldn't take again: failure.

I picked up my ringing cell phone from my Coach bag and answered.

"Hello, may I help you?"

"Hello, sweetheart." G's voice came through over background rap music.

"Hey, G, what's up?"

"Wanna meet for lunch? I'm in a bad mood and need someone to talk to." His voice had a hint of sincere depression.

"Where do you wanna meet?"

"The Cooker Restaurant at twelve thirty."

"No, one thirty." *He don't run shit!*

"Okay, one thirty it is. Carmen, you don't give a brother nothing, do you?"

"Nothing he doesn't earn. Just like I got to earn it, so does the next man. I'll see you at one thirty."

I went to collect from the girls, and before I knew it, I was running late to meet G. So what! You press hoes and clothes. You don't press me. My Chino used to say this all the time when I tried to press him about things. As I pulled into the restaurant parking lot, there was G waiting in his champagne-colored Honda Accord, rims sittin' on 20s, with the music playing.

"Hey, beautiful, you're late." He raised his sleeve, displaying his diamond-studded Rolex watch. Flossin' for fun, I raised my arm, displaying my diamond-encrusted Ebel watch and said, "I know, I know. I had to make some stops."

"How are the girls doing?"

"That's a $2,000 question. Where is the rest of my money?"

"Come on, let's go in. That's what I want to talk with you about." We walked into the restaurant and we were seated near a window. Gazing out, I playfully said, "G, I am starving like Marvin." I noticed he was not his usual self.

"What's up? I like this place," I said, looking around. "Here comes our waiter. We must look hungry." I laughed aloud.

"May I take your order?" the waiter asked.

"Yes, I'll have the lasagna and salad with a glass of your house white wine."

"And you, sir?" he asked, turning to G.

"I'll have a highball of your best Cognac," G replied, rubbing the sides of his face.

That was it? Normally, G gets his eat on. As the waiter left, I kept my eyes focused on G's face. We had grown closer, so I knew his moods. G and I basically came up together on different teams, but we watched each other grow. Over the last couple of months, I watched him go from a Honda Civic to an Accord. He watched me go from a white Jeep Cherokee to a black Range Rover and silver BMW.

G began to shift in his seat. He was obviously annoyed about something. "Carmen, my connect got knocked," he blurted out.

"Okay," I said, trying not to sound upset. "You don't know anyone else?"

The waiter returned with our drink orders. G took a big gulp of his Cognac and continued. "Carmen, I never told you this, but I work for someone else."

You frontin', fake-ass nigga, I thought.

"I had my own girl connect, but he got knocked, too. I didn't do much with him, but what I did allowed me a lil' more freedom. I work for this dude named Jay-Jay. I push heroin for him, and he pays me."

Just to break the mood, I said, "Oh, so you on commission. You a salesclerk." I laughed, but this was serious. "Damn, G, it's not like you'll starve. You still have the boosters."

"No, not really. They work for drugs. They want to unload and score all in one stop, ya know?"

"Yeah, I hear you. It is all about service, convenience and another hit. Just give me one more hit!" He still didn't smile. Shit ain't funny when you on the verge of broke.

"I'm gonna lose them, C. I got bills. I don't know what to do." He finished his drink. "Can I get my $3,000 back?"

I couldn't believe my ears. He looked me dead in my eyes waiting for a response. I leaned into the table and replied through gritted teeth, "Hold up, this ain't no refund counter. You want that, then go to Wal-Mart or someplace." It was time for one of my lectures.

"First, stop all that whining," I demanded. "You've totally flipped on me. Where G at? 'Cause Gregory is trying to fold like a card table. Money don't make you, you make money. Remember that! I gotta go to the bathroom. I'll be right back."

I excused myself, and as I walked from the table, I heard Carmen in my head. *Look, game is sold, not told. Remember the price you paid for it. This is an opportunity, so take it. Fair exchange ain't robbery. This nigga looking for a sponsor, so sponsor his ass 'cause he ain't getting his money back. He ain't your friend. Ain't no friend shit in this. You already know that—don't forget it. You down for yo' crown, fuck da rest.*

"Okay, okay, can I pee now?" I asked myself. My mind was really starting to play tricks on me. I couldn't believe I was really talking to myself. To rationalize is normal. But I was having a full-fledged conversation. *G's a wimp. Who doesn't have problems? Get in line. Nigga crying because the next man really was making him. That's exactly why I chose to help myself.*

I returned to our table and cleared my throat. "Okay, G. Explain to me what you need and what you are trying to do." Our conversation was cut short when the waiter arrived with my lunch order. Although I'd lost my appetite with the shit G had laid on me, the aroma was too tempting not to dig into the hearty pasta.

"Is there anything else I can get you?" the waiter asked.

"No, thank you," I replied. He walked away. I then focused my attention back on G and what he was saying.

"I was getting an ounce of powder, and I'd rock it up and sell it to geekers."

"Okay, how much do you pay for an ounce?" *I don't know what I'm talking about, but he will never know,* I thought.

"Anywhere from $950 to $1,200." He shrugged. "It just depends on my plug. You know how it is."

No, I didn't. I took another deep breath and responded confidently, "I'll see what I can do for you. I'll get my people on it and get back with you. Now, do you feel better?" He slowly nodded as I continued, "Now order. I see you eyeing my food and you ain't gettin' none."

Finally we both smiled.

Four

"Hello, may I help you?" I spoke into my phone.

"Hi, Carmen."

"Hi, whom am I speaking with?" I wondered who this was getting comfortable with me.

"This is George. I've been a very bad boy." I was relieved to know it was one of my favorite clients.

"Yes, George, you *have* been very bad. I want you at Toy's hotel room in ten minutes or you'll really be in trouble."

"But I can't make it in ten minutes . . . I need twenty," he pleaded, getting into the role-playing of his session.

"*No!* You be there in ten minutes, up north on 161 at the Cross Country Inn in room 212—or else. Now go!"

Toy was a dominatrix. George, a very successful investment banker at a prominent financial institution, was extremely generous and loved to be dominated. He liked to play house and would role-play the child in need of correction. He never touched Toy, and she was never allowed to touch him. She only used her whip, belt or paddle. At the end of her session, George would masturbate to satisfaction.

I called Toy to tell her George was on his way before another call came through.

"Hi, Toy. It's Carmen."

"George is on his way over, and he has been a very bad boy. So give him what he's looking for."

"Carmen, I'm getting uncomfortable seeing George. The last session, I beat him so bad that it scared me."

"What's up with him?"

"C, he likes it rough. If it ain't rough, it ain't right for him."

"Just complete this session, and I'll find him a replacement. He really likes you, though, Toy. What does he look like?"

"He's sorta scrawny looking. Very pale like he never sees the sun. Black-rimmed glasses, short curly hair, very conservative in his dress and rather thin. But he's fun, and I do get rid of my frustrations."

"Then there are the tips." The tips always made the session go better.

"Carmen, I know, it's just—let me see how this session goes. Maybe I'll keep him."

"Be sure to let me know so I can find someone else and get them the equipment for his sessions. I'll beat him myself for the right price."

"C, you are wild."

"Yeah, I have a wild side, too. I'll let you go. He'll be there soon, and remember, he's late no matter when he arrives. Here's a new punishment for him: have him drink a lot of water and make him hold his urine. Be creative."

"Okay, C, I'm waiting for him."

"Great! Later, bye!"

Ring . . . ring.

"Hello, may I help you?"

"Carmen, this is Toy. George is here."

"Good, I'll mark it. Have fun."

With a smiling voice Toy responded, "*I* will. But I don't know about him." I heard her snap her whip, getting into the role.

"Call me when he leaves, and I'll get you some regular calls."

"Thank you, Carmen."

"Bye!"

As soon as I hung up, another call came right on its heels.

"Hello, may I help you?"

"Carmen, this is Gabrielle. I have a problem."

"What's up?"

"My client is still here, and his time is up."

"Wait, let me check. Mmmmm. Yeah, it's up. They never stay the full time, anyway."

"I know. Well, he hasn't—you know what yet, and I'm tired."

"I guess so," I said.

"Seriously, C, he wants his money back."

"Whoa! This is serious. Is he threatening you?" I listened intently to Gabby's voice, trying to gauge how she was reacting to the situation. I felt helpless on the other end of the phone line.

"No, but he's not happy."

"Tell him he can have his money back, and I'll still pay you for this call."

"Hold on." I heard her offer the suggestion, then she spoke into the receiver. "C, he doesn't want it. He wants service."

"Put the money on the bed."

"That's not possible."

"Did you hide it?"

"Yes."

"And you don't want to retrieve it?"

"No."

"I understand. Gabby, Renaye is in the same hotel. Listen, tell him I'll send someone else down to the room to complete his session."

"Hold on. No, he wants me. *Jack Ruby*." This was our code word for trouble.

"Gabby, you have to hit the door. Renaye is in room 160, and I'm ringing her room on my other line now. Hold on." I placed her on hold and called Renaye's room.

"Renaye, go get Gabby in Room 180, Jack Ruby." I went back to Gabby's line before she could respond.

"Gabby, she's on her way. Hit the door and call from Renaye's. He's not a maniac or you'd know by now. When you leave, he will, too. Trust me. I'll send someone to clean up your room."

"Okay."

"I'm sending the driver for you both and I'll move you to another place. Gabby, are you ready?"

"Yes."

"Hit the door now!" I screamed at the top of my lungs.

The phone fell and I heard yelling. "Please, God, protect her."

Ring . . . ring.

"Carmen, you paged me?" the driver asked anxiously.

"Yes, go get Renaye and Gabby ASAP! It's a Jack Ruby. They're at the Cross Country Inn. Take them to the Hampton Inn, get them settled and call me."

"No problem."

Ring . . . ring.

"Hello?" When I answered the phone, there was silence on the other end. The silence was finally broken with hard breathing. "Carmen, this is Renaye. I got her," she said, out of breath.

"Good, girls, hold on. Renaye, you pack up your stuff. The driver is on his way to move you. Be ready! Call me."

"We will."

Ring . . . ring.

"Hello, may I help you?"

"I want my money back!" an angry male voice yelled.

"We tried that and you did not cooperate. Use another service." I furiously slammed down the phone.

Ring . . . ring.

"Hello, may I help you?"

"Bitch!" Click!

Just another day on those phones. This kind of thing was happening more often. It made me think about getting out of the business. That was a close call for Gabby.

I thanked God for keeping Gabby safe.

Five

$\mathcal{I}$ found a luxurious condo to rent on the northwest side of the city. I had always admired it when I drove past it and I told myself that one day I would live there. "One day" finally came when there was a sign out front that read: FOR RENT. This was rare, because in that area, condos sold well and were seldom rented.

I called the number listed on the sign and prayed that nobody had inquired about the property. I met with the property management office within the hour, went on a tour and, after the customary credit and reference checks, I moved in within two weeks. The unit included two master bedrooms, a sunken living room with a wood-burning fireplace and a gourmet kitchen. It had a finished basement with a washer and dryer. It was just what I wanted.

The apartment received lots of sunlight, gleaming through skylights throughout the condo. Emerald green plush carpet cushioned my feet in the front room. White marble tile led me to my enclosed patio with French doors. It wasn't bad, not bad at all for a come-up.

T-Love was staying with me as he usually did when

he was in town hustling. We were in my den when he approached me.

"Pammy, this guy I do business with is gonna stop by."

"What do you mean 'stop by'? T, this is my *home*. My
son is here."

"Calm down, he's good people," T told me reassuringly,
"and it's too late to stop it; he's on his way."

"Shit, T, damn!" I guess I had to let T-Love have his
way. Eventually, I knew he'd come off of a favor or two for
me, so I decided to let it go and roll with the flow. We were
like brother and sister, arguing, sharing secrets and playing
cards late at night, talking shit. I knew he wouldn't put me
or my son in any type of danger.

I was upstairs getting dressed when I heard the chime of
my doorbell. I heard T-Love let someone in. Moments later,
I heard my son's laughter. I came downstairs, and that's
when I saw *him* playing with my son. My son was laughing
like he only did with me. The guy was very handsome—
tall, thick and tempting. His presence reminded me of
Chino—the way he stood, self-assured with his shoulders
back. He commanded attention. I observed his interaction
with T and my son. When he spoke, he looked them in the
face. That's how my Chino was, a dead-in-the-eye kinda
guy. The shape of his lips had a look of softness and made
me imagine the feel of them on the sides of my neck. He
was shifting his weight back and forth from one leg to the
other, just like Chino, giving you the impression that he
was impatient or ready to go somewhere. I wondered if his
lips hid a set of perfect teeth like Chino had.

"Out? Please, Chino, don't leave, you just came home." I ran to block his exit but he pushed me aside.

Grimacing, he said, "Every time I look at you I think of you and Erik."

"Chino, please—"

"Out of all the niggas in the city, why you need him for a friend when I was doing my bid?"

"What are you talking about?

"You know what I'm talking about!" He grabbed my forearm.

"No, I don't, Chino! I didn't have any friends because you wouldn't allow it," I yelled at him. "When you were away, he was just someone to talk to." Tears began to well up in my eyes from the pain his words inflicted. This was not like us, not how we related to each other.

Chino tightened his grip on my arm and continued, "Fuck that! Did you think I wasn't getting out? You were supposed to stick to my program and wait. Did you think I wouldn't find out that you was fuckin' that nigga? You just like the rest of these gold-diggin'-ass bitches. Pooh, you will not get another dime. You've played yourself. I do more for you than you can do for yourself. I taught you finesse. I clothe you. I take care of you. I made you. Look at those jewels on your fingers—I put them there. Look at this house—you can't even pay the damn light bill, let alone the phone bill. Bitch, I put you in this place. If it wasn't for me, where would you be?"

Those words cut deeply into my heart . . . into my soul. Chino had never called me out of my name. He knew I was a *virgin when we met and that I had never been with anyone but him. What type of shit was he on?*

"How in the fuck can you say some simple shit like that? I've never been with anyone but you. Can you say the same? Chino, you went to prison, and I was left out here all alone. None of your crew would help me. And muthafucka, you came home from the penitentiary with everything that you left with. Not one lock was changed, not one phone number changed, your clothes hangin' where you left them. I put your precious cars in storage, visited you twice a week. You came home to all your loot. Every stashed dime. Nigga, what? I kept money on your books. I sent clothing and food boxes in your name and any other nigga's name you gave me. I accepted the collect calls and made three-way calls for you and all them other sorry-ass niggas you met up in there.

"Why are you doing this to us? Chino, I need you. Erik was just my friend. You know we went to school together—"

Cutting off my words, he pressed harder to get past me. "Pooh, that nigga getting money in the streets just like me, and you should not have been fuckin' with him like that. Save that drama for your momma. Them tears is because your ass is cut off. You on your own. I can't take it anymore." Then Chino looked me dead in the eye and delivered the final blow. "Besides, I'm in love with someone else."

Chino's insistence to leave and my resistance to let him go stopped. His words brought silence to our home. We both stood up straight, as if a drill sergeant yelled "Attention." The words sobered my mind, and I really looked at Chino for the first time that night and noticed hickeys on the side of his neck and the exposed part of his chest. My mind drew a blank as I felt the blood rush to my face. I wanted to rip his pants off and examine his dick, but the truth was obvious. He had been fuckin' someone else.

"What, Chino? What did you say?" He didn't repeat himself, so I did it for him. "You said you're in love with someone else?" Again, he said nothing. I raised my hand and smacked the shit out of him.

———

At the sight of him, there was a flutter in my heart. It was surprising because I thought my heart was frozen.

"Hi. My name is Delano." His eyes roamed my body from head to toe. Delano began looking into my eyes until I could not hold the stare any longer. I was feeling extremely self-conscious, because I wanted to be as attractive to him as he was to me. Blushing inside, I felt as though I were standing before him in the nude. I began to tingle inside, anticipating whatever words were about to come out of his mouth. With my heart beating faster than an addict's after a hit, I believed that God has placed before me the man of my dreams.

T-Love eagerly said, "And this is Carmen."

"Hi. Umm . . . T, I need to talk to you. It's really important."

"A'ight, no problem. Me and my boys gonna crash in the family room for a couple of days."

"I need to go get my hair done," I told him. "Can you watch the baby?"

"The baby?" He turned, looking at me with surprise.

He was about to get put out. "Yes, the baby!"

"Uh, how long?" T asked irritably.

"Four hours max." I held my hands as if in prayer.

"Well, that's cool. Me and lil' man will watch the Playboy channel."

"No way!" I was worried that T-Love would be irresponsible with my son. He must have seen the concern on my face.

"Nah, we'll take a nap." T smirked as he looked over at Delano. "Can you drop Carmen off?" T-Love, continuing to control the room, then turned to me. "Carmen, I might need to make a run, so I'll take the baby with me."

"What type of run with my son?" I did the sister-girl routine and placed my hands on my hips.

"No, it's not what you think. I had something made by a jeweler for my wife the last time I was here. It's supposed to be ready, so I may just have to run and pick it up. So, D, can you give Carmen a ride?"

D and I both looked surprised, but Delano casually said, "Sure. No problem."

Now, this will be interesting. We left the condo and walked over to a hooptie. *No, this nigga ain't in this shit,* I thought. It was a dingy gray color with dents on every side. The passenger door stuck as he attempted to open it gracefully. None of the tires matched, and the rims were nonexistent. It didn't look like it would get us to point B. "Don't be laughing at my car or I won't let you in," Delano said jokingly.

I thought, *Well, at least he has a sense of humor.* I had

gotten to the point of trying to find anything to amuse myself. Most days I laughed to keep from crying. I hated the streets, the constant lies and mind games. You could never forget that your life was in danger all the time. I was making some money, but it wasn't enough to be out of skid row's reach. I had to keep stackin' dollars. I didn't want to get hurt out there in the game. And I couldn't imagine life without my son or doing time behind bars. Noticing the manicured lawns that covered my neighborhood, I had the urge to knock on the doors of these homes and ask the question, "What do y'all do for a living?" or "What kind of job you gotta have to live in a place like this?"

As we rode, I thought of my Chino and realized all he went through to provide for us.

Well, many nights, Chino and I would talk and talk. He was so wise and would use stories and parables to teach me life lessons. One of the many memorable stories that he shared with me was about the loss of a friendship. Chino was around eight or nine and was playing with a kid from a financially secure family. During one of his playtime visits, Chino decided to take something from the home that didn't belong to him. As a punishment, the parents of the kid forbade him from playing with Chino. Chino related how painful this was for him and how his actions were definitely not worth the loss of his friend.

His lesson was that you have to weigh the consequences of your actions. Nothing is worth the loss of a true friendship. I also was learning every day that all that glitters wasn't gold. Now I was beginning to make sacrifices and overcome the same challenges Chino faced to provide for my son. Although I was making a little money, I had to be careful because one slipup could cost me my life. I was entering another level. The same level that sealed our fate.

"Carmen . . . Carmen! You're in another world. Can I give you a penny for your thoughts?"

I snapped out of my daze. "No, I'm sorry. I was just daydreaming."

As I stared out of the small Honda window he continued, "Are you married?"

"Why?" I asked defensively. *Do you want to marry me? Did you know that I was almost married, was going to be married in two months before the drama?*

"Because I want to know if you're available."

"You're very direct."

"I believe honesty is always best, and distrust is the number one reason relationships fail."

"Well, I'm just getting a ride from you, and I *honestly* need to get my hair done."

We both laughed. Just like pieces of a puzzle, we fit so easily, like we had known each other forever. I hadn't felt this comfortable with anyone since I met Chino years ago. Delano was handsome and had beautiful eyes. They weren't beautiful because they were another color besides brown; they were beautiful because they were full of sparkle. The eyes are the windows to the soul. He was so much more than his outward appearance, and his vibe just felt right to me.

"Hey, that's a nice reggae tape," I whispered.

"Don't tell me you like reggae."

"Yes, I do."

"I know a reggae spot that's open late on Fridays and Saturdays. You want to go tonight?"

"D, it sounds good, but no thanks."

"No?"

"Yes," I looked at him with a puzzled expression on my face. "Have you not been told *no* before?"

"Yes, I have, but when it's something I want, I won't take no for an answer."

Time to change the topic. "Where are you from? You drive like a maniac."

I clutched the dented door panel as he glided around the corner with one hand on the wheel and replied, "Brooklyn."

"I knew it. You drive like a wild New Yorker."

"What do you have against New Yorkers?"

"Nothing," I said defensively.

"Do you want me to come and pick you up?" He pulled up to the curb in front of the salon and the car backfired loudly. Neither one of us said a word for a minute.

Reaching for the door, I responded, "No, I'll get a cab or call T-Love for a ride. Thanks."

"Page me when you're done."

"I'm okay, really. Thanks. Drive safely."

I gave him a wave, then dashed across the street, already twenty minutes late for my appointment. I prayed that nobody saw me get out of that death trap.

Three hours later, I was under the hair dryer reading a magazine when my hairdresser, Tiki, came over. "I think you're finished and you have a phone call." My first thoughts were of my son. T-Love would have paged me, though, if something were wrong. As I walked to the phone, I checked my pager: no messages from T.

"Hello?"

"Hi, Carmen, almost finished?"

"Who is this?"

"You know who this is. I'm on my way to pick you up, so don't call anyone." *Click!*

I couldn't believe he had the nerve to hang up on me, but it felt good to be waiting for someone to come get *me*. My hair looked great, every strand in place. I decided to put makeup on, but I changed my mind because this time around I wanted a man to accept me as I was, this time around. *If he can take me at my worst, then he will appreciate me at my best.*

Delano finally arrived, and his entrance into the salon caused collective murmurs and heads to turn in his direction. He walked over to me, admiring my hair, and said, "Carmen, you look good, girl."

The patron seated to my right leaned over and whispered into my ear, "Girl, where did you get him at? He got a brother? Is that a sock in his pants or what?"

I blushed and responded to Delano, "Thanks." I turned to my hairdresser. "Tiki, how much I owe you?"

Unexpectedly, Delano said, "Don't worry, I got ya. How much, Tiki?" In my peripheral vision, I noticed women applying lipstick and walking, no, sashaying past Delano to the magazine rack attempting to catch his eye. However, this gentleman kept his eyes on me. Tiki did a pretend calculation of my bill.

She taxed him. She charged him $95. Delano flipped out a crisp $100 bill and added a $50 bill on top of it for a tip. Tawanna, Tiki's assistant, and Tiki gave each other the eye and looked at me like, Damn, can I be you for a day?

Tiki Baytops, a hair designer from Jersey, was the best stylist in town, and she knew it. You paid for her expertise and she cut and styled your hair like no other. I even purchased the same sort of hair comb she used, trying to duplicate the style at home. Tiki styled hair with soft, flattering layers that framed your face and complemented your personal look. My appointment was standing twice a week, on Tuesday and Saturday, and I had a guaranteed three-hour wait. Insanity, but you gotta do what you gotta do.

During my wait, it was business as usual. I would sit in the reception area, telephone and notepad in hand, answering calls and arranging dates. G would come up to the shop and bring me lunch, then we would sit in the parking lot rappin' about getting money while I sported a shower cap getting my locks deep conditioned. I definitely did not do split ends, dry hair or curls out of place. G would say, "Damn, Carmen, it takes all this to look good? You need to get a fro or some damn braids. You *live* up in this piece."

Beauty is pain sometimes. But I got the absolute best fashion tips from Tawanna, who was from Detroit. During my wait, she would try to sell me something or up me on the latest styles. Tawanna would shampoo me wearing her Gucci boots and Prada jeans. She kept me laughin' while

I waited my turn in Tiki's chair. But if they smelled drug money, they upped the prices. Who could blame them? Everyone wants a piece of the pie. If D wanted to be Big Bank, then he could be Big Bank.

"Delano, thanks for my hair. You didn't have to."

"I know I didn't, but I wanted to do it. Your hair needed some help, girl." We smiled as we walked to his car. "Are you hungry?"

"Yes."

"I know where we can get some delicious food made like Mom makes it." *Wow, is he asking me out on a date? Courtship isn't dead, huh? In his presence, I feel special.*

"Now, that's good because my mom can cook. Let's go."

"They also have good music. One concern, though."

"What's that?"

"It's in the hood. Is that a problem?"

"No, just as long as I don't get shot."

"I'll protect you."

The food at Boopsey's was great and the music was good. They had a jukebox that pumped the latest in R & B. There was a row of booths for seating to the left and a bar equal in length to the right. They also had pool tables toward the rear of the building near the restrooms. It was a smoking environment, and I got a breathful of indo. The tables were equipped not only with salt and pepper shakers but with all the necessary condiments for the soul-food menu—hot sauce, mustard and ketchup. D and I played a few games of pool, and he gave me some quarters to play the jukebox. I felt like a schoolgirl on a date. He led me to our table.

"Well, you already know from my driving that I'm from New York. I'm also the proud father of two sons. They're by two different women from my younger heyday." *I knew it was too good to be true. Not one, but two baby mamas.* "I have a nice friendship with them, and I spend a lot of time with my sons. I'm single and have been for some time. I'm looking for Ms. Right. Well, not actually looking, but I asked God to bring her to me. Carmen, I see something in you that I like."

"Oh, really?" I gave him a screwed-up face and raised eyebrow.

"Yes, really, despite your attitude."

Keep your guard up and keep your heart locked.

"Life has taught me that the things worth having come with a challenge, and I'm very patient," said Delano confidently.

"How old are you?"

"Thirty."

Great, a man with a little bit of wisdom. "Well, I'm not interested in being chosen." I needed him to understand where I was coming from.

"You always talking fly. Carmen, you need to understand that I'm in the streets on a mission, but I'm not classified by baller, player—none of that stuff. So talk to me like you talk to a man because that's what I am, and in turn, I'll always talk to you like you're a woman."

"Will you stop talking so I can eat, sir?" *I don't want to like him, but I do.*

We sat, ate and talked for hours before I realized I'd

been gone from home longer than I wanted. It was my first time being out on anything close to a date since Chino and it was fun. D dropped me off at my condo. I told him I would call him, though I knew I would not. Well, I knew I didn't want to. I was on a come-up, and love wasn't in the equation.

I walked into my den a little after 9:00 p.m. and found T-Love and my son asleep. Music videos were playing low on the TV. I took my son in my arms and kissed him as I walked him to my bedroom. He never really slept in his room. We always slept together. My son was my life, my force and my motivation. For me, he represented all the good in the world. He was my blessing from God. I just wanted his life to be better and wanted to give him the best.

I went downstairs to talk business with T. I really didn't know what to say to him. Although I had been exposed to it, I knew nothing of the dope game. I knew G purchased O-Z's. That was it. I had an outlet and was determined to find a resource. That resource was T-Love. I touched his shoulder.

"T, wake up. I thought you had a date."

"Yeah, I did, but you jetted. You were gone forever."

"Well, I didn't mean to be late. Thank you again 'cause I really needed to get out."

"Watch yourself with Delano. He has a lot of women interested in him. Plus, I hear his babies' mothers are crazy."

"Don't worry. I will. It's still early if you wanted to use the Jeep to go out. Were you at least able to make some runs?"

"Yeah, but Abdullah and 'em are coming over, and I

need to be here at the house to get his page and give him directions to your new, fly-ass condo."

"T, I'm going to stay up and watch a movie. I can get his page, return the call and give them directions for you. I can wait up for them, get them settled and squared away. You leave your pager and take mine. I'll page you when they get to the house. Go out and enjoy yourself. You go back home to your wife in two days and you know you wanna get your freak on. Besides, I need to take some calls and make some money."

The more I talked, the faster he moved. All T saw was ass and all I saw was opportunity.

"Mmmmm, T," I said as I followed him around the house, "you know I'm a single mom and out there hustlin'."

"Right, right." He nodded in agreement.

"Well, I need to buy some girl. Can you help me?"

"No way!" He looked at me and shook his head in disbelief. "Keep your service."

"I need a house for my son and me."

"You living nice, you're making money. Shit, I want to leave my wife for you. What's up?" he said, smiling sheepishly.

"Yeah, silly, but I spend a lot of money, and I'm renting. I need security."

I quickly saw that I could not get any sympathy over my situation, so I went for the jugular: his pocket. "I'm talking about making real dollars." Aw! A raised eyebrow. Now I had his attention. "Listen, whatever you're movin', I can help you move double."

"I'm moving a kilo to a kilo and a half in a week, no problem," he stated proudly.

"Next week, bring me one," I pleaded.

"Umm. I need some money up front," T responded, staring me in the face.

Damn, he's sleepin' in my den, driving my Jeep, and I've never asked for anything. I was hurt and about to cry because all this time I was thinking that we were closer than that. I knew he didn't get money up front from the other people he dealt with, so why me? At that moment, I vowed to get independent, so I'd never need anyone.

My anger brought out both strength and weakness. In my strength I said, "No problem, but tax me and I'll tax your ass."

"A'ight, next week it's on, and I'll see what you can do."

With that we exchanged pagers. I handed him my car keys and waved good-bye. *Yeah, T can bounce my Jeep around town and make it hotter than a firecracker, tryin' to use me. Okay, T-Love, everyone gets a chance, and my chance is coming.* As I ended that thought, I turned my phones on and settled on my couch watching TV with my pencil and notepad. I paged some of the girls for their locations, then got down to business.

Ring . . . ring.

"Hello, may I help you? . . . Yes! Renaye is 36–24–38 . . . Outcalls are $175 . . . No problem. She'll be there in thirty minutes." I verified his number and address.

Click!

I called Renaye to set her appointment, as something

on TV caught my attention. A video by Janet Jackson had come on. It was the same song that I heard in Boopsey's when I was with Delano. I couldn't stop thinking about him, no matter how hard I tried. I paged him, even though I told myself earlier that I wouldn't.

In fifteen minutes, he called back.

"Someone call a pager?" He sounded anxious as if this were a call for a potential buy.

"Hi, it's me. You don't recognize my number?"

"No, but I recognize your voice."

"What's up?"

"I've been thinking of you," he smoothly responded with that Brooklyn accent.

"Yeah, right." I twisted the cord of the phone as I was mesmerized by his soothing voice.

"No. I really was, but hey, I'm at Boopsey's playing pool and I'm at the outside pay phone. It's cold."

"Well, I can call you later." I didn't want him to hang up the phone, but I couldn't let him know that.

"Can I come over?"

"No. I just wanted to call and say hi. Maybe we can do lunch this week. I'll call you."

"Carmen?"

"Yes?"

"Good night."

I smiled. "Good night, Delano." His Brooklyn accent sent chills up my spine, and I longed for him to be sitting beside me on the couch talking to me as I laid my head in his lap.

My phone rang.

"Hello?"

"Hi, sweetheart."

"Hey, G."

"Can you help a brother out? I'm pressed."

"Yes, it's on for next weekend. I'll see you then and we will discuss more about it."

"Thanks, C."

Now, how in the hell could I sell a kilo? More research was needed. It would all work out somehow. It had to. If not, I'd be out of my savings and on skid row again with enough coke to snort for a year. The deck was definitely stacked against me. I had come so far, and the escort and fencing were slow-roll hustles. The potential earnings thrust me into belief in the unknown. I had to take a chance and ball. The come-up is always the greatest challenge, and I loved a challenge.

"Oh, shit!" The beeping of T's pager startled me. "It's them." I'll never forget it. Abdullah and the fellas from New York—my entry into the dope game.

Six

"Hello, Infa, this is Carmen. T asked me to give you directions to my home."

"Where he at?" asked Infa.

"Where else?"

"On a booty call." We faded in like a rap group.

"You got anything to eat?"

My grocery bills alone supporting this crew were in the four figures. Damn!

"Yes. My fridge is full. Want me to fix you something?" I knew he did. They always wanted service.

"Yeah. Do dat," said Infa.

"How about some Philly cheesesteak sandwiches with onions, peppers and mushrooms with some Heinekens to wash it down?"

"Sounds good," he told me. I gave him directions and the line went dead. They were on their way.

I grabbed my cordless and went to check on the baby. I enjoyed just watching him sleep. I gave him a tender kiss on the side of his face as I traced the outline of his eyebrow, down the middle of his little nose and over his lips, where I noticed his first teeth coming in. I smelled his scent on his neck.

After going downstairs to the kitchen, I got all the items out of the fridge. I got a bowl and put some chips in it, then got some blankets, linens and pillows, and stacked them by the stairs.

I saw the lights from the kitchen window as they pulled into my garage. It felt like déjà vu because I had gone through this with Chino and all the fellas. I did the same things for them; then they turned around and cut my throat. I was not about to forget that. I told myself this go-around would be different. I would not get hurt this time, nor would I be forgotten. Carmen would make sure of this. It was all about me and stacking some dollars to buy us a new home.

For a split second, I was standing in my old kitchen, Chino's and mine. I could see a pile of tennis shoes next to the door to the garage off the kitchen. I really missed the fellas.

They would watch basketball game after basketball game. There was Rock, the athlete of the crew. Wherever you saw him, a basketball was nearby. He would dribble and talk, talk and dribble. Getting down on the court was his thing. Chris J, the tallest of the team, standing six-four, was thin, gentle and a definite follower. Ant, the model type, had good looks that only handicapped and confused him. All he wanted was some money. Cory, nerdy, reared for more out of life, chased the excitement of the streets. And my Chino, the leader of the pack. Talk about some niggas looking good ridin' five deep in a 500 SEL.

Just when I began to feel a sudden sadness inside of me, Carmen popped back in and greeted Infa at the door and took control of the night. Infa was sexy. He was half-black and half-Panamanian. His skin was smooth and cocoa brown, and his jaw was outlined by a thick, trimmed beard. His thick mustache accented his thick, kissable lips. I thought, *Ooh wee*, when I saw him. He was also married to a Spanish *mami* who would definitely kick your ass for thinkin' about her man. So I left that one alone and gave him the utmost respect because of her. All the women lusting after Infa were afraid of *mamacita*.

They came, and we kicked it, hitting the club. We arrived in a white Lincoln Navigator limo with chromed-out rims, black piping on the seats, TVs in the headrests complete with PlayStation and a fully stocked bar and fridge. We were flossin' and profiling as we pulled into the valet section for drop off. Infa handed me his nine to place in my purse to get past the security pat down. Problem was, my shoulder-strap purse was too small.

Infa started cursing. "Why in the fuck you carry such a small-ass bag? You know the drill. How am I gonna get my piece up in the spot?"

I ignored his complaints and looked at Abdullah, whose nine was now sitting in his lap as he thought about how he would get it up in the club. "Okay, my fault, but do you got beef with anyone? Y'all from Uptop, and we in Ohio. Let's just stay for a couple of hours." I convinced them it was cool. This was a new nightclub that didn't have a notorious rep for violence yet. They stashed their nines underneath the seats.

I emerged from the limo sportin' Versace white leather hip-hugging shorts and knee-high white Durango boots with three-inch heels. My matching white halter rested against my skin. The leather was so soft you had to get up close to determine if it was fabric or leather. Infa bounced from the limo wearing a black Armani suit, and Abdullah followed wearing the exact same suit, only in white. All eyes were on us as we strolled into the club giving shout-outs to people that we knew.

The Pulse nightclub was on jam. Swinging my hair from side to side and pulling it behind one ear, I sipped on my drink, listening to the music. The club was sponsoring an open mic contest, and the contestants were going for the gold, rippin' shit up on the mic. I ignored the stares from the jealous females wondering how I had it like that. I was enjoying the men's eyes glued to my backside. We were having a good time. Abdullah motioned for two nearby chicken heads to join us. He pulled out a wad of cash, and I was sure I heard one of them cluck. I looked at his wad. *I want my wad to be bigger*, I thought. *And better yet, I want it to be all mine.*

"How about some bubbly?" Abdullah motioned the bartender over.

I didn't get any play due to the fact that Infa stayed glued to my side with a mean look on his face. He called it his club look. Any interested suitor knew that to approach me was to approach Infa. He felt he didn't have time to get played anywhere, especially up in a club with an audience, so we stayed up in the place for about two hours, then began making our way to the exit. Abdullah smacked a C-note on the photo booth counter, and we began a modeling session. We clowned and hammed it up for the cameras. I gave up some booty shots, and they broke out with some penitentiary poses. I got tired of being silly and just stood on the sideline as the chicken heads joined them, allowing total strangers to cup their booties and tah-tahs. Infa even stuck his tongue down one girl's shirt. I stuffed the photos in my purse and headed for the exit.

We returned to the limo and headed downtown for dinner at Morton's. We ordered steak and lobster and drank bubbly all night. After the third bottle of Cristal, we started crackin' on T-Love and his booty-call adventures.

Abdullah got it started. "Why won't T-Love use some of that money and buy his girl a new hair weave? Or at least get it the same texture as her own hair."

I elbowed him in the side and said, "When I first saw her, I wanted to reach over and feel T-Love's forehead and take his temperature, 'cause his ass must have been near death and desperate when he picked that one out of the bunch. And you, you can't talk. Don't your girl got a weave, or do you not think that latch hook is fake?"

Infa started on me. "You the only girl I know who wraps her hair up at night so damn tight that you got lines on your forehead and have to press your face in the morning. What the fuck is a wrap anyway?"

I got an attitude and said, "Oh, please, if you dated black girls, you would know what a wrap was."

Infa responded, "It ain't enough aspirins in a bottle of Tylenol for me to date a black girl."

Abdullah took another sip and continued, "Shit, I don't see how T-Love dates LaShonn. Her damn voice is irritating."

"Playa, he ain't dating her voice, and I don't think her pussy talks back," Infa told him.

"Well, she getting paid," I confirmed. "Don't T know that they call it trickin'? How does it feel to have a brother out there trickin'?"

Abdullah spat his bubbly on the table. Infa and I both screamed, "Damn, nigga!"

He began to wipe his shirt and said, "Ms. Heidi Fleiss imitator talking about trickin'. You run an escort service. Come on, tell us, do you be doing them dates?"

I replied with a raised eyebrow, "You really wanna know, don't you?" I smiled at him. "You can't afford this." I pointed between my legs and traced his lips with butter from my little finger.

The waitress approached the table with a monster-sized dessert that Infa had dreamed up.

"What the hell is this?" I asked after she left it sitting in the middle of our table.

"Look, Wrappy." Infa chuckled. "Just eat it. You ain't never turned down chocolate."

We grabbed our forks and dug into the plate and all started nodding. "This some good shit," Abdullah said.

We closed the restaurant, and when the bill arrived, we kept passing it around and around the table like no one wanted to pay for it. Abdullah was so drunk that I slid my hands into his pants, clipped him for $300 without him noticing, and paid the tab. Infa saw every move, and we just laughed at his drunk ass. We hoisted him into the limo and headed back to my place to crash. The following morning, they were back on the road, headed home to New York. It was a fast weekend.

—

The next morning, I got my son dressed and ready for day care. I always hated saying good-bye to him, but I'd learned you had to do what you had to do, and that's just how it is. Because I was seeking knowledge, I went to the place knowledge is found: the library. I didn't want to ask anyone for anything. I got a book on weight, then read and copied all the things associated with a kilo. I learned that there are twenty-eight grams in an ounce, and I learned how many ounces are in a kilo. It wasn't difficult to figure out a big eight's amount. Then I went to a drug paraphernalia store named Cloud Nine on Cleveland Avenue and purchased a scale for about $100.

I reminded myself to stick to the rule of keeping the scale in the kitchen. Rumor in the streets said that if the po-po found a scale in the kitchen, they'd think you were weighing food with it, not drugs. I also purchased some rubber gloves and plastic baggies. Shit, Chino used to count money in gloves, his ass was so cautious. I had everything I needed—I hoped.

As I began cleaning my house to music, the pagers were buzzing off the hook. I ended up checking messages and answering phones, the usual hectic day. Hustling is very hard work. Most people don't know this. They think it's easier than working a real job, but it's not. My nerves were a wreck. The only soothing balm is the money. So I hustled harder to get more of that soothing dough. But I would soon learn that even the money came with it's own drama—muthafuckas makin' my money short.

Short money brought bullshit excuses. "See, see what I'm sayin'. I got stopped by the police, and the money was in the trunk of the car, and the police towed my car because I don't have a valid license, and when I went to pick up my car the next day, the money was gone, so I'm short, but I'm gonna make it up."

Or "I was gonna pay you, but my mom had an operation," while I knew good and well their mama died a year ago. Or a whore talkin' about, "I can't fuck 'cause I am on my period," while I knew she had a hysterectomy. Or an escort talkin' about, "I got a headache, so I can't fuck."

Then come the friends who think since you gettin' money it's okay to borrow money, knowing full well they won't repay. One time, a heroin-addicted booster stood on my front porch ringing my bell for hours in the rain until I let her in to sell her wares. There was the salesman at my favorite sound-system store, trying to upgrade my shit so his commission was higher. If you check out Pretty Toney at Mobile Electronics, his ass is the bearer of bad news: "I'm afraid to tell ya, because you own a BMW and are a drug dealer . . . oops . . . I mean, you have an expensive car, it will cost you triple to install your system."

Then there was the rival drug dealer worried about you tryin' to get their block. I wasn't interested in no blocks or territory. I wanted to sell weight and let them worry about where they sold it. I intended on being that girl. Do me, be loyal to myself and get paid.

I was a madam, or more like a "pimpadam." My criminal résumé was growing. I was a fence, and now a drug dealer. This was not how my life was supposed to be. I just sat on the floor and tried to suppress the tears as best I could. Things were going better for me financially, but I was sad inside. I missed my Chino. It wasn't supposed to be this way. Before many tears could fall, Carmen chimed in. *Snap out of it and get over it.* That voice and the ringing of the phone snapped me out of it. I suppressed the pain.

"Hello, may I help you?"

"Yes. Do you have girls who speak Greek?"

"Yes, I do." I now knew that "speak Greek" means anal sex, or the Hershey Highway, as they say. Most men like to get down like that. Responding to the caller's question, I chimed into the receiver, "They are fluent in it, and for three hundred dollars, you can be tutored." I set the appointment and told myself China's line: "Let that be the reason I get over my past."

The weekend was here before I knew it, and I was ready. T-Love arrived late Friday night, so I told G-Money I'd meet with him early Saturday at the hotel after I collected from the girls. T-Love was very anxious. He gave me my package and told me my ticket was $24,000. Twenty-four Gs. I couldn't believe it, my own bird, my own brick. I had seventeen Gs in a shoe box upstairs, but I was thinking, *Now what? I'm short, so I have to think fast. I've got to make some moves.*

I impressed T-Love with my confidence and shiny new triple-beam scale. I had practiced using it. All I knew was I had a sale for a big eight, and that four big eights equaled a half a kilo. So I could package four big eights. I weighed and measured as T watched me. I was very nervous but tried not to show it. This was my prerequisite for tomorrow's performance with G-Money. Yes, I was ready, as ready as I could get. I immediately took the conversation to one of his booty-call adventures. I was hoping he wouldn't ask for the money up front.

"So, T, when are you leaving? Sunday night or Monday morning?"

"I'm bouncing on Sunday night." He continued to watch me.

"You didn't finish telling me about your hoochie LaShonn. Why she be tryin' to pronounce her name 'LaShone' like it got an 'e' on the end? Like her shit is French or something. I call her LaShonn. Which is it? When she call, she be like, 'Tell him LaShone called.'"

T laughed. "Yeah, she be trippin' about her name. I just call them all boo. You can't never go wrong with 'boo' or 'shorty' because it's easy to remember and you won't be mixin' their names up. Every girl I date is shorter than I am, and everyone is a boo, but they all chicken heads. But

LaShonn got something special. She's not as pretty as my wife, or as intelligent, but I kick it with her because of how I feel when I'm with her. LaShonn swallows, if you know what I mean, and wears some sexy-ass lingerie. Have you ever seen those bras that got the nipples exposed? She rocks those joints," he announced, fidgeting with his jean outfit, smoothing the jacket as he laid it on the couch.

T-Love wore jean outfits every day of the week with matching Timbs. He was the type of brother who sent his jean outfits to the cleaners after wearing them one time as if they were business suits.

"Well, I'll have everything together by Sunday."

"No problem. I've given you the very best flakes so your custies will be pleased. Curiosity killed the cat, but satisfaction brings them back all the time. As China would say, 'Let that be the reason.'" Our eyes met and we laughed together. The friendship was restored.

"I need to use your Jeep. Every time we ride around in the rental car with those New York plates on it, we get pulled over."

"I understand, T, I got you. I know one slip is a prison bid waitin' to happen."

"C, give China a call. I feel like eating some Chinese tonight."

"You are so nasty." I laughed. "China will be glad to see you. She said you're a good tipper. That'll be two bills. I'll take it off my twenty-four-grand ticket."

"No problem. I'm going upstairs to take a shower."

I called G and told him to have the boosters get me

some fly men's gear and that I'd take it off *his* ticket the following week.

"G, one favor deserves another," I pleaded into the phone.

"Carmen, it better be worth it."

"And you know it will be, man. Hook me up. I need it tomorrow. You bring yours to the table and I'll bring mine."

"Okay let—"

I cut G off before he could continue and completed his line. "I know—let that be the reason. Bye."

I packaged everything and went to sleep. I said a prayer. "God, direct my paths and forgive me. Watch over my son and protect me."

The following morning I told the girls I needed to use the hotel that night. I had rented a town house suite at the Residence Inn. It had an upstairs and downstairs, two full baths, fireplace and kitchen, a bedroom upstairs and one downstairs, both with large TVs, VCRs and cable. Damn, this place was nice. Perfect for setting a comfortable atmosphere. After all, in the streets you never take people to the place you rest your head.

I brought my clothes and I took a long bubble bath to kill time. I decided to wear a beautiful white linen Armani pantsuit. Chino had purchased it for me. It was another "just because" gift. He had it custom-tailored by his personal tailor, Stephano, who had a shop on High Street. There is something about a woman in a tailored pantsuit.

The fabric rested against my cocoa brown skin, hugged my waistline and accentuated my hips.

I was nervous. It was six o'clock, and T-Love wouldn't miss me until later. G finally paged me. This meant he was ready for the sale. My first drug sale. I called him and told him to come on through. I had his package all prepared. The dope looked great. This really was some high-quality girl. I had two big eights with me and still hadn't figured out what to do with the rest of the kilo I had talked myself into. Anyway, there was the bell, so out of the corner I went. I took a deep breath and opened the door.

"Hey, G. Want a drink?" I said, smiling.

"Sweetheart, you look fabulous. This spot is tight." He looked around.

"Yeah, yeah, let's do this. I'm expecting others and my schedule is tight tonight." I focused on being calm and not exposing myself as a novice drug dealer.

"I thought all this was for me, for us."

"Well, it's not, so come on." I pulled out the package and his eyes widened at the sight of the chunks.

"Damn, C, I always get shake, you know, powder. This is lovely."

"I'm glad you like it." Next, he pulled out the money, and I began to count. I still didn't know the price, but I counted $3,800 for four and a half ounces. I took the money and prayed this was the going rate. I was so relieved it was over, I rushed G out the door. He hesitated before exiting and asked, "Sweetheart, is there more of this?"

"Yes."

Nodding his head in approval he said, "I may be back."

"Just page me." With that, he turned to leave. I sat down and poured myself a glass of wine. I did it! I did it! If only my Chino could see me. A small tear fell from my eye. I quickly wiped it away, and I went for my pen and paper to do the math. *Okay, I can get $15,200 for half a kilo, and for a kilo I can get $30,400. With me paying $24,000 for it, that's a $6,000 profit. Great! I can do this.*

Forty-five minutes later I got a page. *Beep . . . Beep . . . Beep.* It was G paging me again. "What's up, G?" I confidently whispered into the phone.

"C, it's great, baby. It's nothing but 'butter.' I'll see you in five minutes."

He came back and got some more. This was perfect.

My client Terrance and his wife, Tasha, wanted a lil' somethin'—an ounce. They were faithful customers of the escort service. They gave me $1,000 for an ounce—unbelievable. T had always said the prices in Ohio were sweet. I could see that. Later, I got a page from Tasha and Terrance. I returned their call, and Tasha answered on the first ring.

"Yeah, C, there's a lil' problem. Let's meet at Damon's for a drink."

"Okay. In fifteen minutes," I said. Hanging up the phone, I paced back and forth, feeling some of my nervousness leaving. I regretted not learning more of the drug game from Chino. Then I would know how to handle this and not just have gut feeling to rely on. Shit!

What am I getting myself into? How do you know if the drugs are real? I know Chino used a tester from time to time.

A tester is someone who is an addict, and they sample the dealer's purchases for them to test the quality. There were heroin testers whom one could hire for a sample; they would shoot up a sample to tell if it was good or not. They welcomed the thought of a near-lethal overdose of something strong, which had no cut on it. If a heroin addict read in the newspaper about a person being found dead from an overdose, the first question they'd ask was, "Where did he cop at?"

There were also cocaine samplers who gave a firsthand count on the quality of the coca. I was winging it, and hopefully not so much that I'd gotten myself into trouble. Getting myself together, I took a sip of water and left the room, walking at a slow pace trying to keep calm.

Damon's Grill was directly behind the hotel. I decided to front G two more big eights since he had paid me for two. This way, half the kilo would be gone. I paged G and invited him to meet me at Damon's ASAP. I went through the back parking lot leading to Damon's. It was a beautiful summer night. Not too hot, not too cold, and I was enjoying the walk. Tasha arrived first.

"Carmen, smooches," she said, giving me play kisses on both cheeks.

"What's up?" I said, backing from her embrace and trying to read her expression.

"What are you drinking?" She waved the bartender over.

"Kahlúa and Cream. Is there something wrong?"

"Well, yes and no."

Oh shit! Was it real dope? I didn't test it.

Climbing up on the bar stool, I replied, "Yeah, let's talk. What's up?"

"Carmen, it's too strong. It's making our noses bleed. We didn't want to try and cut it ourselves because we don't know what to use. We've heard of using baking soda, but we don't want to mess this up."

Now what should I do? I don't know what to use. I don't know how to cut this stuff. I'd learned in my research that powder cocaine was most often cut with acetone to either stretch its volume or dilute the potency without changing the texture, whereas baking soda was generally used in rocking up cocaine. But due to our collective ignorance, I elected to advise Tasha to cut the powder with just a little baking soda.

"Well, just use a little."

"We did, Carmen, and we are still high behind it. Terrance will probably be dead by the time I get back home."

"Please, don't say that." I placed my hand to my chest.

"No, he's okay. He has one of his friends over."

I am going to silk it. "It's like this, Tasha, I don't cut my packages. I don't deal like that. So I honestly don't know about cutting. I give it like I get it. I like quality. Ask Terrance about my quality." I winked at Tasha, and she gave me her dentured grin.

"C, that's why we like you so much," she replied after gulping her drink.

"But I'm meeting someone, and I can ask him what he uses, if you want."

"Yes, please. Terrance will wait. I'll finish my drink 'cause I want to get my snort on. Let that be the reason I wait."

That damn China got everyone saying that line. China had seen Tasha and her husband the night before. Tasha and Terrance had a great relationship. They did everything together. I guess that was why they'd been able to make it work for eighteen years. That's what I'm looking for, an everlasting love. We noticed G-Money walking toward the bar.

"Hi, sweetheart." G reached to hold my hand and I raised my hand to introduce them to each other.

"Hi, G. G, this is Tasha."

G reached down and kissed her hand. He was such a flirt.

"Tasha, excuse me," I said, and G followed me over to the phone area.

"G, I've got a lot of running to do. I want to leave you with nine ounces, and you work it during the weekend. This way, you'll be covered. I promised I'd do all I can to help you. So I'm trusting you."

G gave me a big hug and said, "C, I won't let you down." I could tell he appreciated it. I was not certain on the "let me down" part. I knew men were not reliable. I also knew G had been through some problems in the street. Plus, he'd recently gotten out of jail. He was doing everything he could to make it, and in this way we were very similar. Nevertheless, I just didn't trust his ass. I didn't trust anyone anymore. Shit! I didn't even trust the weatherman; I always kept an umbrella in my car.

"G, my associate Tasha snorted her purchase, and she said it's too strong. It makes her nose bleed and I don't cut my packages."

"C, your package is straight. When I rock it, it comes back even more. My pager is blowing up over this. Don't start cutting it, please. Tell her she can go to Cloud Nine. They have all sorts of stuff to cut with there. She can try baking soda, but it will mess her nose up. I have some one-hundred-dollar packs of powder of some old, weak bullshit that ole boy gave me. It may be good for snorting."

"G, check this out, I'll turn you on to her." *Good. I won't have to see her for ounces. I'm not about to start selling O-Z's.* "I'll turn you on, but you gotta treat her right. Tasha is good people."

"Great! I'll take care of her. I'm trying to get paid."

I gave him a wink, then we walked back to the bar.

"Tasha, G can take care of your needs. I'll let y'all talk. I've gotta go."

"Wait, Carmen, I want to ask you something." Tasha was whispering in my ear. "Is he with your service?"

"No. He'll probably do you for free, but probably not your husband."

"You know we do everything together. Terrance wants what I want."

I just laughed and whispered, "Good luck." Then I turned to G and asked, "G, you got my tab?"

"Of course, C. Good-bye."

I looked over my shoulder and saw they were getting along great.

My Jeep's clock read 9:30 p.m. Time to go home. I had to get T's money together by Sunday night. I hoped his booty call lasted for another night, but I was living for today, and today I was all right. After all, it gets greater later. I was at the bottom, but I was also on a come-up. I popped in a Sherry Winston CD, and I knew I would somehow be fine. Nothing on my mind but my son and our new life. Safe in a suburban home, streets lined with mature trees and me greeting his school bus at the corner. Dreams can come true.

Seven

Sunday morning and there was still no sign of T-Love. Different scenarios were racing through my head. Was he hurt, did someone jump him or worse . . . did his wife make another surprise visit? I shook my head to clear the last thought. *Well, while the baby is sleeping, I might as well do my usual Sunday errands.* My son fell asleep. I placed him in his car seat and decided to go to the grocery store since I had some money. I was gonna splurge and purchase some red snapper. It seemed like just yesterday I was preparing some for Chino and the fellas.

Yeah, that was the first meal I prepared for him and Joe Bub. Old Joe Bub Baby, standing six feet even, with brown skin, a large nose and a dazzling smile. Clothing was this man's best friend. If you looked in the dictionary under "dapper," he would be standing there, suited in Armani with a cane, smiling and smelling like Cool Water cologne. He was Chino's first partner back in the day, but they fell out over some bullshit. The same old shit we all promised on our lives that we'd never fall out over.

Damn, Chino, why we gotta hate each other? Forget it! I'll pass on the snapper and take my boo to Chuck E. Cheese. He'd really love that, and so would I. Forget red snapper. Forget Chino. And forget the memories!

My beeping pager brought me back to reality. It was G-Money paging me. I turned down the music before I called him back. *Dear God, please let it be good news.*

"Wuz up with ya, baby?" I confidently spoke into the phone.

"Hi, sweetheart. How are you?"

"I'm well, and you?"

"I'm sitting on top of the world."

"Oh, really? Do tell." I listened closely for a juicy come-up story.

"Well, not yet, but I will be. For real, though, I need to see you."

"Well, today is Sunday, and you know what that means."

"Yes. You and your boo will be together."

"Exactly."

"But this is really important."

I paused for a moment and wondered what was so important that it couldn't wait until tomorrow. "Check this out. I'll see you at Chuck E. Cheese up north at two p.m." There was silence on the other end. "Hello?" I called out.

"You're kidding, right?" This time, there was silence on my end. "Aw, come on, C, why there?"

"G, you the one who wanna see me. You getting real comfortable, especially when you know my time goes to my son first. Don't press me, G," I warned. "Not now, not ever."

For a minute neither one of us said anything. The

silence seemed to go on forever. *Good. Screw him and any-one else. I've got enough stress. I don't need any more.*

"Okay, Carmen, you drive a hard bargain. Two o'clock it is."

"Oh, G," I called out, making sure he was still there.

"Yes, Carmen?"

"Don't page me this early again unless it's an emergency." And I hung the phone up. *I've turned into a real bitch!*

I had to come down on him like that because I couldn't be soft. Only God had my back, and He was kinda up there moving on the slow side these days. It was time to get the baby and me dressed to get some playtime in before the day got away. One o'clock and still no sign of T, and no page. He must have really been getting his freak on, and I wasn't mad at him, that's for sure. Not that weekend. I needed all the time I could get. I wondered if I should call him just to make sure everything was cool.

I decided to call him later. He had my pager number if he needed me. Besides, if he wasn't worried about this kilo I had, why should I be? I had been thinking that I really needed to get out and mix it up a bit and set some goals for this lifestyle, because I wasn't trying to do this forever. I decided to pray about it, making excuses for myself to the man upstairs.

Dear God,

When I make fifty thousand dollars, I will stop the street life totally. Just nineteen thousand short. Okay, God, I just need some things for my son and me. I mean, after Chino reached in his pocket and gave me two twenty-dollar bills for the baby, I swore I'd never need him or anyone else again in this lifetime. Piece of shit! Driving a brand-new convertible Corvette and this punk gonna give me two twenties. The sad part of it is that I took it. I needed the money. So I've got to get myself established and together.

Amen.

"Boo, we're going to Chuck E. Cheese." My son started clapping his hands, and so did I. It felt so good to be able to go out somewhere fun with him. I looked at him in his car seat as we bounced the Jeep down the street to see Mr. Chuck E. Cheese.

My son loved to play in the colorful balls there. It didn't look like too much fun to me, but the kids love it. I was tempted to get in them myself just to see what the big deal was. The children were running and screaming. Although I was sitting all by myself eating pizza and sipping on a beer, I didn't feel lonely. Actually I was very content. Money makes the stress go away.

It was time for the Chuck E. Cheese's stage show, and the kids were going nuts. Throughout their excitement, I heard all sorts of sounds coming from a variety of video games and music over the speakers. My son always wanted to run in the other room to see the big-ass rat, but when the rat came over to him, he started crying and wanted me to pick him up. I still couldn't figure that out, but I could go through it as many times as he wanted to because one day he wouldn't be afraid of the rat. One day he wouldn't even want to see the rat, or spend Sunday with his *mom*, so I knew that we'd better enjoy it together at that moment. In walked G-Money.

"Hey, G, what it be like?" I extended a 1970s handshake to him and he laughed.

"I didn't know what to expect from you, another cursing out or what."

"You know we all right. We in it to win it!" I extended my arm for some dap.

"You be acting crazy. Carmen, you won't let anyone get close to you, will you?"

"You're as close as close gets to me. What more do you want?"

"You know what I want." He gave me that supposed-to-be-sexy look, rubbing his silk shirt. He didn't know that I hated silk shirts.

"Yes, I do. Money. I do, too. So, how's it going?"

"Well, girlfriend, I have all your money, and I thought you would want it. I promised to be straight with you. I've hooked up with someone, and I'll be able to do more if you can handle it."

"You know I can, man. What is more?" I replied, feeling like a baller for the first time.

"Maybe a kilo a week."

"Good. Right, right. Let that be the reason."

G smiled, proud that he was able to do something for me.

"Check it, G, I'll need money up front or at the time of purchase."

The expression on G's face was priceless. *Yeah, nigga, that's what they told me.* "I still may be able to front occasionally, but it will go better for us both if you begin to save your money."

"The guy I used to work for wants to know if you can get some dog food?"

Swallowing the last of my slice of pizza and washing it down with cold beer, I thought about what he asked. "Maybe. Who have you been discussing me with? Who did you say you work for again, and why didn't you tell me this up front?" *Time to put the baby back in the balls.*

"Well, he doesn't know that you're female, and I never told you I worked for someone because I didn't know how to tell you."

"G, it's really none of my business. I'm just messin' with you. We all work together in the streets. Be careful because you never know who's watching. Just have your own terms and do the best you can for self. That's what I do."

"I think things can work out for us," said G.

"I think things can work out between us, but ultimately, for each other." He had that hurt look on his face. I wasn't being a partner with no one.

"I hear ya."

"Yeah, G-Money. *Solo l'uomo* is the only way to go."

"Well, Jay-Jay knows I'm seeing someone, and he wants in on the mix of things. He's really looking for a good supplier of heroin. That's his thing."

"So, tell me about your arrangement with this guy and more about him," I said.

"He and I did time together. He sold lots of drugs in the joint. He got out before a lot of us and set up things. So when I got out, along with some other guys, he gave us some work and put us on his payroll. The problem is, he won't sell to me, but he will front me, and this keeps me under his thumb. He's controlling. I know this sounds weak but, C, that is how it is when you want to be put on."

"G, baby, I understand because I've jumped through some hoops myself and still may have some more to jump through. So don't even knock yourself. I see a lot of me in you. I heard some stories about the time you did and about you working for someone else."

"So you already knew?" He looked embarrassed.

"Yes. I just waited to hear it from you. That's how I am. I've never been one for rumors."

G nodded in agreement. "I can respect that."

"Good, just save your own money because that's what makes you your own man. When you're able to pay up front and not be fronted, it becomes your shit and not the next man's.

"So, G, I really need you to be able to purchase your items. This will keep it all good between us and not place me in a position over you. I don't want you to owe me anything. We simply workin' together, trying to make our money. Besides, no man wants to answer to a woman. Money will make you fall out real fast. I'll be ballin' until I reach some personal goals, and then I'm out of this business and out of this city. Let me check on some things, and I'll decide if I want to deal with Jay-Jay. If I do, the first round will be on you. This is the only way I'll do this, and possibly your boy Jay-Jay will appreciate the favor. It may put your relationship on another level. You got the plug. He could be coming to see *you*. Imagine that.

"But listen, please don't bring me any more people or inquiries because we're not partners in this game. If you see some moves, please use some courage and faith in yourself to do some things for yourself and not for me, or through me. You know a lot of people and have a lot of opportunities for yourself. This is your city. It astonishes me how guys will let out-of-town people come into their city and take over. New York boys come in and have shit on lock."

"They got all the connects," he responded defensively.

"So what? This is still your city, and can't nobody do it better than you. Use your opportunities. You plugged in now, so get the ball and run with it. You big baller, baller." With that I punched him in the right arm to end my pep talk. I could tell that I had encouraged him. Either that or sold him a dream.

In the streets it's either one or the other. Nothing in between. I was just trying to keep off ties and keep people up off me. No time for the clingy hold-me, grab-me type bullshit.

"G, this your last free conversation. My game is sold, not told. I'll talk to you later in the week. Take care."

"Bye, C. Later."

I knew I was taking a big chance in my demands, but I refused to be looked at as just another female in the game. Even though I had been doing this for only a week, dealing with men, I had to have everything on point and had to stand firm on what I said. I realized I was doing something right when those who had been in the game longer than me followed my direction.

I said good-bye and turned my thoughts back to my son. Where was he? He was going to be worn out in those darn balls. *God, I thank you. It seems like some things are working out for me. If I can only reach my goals.*

Once I got back home and put the baby down for a nap, I noticed that there was still no sign of T-Love, but there were quite a few messages for him on the answering machine.

Beep . . . beep. China was paging me for some calls. I hadn't answered the phones since this new gig opened up. I needed to get settled and get her some calls. I needed to get all the girls some calls before I pissed them off. I knew they had been using other services since I had not been working the phones like I used to, and they needed money just like I did. They were very faithful to me, and I tried in every way to show that I appreciated them also.

Last week, Toy had gotten a little anxious because I didn't send her any calls in two days. I stopped by the hotel and gave her $300 as an incentive to hang in there with me. I didn't want her to bail, and I knew the girls liked my clients because I mixed it up, and we had fun. I'd been plugging in the ballers with the service, and it was refreshing for the girls to date some young, money-getting niggas instead of all those older white-collar workers. The other services didn't have the flavor I had. The ballers went to the titty bars 'cause they wanted to see the girl next door, but I was giving them Carmen's "girls next door"—for a small fee.

I thought I'd give Gabrielle a birthday party at the hotel the next weekend. She would be nineteen, and after all she had gone through, she really deserved to have something special. If it were not for her 44 DDs, I would have starved, and she really helped me when I needed it. I decided to work on that and call all the girls with my plans and catch up on some chitchat. I would send the driver and have him pick up the money from the previous night's calls.

The vibration of my pager interrupted my thoughts. It was T-Love, finally. I was relieved that he was okay. I began to think of the proper way to approach him before cursing him out for not calling sooner. Immediately, I called his number.

"What's up? T-Love, lover, player, big baller, baller. Nigga, where you been? I got a message from your wife on the machine and a message from her brother. He wants me to call him, said it was urgent. If you expect me to keep having yo back, you need to let me know something. This shit ain't cool, man."

"I'm sorry, I should have called." His little apology sounded sincere, so I couldn't help cutting him some slack. "I just talked to Erik and he's hot, so I need to speak with you about a few things. I'm on my way to the crib. Will you be there?"

"Yes. I'm staying put and answering some calls."

"Good. Peace!"

I also had to call my mom. We talked every week. If she

didn't hear from me, she would think something was wrong, so I called her. If my mom found out about my life, she would hit the ceiling, drop to her knees and call on Jesus. I wished I could tell my sister, Lori. Lori was my big little sis. I called her that because I got all the height in the family, and Lori was short and petite. She was six years my senior, but I still acted as if I were older. Lori would listen, but not keep my confidence. The things I was into were too deep, and she would tell our mother. Not out of betrayal, but out of wanting the best for me. Every day I stuffed one more bone into the closet. I phoned my mom, thinking about how she had had the same phone number for almost twenty years.

Ring . . . ring.

"Hello?"

"Hi, Mom."

"Hi, baby. How are you and my grandbaby?"

"We're well. We just got back from Chuck E. Cheese and he played himself to sleep."

"When will you send him up here to see me? I miss my baby. Actually, I miss both of my babies, so when can you visit, too?"

"Soon, Mom. As a matter of fact, I got some things I'm working on."

"Well, has Chino seen the baby?"

"No." The baby-and-Chino subject was my Achilles' heel. I hated to go there.

"I told you he wouldn't care where you were. A sorry-ass man is going to be sorry no matter what. He really doesn't deserve to see the baby."

"I know, Mom, but I'm just praying he'll come around and be there for him and be a father. I never dreamt in all my life that he would act like this."

Seeing the look on Chino's face after I stabbed him filled me with fear. I turned, moving just in time to get out of his reach, and ran toward the stairs leading to the lower level where the pool table was. With Chino in pursuit, I jetted toward the pool table and remembered what I had placed underneath the pillow the night before: a .380 with hollow-point bullets.

"You stupid bitch! You just made my day. Oh, now you wanna be a man? You wanna fight?" He started to act on pure adrenaline. I ran around a chair for the pool table. I thought of grabbing a pool stick, but I was afraid that he'd use it to crack me upside my head. I was dancing back and forth around the table in my bare feet, almost sliding on the ceramic tile, while he continued to rant and rave. Then suddenly he became calm and removed his shirt in order to get cool. The removal of his shirt exposed his thick frame, which held a slightly pudgy dope boy midsection from one too many good meals. My eyes watched his face, then traveled downward. In his waistband I saw the handle of a shiny black 9 mm.

Chino had never brought guns into the house. The rumors of him out in the streets wilin' were rampant. This was one of the reasons I had secretly propositioned my brother for the purchase of a small .380. I wanted to feel protected. He added the hollow points, with the premise that if I shot anyone with such a small caliber gun, I needed to take them out or they would beat my ass for not killing them. I began to plead as the look on

Chino's face announced war. "Okay, Chino, stop playing. Can we talk about this like rational adults? Damn, I'm sorry." We continued the game of chase around the pool table as he breathed harder, getting angrier by the moment that he couldn't catch me, but I'd be damned if I was going down.

My mother said, "I know, baby. No one could have told me this either, and I've been around for a long time. I'm praying that the two of you work out your differences and come to some agreement for the sake of the child. He is a beautiful baby and looks just like Chino. Like he spit him out. The child doesn't deserve this. He's caught in the middle of the problems you have with each other."

"I thought we were closer than this."

"Like my mama always told me, 'Teeth and tongue will fall out, and you can't get any closer than that.'"

"I know. I've turned it over to God. If it's meant to be, then so be it. Sooner or later, something will give. I'll either give up or he will give in to his responsibilities." At that point, I felt it might be a lost cause.

"I'm always here if you need to talk."

"I mean, I thought for sure someone in his family would have made it to the baby's first birthday party, but they didn't. If Chino is mad at me, then they all are."

"That's just the way it is with them people. But God don't like ugly, and you don't make differences over children. It's not right," my mother contributed with extreme bitterness.

"I know. His family never did try to get to the truth.

One day they loved me, the next day I was hated, and so they rejected my son. But, Mom, I thank God for my child even if nobody else does."

"Amen!" said Mom.

"And I heard it on one of those rap records that you don't like. Imagine that."

"Pammy, remember the baby isn't missing out on anything with relatives like that. Children are a blessing. They come when God tells them to come. Why can't people understand that? People love you in good times and leave in bad. That's how friends do you, but remember, I'm not your friend. I'm your mother and I'll be here until the end. You can count on me, Pammy, and you can always come home." I detected a hint of sadness in her voice.

"I believe they never cared for me and only dealt with me because of Chino. I never listened to you about that. I'm trying to do better now. See, I am growing up, Mom. I'm just trying to go on with my life, make some sense out of all I've been through and all I must go through."

"I understand. Just make sure you bend those knees and pray. God will see you through this. He never fails."

"What's for dinner?"

"I'm cooking your favorite, barbecue chicken with my special Star sauce. I got my potatah salad and some greens with a side of macaroni and cheese. Want some?"

"Yes!"

"I wish you were here. I worry about you all the time."

"I miss you, too, Mom. I'm being careful and trying to work out some internal and external issues."

"Remember to let God help. He is the Master! Have you gone past the hair salon? Who owns it now?" asked Mom.

"No, I haven't had the courage to go past the shop yet. I will one day. This guy named Ricky has it and I hear it's not the same as when I had it."

"Of course, my dear, no one can do it like you."

"Mom, you always know what to say."

"If you would only talk more, I could help you a lot more before your concerns become problems. Promise me you'll talk to me more."

"I promise that I'll try. So, what's up at work? How are your students?"

"They're fine. These kids are getting bigger every day. It must be the fast food."

"Speaking of that, the baby has more teeth and he's trying to swim in the bathtub. One day I'm going to buy him a swimming pool, and not a lil' plastic one."

"I know you'll be fine. Do you need anything?"

"No, I'm fine. T-Love just pulled into the garage."

"Oh, he's there again? Where does he work?" questioned Mom.

I didn't answer.

"Pammy, be careful. Don't get into that same messy stuff again."

"I'll call you tomorrow, okay?"

"Okay, baby. Kiss my grandson for me and yourself, too."

"I will. Mommy?"

"Yes?"

"I love you."

"I love you, too. Remember to pray."

"I will. Good night."

I heard the garage door raising, followed by the sound of the security system being disarmed. Attempts at gentle footsteps glided across my kitchen floor, but T-Love was too heavy for gentle steps. I knew the sound of his brown leather Timbs anywhere.

"Look at you. T-Love finally home. You'd better call your wife. She left three messages on the machine."

"I know. She's been blowing my pager up, but first we need to talk."

"Okay, but remember the last time you didn't call her back? She got in her car, drove all the way here from New York, caught you in the bed with that sack chaser and beat both y'all's asses." I laughed at the memory.

"Well, those days are behind me. She wasn't my wife then; she was my girlfriend. Now she's my wife and driving an Acura Legend, so she'd better sit her ass still, keep counting them dollars and take care of my son."

"So, what's up?" I asked curiously.

"Well, C, Erik doesn't want me to deal with you. He found out that we did something this week, and he's crazy mad, so we ain't gonna be able to do this drug thang. You know what I'm sayin'?"

"Oh, really?" *Stay calm.* "Erik has mo' money than God, but he wants me to starve, right? This shit is crazy. I don't understand, especially because I've got your money."

"I don't understand either, but he just feels like I shouldn't sell to you. Why can't you go to Chino? He's in the same game."

"You know why I can't go to Chino. I went to him for help and couldn't get it, so you think he's gonna give me some dope? Been there, done that with him and I ain't goin' back."

"I don't know what else to say, Carmen."

"So now you wanna dump me, too?"

"Erik thinks you're getting it for Chino."

"Oh, yeah, right. One kilo? What is Chino going to do with that? Erik hates Chino just as much as, if not more than, Chino hates him over that fake affair he accused Erik and me of having. Look, I've got to take care of myself. No one is helping me—not you, not Erik, not Chino. So I must help myself, and that's what I'm doing!"

"I know, but Erik said no!"

"So, is that what this is? Fuck me? Take your money and your shit and get the fuck out! I'm not gonna beg your fake ass! As a matter of fact, give me some money since I can't work for it."

Silently, T just stood in place, unable to look me in the face. He stared at the walls, then the kitchen floor. Here I was ballin' for mines. He knew I had no one, and now he was turning his back on me. Just when I had begun to trust again. Just when I had begun to think things could be different, this shit happens.

"That's what I thought. Fuck you! I'm an entrepreneur, and I'll survive all of this shit! Trust and believe."

Eight

$\mathcal{I}$ ran to my room and started crying. All I saw was opportunity going down the drain, and that was when Carmen kicked in.

Look, dry those fuckin' tears. He ain't the only store in town. You gotta campaign, not complain. What's really the deal? Obviously, T ain't his own man, but Erik is. So fuck it, go kick it. Money talks and bullshit walks. Go spit it at him. This ain't nothing but an illusion.

I rose from my bed, dried my tears and got his money together. He was in the basement watching videos when I said, "Okay, T, here's your money, and thanks for everything. When you get your own connect or become self-sufficient, then I'm here to deal with you, but until then, I'm getting my serve on, with or without you. You ain't bringing no drugs or flopping on my couch no more either. I'm all for self, and actually, I've got work to do. I've still got my phones. Who needs Erik?"

I just made his fat ass money, probably twenty grand more than he had, and that had to be worth something. In the streets, money is worth everything. I knew there was no use in calling Erik. He was a Taurus just like Chino—stubborn as hell. They were so much alike, and I knew once his mind was made up, that was all there was to it.

Erik believed that one day Chino would come around and help me with the baby. I too believed that shit, but after a year of no help, I was seeing him for what he was worth. The nigga shitted on me and I was on my own. While Chino was driving around sporting the latest in everything, I still had nothing but what I gave myself. Nobody could pay me like I paid myself, and I liked paying myself. So I wouldn't try to call Erik, but I *would* try to work T-Love.

See, Erik came to Columbus from New York for school as an engineering major. He more or less pioneered this area with the New York trade, and the same custies that T now had, were once Erik's. While Erik was in New York with the connect, he sent T down here to keep the hustle going. T didn't have his own customers, neither did he have the plug. He more or less worked for Erik, and all the money T made was split with Erik because of what Erik had established. If you look and listen, you learn a lot. Not to mention if you get played the way I did, you learn even more. I knew what time it was. I just needed T to know he could be his own man if he wasn't so fucking lazy and content with being the middleman. So I figured I'd take a chance on some convo. The way I saw it, they were trying to dismiss me, so I might as well give them something to dismiss me for.

I sat next to him on the sofa and calmly said, "Okay, T, check it. I know you share custies with Erik, but I can be *your* new custie and give you an opportunity to make money on your own. I can do more. In fact, I need some heroin, too. A couple ounces of it."

He sat up and I continued, "Yeah, I know all about your clients and how y'all got them and what's what. You can keep tearing off Erik, but tear yourself off on some things you put together. Would you like something to eat?"

"Yeah," he responded eagerly. *Look at him rubbing that stomach of his.* "Come on, let's go into the kitchen to talk." *I will not be cut off.* "Let me fix you something while we talk about this." *At least I've got his attention.*

"C, you trying to get me cut off?" he asked, opening the cookie jar filled with chocolate cookies. "Erik said *no*, and I can't get cut off." I poured him a glass of milk so he wouldn't choke. T popped the miniature cookies into his mouth.

"How he gonna cut you off? That's your partner."

"I know, but you don't really understand."

"Well, explain it to me, and make me understand how it really is. Don't you know the connect?"

"Yeah, but Erik mostly deals with him." He spoke like a scared kid who wanted no part of that adult responsibility.

"Well, all you have to do is talk to Erik. I'm not saying to cut his throat; all I'm saying is that I need money and so do you. That's why you out here, right? And I feel you owe me that effort. Talk to Erik." I looked directly at him. "For me. You know I can't talk to him. You know how he feels about me and the streets. He don't want me in them."

During Chino's incarceration, Erik and I spent time

talking about the streets, and he was sympathetic to Chino's imprisonment. He understood it to be a price you paid in the game, but he couldn't understand my willingness to wait on a nigga behind bars. He constantly tried to get me to leave Chino, saying things like, "You too pretty to struggle. Another nigga can pay your bills just like he was." He couldn't see that Chino was not just a nigga paying my bills; he was my friend, my first love, and I would wait on him for as long as it took. I resisted his advances, even though I enjoyed hanging out with him, but he definitely didn't want me in the streets. He wanted more for me.

I kept trying to convince T-Love by adding, "I can move more dope and I need a connect. If not, take me to New York with you, give me my own plug." I didn't fully understand what I was saying, but I was desperate and willing to try anything. "Now eat." I put a T-bone steak and fries in front of him. "Here's a nice cold beer, too. Count your money . . . all of it." I leaned against the breakfast bar. "How did you explain the extra kilo?"

He looked startled.

"Ahh." I said when T was speechless. "I understand. Why can't it be a secret between us? Okay? Also, call your wife and give her my love. I never tell Erik about any of your booty calls, so why tell him any of my business?"

T-Love knew two things damn well, and they were: one, not to mess with Erik's money; and two, not to fuck around on his sister Deidre. Erik had hated him dating his sister because of how loose he was with his dick. But against Erik's wishes and warnings, his sister fell in love with T. Blind love; she couldn't see shit and hear nobody but T-Love. Now I had his attention, taking the fight out of a now weak argument.

"But Erik knows how much of them thangs I get."

I got confident and said, "Well, tell him whatever. But T, I don't want to see you again without two kilos for myself and an ounce of your best heroin. Perhaps LaShonn would like to come over for a movie. Maybe you should take that extra money, go to the mall and get her a gift. I can go for you." I folded my arms and gave him a wink with a sly smile. Then I showed a little cleavage and whispered, "T, baby, we can do this."

He gave me five grand and told me to spend it on that bitch. I knew it. He really liked that girl, and people always love it when they have someone to be deceitful with.

I ran to the mall around 8:00 p.m., rushing against closing time to a store called Diamonds, Pearls & Jade. I talked with my favorite jeweler, the same one who crafted the beautiful engagement ring Chino got for me. I saw the perfect gift for Ms. Bitch—a lovely tennis bracelet made up of solitaire and baguette diamonds with a beautiful clasp. The ticket was about four grand, so I gave the jeweler $3,500, had them gift wrap it and signed a card for T-Love. I only wanted to give her some earrings, but sack chasers always want a tennis bracelet. It was a status symbol for them.

The gift was beautiful, and I was keeping the change.

On my way home, I also got some flowers for his girl. I could spare $35 for some roses. *One day someone will buy some for me. If not, I'll buy them for myself. Yes, I'll lace my home with flowers in every room. I can look around and remember that I got love for myself.*

Rushing home, I tried to beat an amber-colored light, but thought against it. "Shit!" I said as I applied my brakes, hoping no policemen were around. The last thing I needed was to get stopped by the police over some stupid shit. I glanced over and saw the gift resting on my leather passenger seat. It was like déjà vu. The wrapping looked exactly like what had been on my engagement ring from Chino.

I was so surprised and happy to get engaged. It was not really a proposal because we always claimed each other as husband and wife. It was more like the final touches to our relationship. He'd kept saying, "I don't have the money to get a ring yet."

Not that I ever pressed him, and we rarely discussed it. The only time we ever talked about it was when I was visiting him at Orient prison on his first drug dealing bid—on the visiting forms, I had to check the box marked FRIEND all the time. He said, "Pooh, that's crazy. You coming up in here as my friend. You're my wife, and I'm sorry I put you through all this, but I realize you really love me, and as soon as I get out, we're getting married. I promise."

"Chino, whatever you want is fine with me. Besides, we have to really budget our money. This trip to the pen almost made us fold."

"Ain't no folding with us," he told me assuringly. "We got love on our side, so it will be all right."

And somehow it always was. We didn't lose anything. We thought of selling the salon but decided against it. Even though times had gotten really rough, I hired more staff, and customers kept pouring in. The salon really began to boom and do very well. We lived by faith, not by sight. Just keep on going and striving.

Honk honk! The loud honking of an irritated motorist snapped me out of my daydreaming.

When I arrived home, I found T and the baby playing and having fun. He decided to give him a bath for me, which I really appreciated. T was all right. It's just that the streets will change people. I knew they had changed me a lot, and the influences I'd been around had really done some lasting things to me and affected my life in profound ways.

"Carmen, I love this wrapping paper," T said as he fondled and admired the gift.

"Thank you. Your girl will love it."

"What is it?" He began to toss it up in the air.

"I won't tell you. You both will be surprised. Here, I'll finish up with the baby while you get ready for your date."

I knelt down next to the tub and began to lift the bubbles from the tub with my hands and blow them into my son's face. At first, he cringed and waved me away, but when one of the bubbles popped on his cheek, he began to smile. T-Love looked through his jeans pocket. There he go with another jean outfit. This one was gray, black and white, with matching Timbs.

"I have some last-minute errands I need to run, or could you help me out like you did last time?" he asked. "I need you to get some money for me from Delano and Paul-P. You remember P?"

"Yeah, I remember him from when Erik was up here last summer."

"Well, if you could do that, then I could go out."

"I can do it first thing in the morning because I'm in for the evening. I'll page the fellas and arrange something with them."

"Cool," T said. Truth was, T was a lazy muthafucka. Anything goes as long as he doesn't have to do it. "Also, I'm throwing Gabrielle a birthday party."

"Who?" he asked, like he had never heard of her.

"Your favorite, Gabrielle."

"The one with the big titties?" He began to lick his lips.

"Yeah, that's her. She'll be nineteen, and I want you to invite some of your fellas. My service could use the business, and we could mix it up a little. Sort of a toast to our new business venture. Besides, I want it to be nice for her. I'm gonna invite Delano, Paul and his boys, if that's cool. I'm renting the party house at this one spot and making it like a pool party and cookout with music. We just gonna get fly. Bring your wife down here so she won't get too mad about things. I need you to go back to New York and arrange things. You need to keep everyone happy so we can get down."

"I will, but if I start bringing kilos down here like that, I gotta do something different. I can't bring them in the trunk. It's too hot. But old dude that we see has these vans with hidden compartments and shit."

"Maybe we can hook up with him and start using his vans. If you start moving things and let *me* spit it at him, then he will. Yo, T, bring him to Columbus. Bring him to the party this weekend, and I'll talk to him. Bring Erik, and I'll talk to him, too. Or better yet, if you hook it up, I can go to New York for the day on Wednesday and talk to whomever." With every word, my fingers were crossed.

"I don't know." T spoke cautiously. "Erik said you were very manipulative and not to really mess with you. He ain't stupid, he knows Chino has schooled you."

"T, life has schooled me. Chino taught me a lot, but not too much about the streets. He taught me about people, and I'm not trying to take anything from you. I'm just trying to make some money. You got the plug, so let that be the reason we get paid."

"Is China gonna be at the party?" He moved his hands down to his pants and started rubbing his dick right in front of me. Nasty bastard. I ignored him and started polishing my toenails with my favorite cotton candy pink polish thinking, *Horny-ass nigga.* The service just well may be easier than slangin' them thangs.

"You know she would never miss it," I said.

"Bet! Carmen, this shit just might work."

"T, I know it can. If only you just believe and have some faith in yourself and in what we're doing. Look how far faith has brought me."

"You've got a point, because we've seen you have everything, then go straight to nothing. Now you on the come-up again."

"That's right, T. Maya said it best: 'Like dust, I'll rise.' It always gets greater later." My son is the reason why I've got to get mines and move out. Ain't no man gonna do it for me, and ain't no man gonna ever again take anything back from me that he gave. Been there, done that shit, and I ain't even interested no more. Now, go on and get changed. I'll take care of Delano and Paul tomorrow. I'll spit some words at them, then give you a total to take back to New York. T, have a nice night."

"C, I sure will. Peace."

Nine

$\mathcal{I}$ woke up early Monday morning with my mission on my mind. I'd been listening to rap music more and more since I started hustling. It motivated me, because it was talking about things close to home—the struggle, the streets, death and loss. Those who couldn't relate knew nothing of the streets. It was good to know hustlers weren't alone. Unlike how the media portrayed rap music, it didn't hype us to kill. What it did do was motivate us to keep on keepin' on. The shit was real when Tupac said, "keep ya head up" and "trying to make a dollar out of fifteen cents." When I heard the *Above the Rim* soundtrack, it seemed to play out my life. Rap was the grim reality, no matter how you looked at it.

Now, there was the new-school rap and the old-school rap. Some of those rappers were kickin' straight knowledge, and some was straight bullshit. Like Ice Cube, he was my boy. His rap was almost a form of gospel because it made you feel stuff. That shit made me want to jump and say, "Ah yeah, ah yeah. Say that shit, say that shit!"

A couple of years before, I was an all jazz kinda girl, and Chino was the one into the rap scene. We were on different pages. I couldn't understand why on our cross-country road trips he needed rap in the CD player and nothing else. But now I understood. If only I could tell him. Every day in the streets brought me to a closer understanding of his work and all he went through to provide for himself. It's hard in the streets and this is a real job. People in the streets ain't people with no brains and no skills. On the contrary, you got coaches, organizers, sponsors and CEOs, just like in corporate America. Only problem is, corporate America ain't trying to give a brotha or sista a chance to really express themselves. Especially with no background or legit papers.

When Chino got out the clinker, or "the belly of the beast" as some Muslims call it, he got hired at MCL Cafeteria as the conditions of his parole. The bosses gave his ass a hard time, although he had more knowledge of being self-employed than the ones who were in charge. The work was demeaning to say the least, but Chino never lost focus and didn't allow them to bring him down. Unfortunately, African Americans put up with more bullshit on the job than any other race because nobody thinks they're capable of doing anything else. I know Chino felt belittled but that made me strive for more. The American Dream. Yeah, I want it. Maybe that's my problem, but I'll figure it out one day.

Paul sounded upset when I woke him, but he still spoke to me. Most of T's people were lazy and spoiled just like his fat ass, but Paul was far from that. He had it in him to do some thangs and I could spot a winner when I saw one, so I was gonna focus on him. Delano had it in him, too. I felt encouraged to work with them to inspire them to reach some goals, thus reaching my own.

P was to meet me at the bagel shop near his house, even though it was out of my way and he owed T money. It was all good because one day I would have it my way, and that day was coming. I ordered iced teas for us as I waited.

He finally arrived, and he was still *fine*. Silky chocolate skin with wavy hair and the voice of a Temptation. He had a luscious smile, perfect build and he always wore a platinum, diamond-filled cross on his chest. His trendy framed sunglasses complemented him. He had a wife, and I think three or four kids. Too much baggage for me, but it wasn't even that type of party. Besides, I didn't want no man, but it didn't hurt to look. I hoped he would smile a lot because he had a nice smile. I liked P so much because he had a gentleness about him and I really trusted him. There were not many people in the streets that I trusted.

"C, what's up?" He pulled out the chair, glided into the seat and scooted in close to me. I moved in closer for privacy.

"You, sometimes me. How have you been?" I asked.

"Just chillin', just chillin'," he remarked, slowly rubbing his chin.

"We need to talk about business. There's gonna be some changes. You bring the money?"

"Yeah, but I normally don't deal with anyone else, especially women. No offense."

"I know," I said softly. My mind wandered to one of the many memories that I'd experienced as a female in *the life*. Men were so threatened when they saw a woman getting money 'cause that same money was what they used as a stronghold with women. When a woman has her own money, a weak man finds it challenging to gain a hold in her life. If she ain't dependent financially, he feels weakened.

The previous Friday night had been the ideal summer night, so I rolled up to St. Adalbert Parish to watch the fellas play ball. A couple niggas started hatin' on me because they knew I was out there tryin' to be that girl, I was fine and I wasn't falling for that weak holla they was throwing.

This one known baller walked over to my Jeep and asked me to step out and talk. I knew he was hatin', but I stood outside the Jeep to holla because I was in a position where I had to mix it up to gain my own rep—a rep of handling my business and myself in any situation. Not by murder or sexin', but by finessing.

So I was talking to dude, just kicking game, when I noticed that we had drawn a light audience as he tried to play me.

"What you driving, baby girl? Is this a new ride or a used one?"

I kept my cool and responded by saying, "Baby, it's transportation for now, but it is mine and I didn't flat back and fake it to get it, you know?"

Everyone knew he had purchased a high-price piece of pussy with his gold-diggin' dress-n-rest whore he was sporting. She was pretty all right, pretty damn expensive.

"You out here kickin' it with the men, why you ain't ever with no man? Can you keep one or is another kitty your preference?" He flicked his tongue.

I calmly replied, "Love, I don't do women, and a broke-ass man ain't in my vocabulary, so I'm out here paying myself."

Since I was holding my own, all he could do was some foul shit. He stepped to the side of my Jeep, unzipped his pants, pulled out his dick and started to pee, saying shit like, "Can you do this? Can you write your name with your dick?"

He entertained the crowd with his stream control and aimed the urine toward the edge of my shoe, with one drop landing on the tip of my sandal. He knew this was provocation for a fight, or better yet, a way to welcome death. But because I was female, he just wanted to offend me and teach me a lesson about coming to the court alone.

I stepped back, and he missed his target.

"Your turn," he said, zipping up his pants. I peered at him with malice. He looked at the tip of my sandal. "Oh, let me get that." He reached into his back pocket, acting like he was going to wipe my sandal with the T-shirt he had in his back pocket. I waved him away, saying calmly, "Not a problem, boo."

I bent down and took off my sandals, exposing perfectly pedicured feet that had all eyes on my toe rings. I walked over to the garbage can, tossed the barely worn sandals inside, then walked over to my Jeep, reached in the backseat and replaced the sandals with a pair of stiletto-heeled pumps. I always kept a change of clothes in my car. It's called being prepared.

I winked at the guy who did the piss performance and told him, "It's okay, baby. I only wear my shoes one time anyway." I looked over at the fellas, who now were smiling and giving me the nod.

"Stay up, ma," I heard one of them say, while another exclaimed, "I should have put some money on that shit!"

I hopped into my Jeep, applied some lipstick, picked up my cell phone, holding it with one shoulder, turned up my bumpin' sounds and drove off. The next time I went to the court, they gave me my props, and I just sat in my Jeep waiting for the right time to make my move and let them know that I was that girl and I had the weight.

"I heard that you were into this escorting service," Paul continued, interrupting my thoughts. "Nothing else?" He held a look of seriousness on his face while he listened for my reply.

"Well, it's like this. I know a lot of people and I mix it up. I'll be the one you'll most likely be dealing with in the future, so I need to know what's up, what you're trying to do and what you're looking for in a supplier," I said sternly.

He looked spooked, but I'd found on the streets that the majority of people didn't have an agenda. Prime example: G. All he wanted was the money so he could have the *honeys*. His motivation went no further.

He was also turning into a big gossip. If he told me one more tale of his threesome fuckfests with China and Ashley, I was going to scream. Every time we met, no matter how many times I checked his ass, he wanted to broadcast how China sucked his dick while Ashley ate China's pussy. Or how Ashley sucked his dick while he watched China eat Ashley's pussy. Or how he watched China and Ashley eat each other's pussies for a hit of dope. Now, why would he brag to another woman, especially about fuckin' a sex pro like China with no protection, no condoms, no nothing. One day G would cost me. I felt this, and I needed to do something about it. He had female qualities, and females will fuck you every time.

"C, I ain't trying to be no drug dealer all my life. I'm in college and studying business. I hustle to support my family and stay in school, but I don't really make a lot of money. I basically turn others on because of my relationship with Erik. Some of my cousins and people I grew up with mostly benefit from what I get from T."

"No, it's not about me. We do this together." *I knew I liked him. He understands the group and the family concept of things.*

"I'm making about four grand on each of them thangs I get. If you could get Erik to lower the ticket, I could do more."

"How much you paying now?" I asked this praying he would provide some answers.

"I'm paying twenty-five for a kilo, and I let it off for twenty-nine."

"That's it?" I asked, trying to hide my disbelief.

"Yeah, because I'm not breaking it down like I used to."

"How are you driving a Land Cruiser making four grand with three children and a wife?" I smiled, but was curious as to how he was doing this, because I wanted to work my hand the best way I could. Perhaps I could learn something from P.

"Carmen, you funny as hell. That's my business. I'm trying to stick and move, and to be honest, it just ain't worth it."

"Well, what *is* worth it? What if the ticket was lower? Could you move more then?"

"Well, I do about five a week from various sources. So if I could get a new price of, say, twenty-four or even twenty-four five, I could do a lil' more." *Wait, so he's making $4,000 five times a week. So $20,000 a week. How is that not enough to support a family? Am I missing something?*

"Have you ever talked to T or Erik about this?" I quizzed. "I tried to talk to T, but he never has the time to really discuss it, and you already know that Erik ain't trying to come up off of nothing. In fairness, the price is not that bad because it's delivered to you in Columbus—"

He cut me off, waving his hand to silence me and began explaining his view. "Look, you don't have to go into all that. I know you got some debate skills. T has mentioned you a lot. He really respects you. I'm not complaining or trying to get hemmed up in a debate with you. I could make more. I'm just keeping it real."

I wanted to keep his interest, so I calmly responded, "P, I ain't here to work you over or debate your position. I really like your style, and I think *we* could do better. Why risk yourself for four grand when you could risk yourself for double that? What if I give you a ticket of twenty-three grand for less than ten of them thangs and twenty-two five for ten to fifteen of 'em?"

His eyes opened really wide.

"How can you do this? Erik and T tell me they can only bring so many."

"I'm not Erik or T, and this is what we on today." I felt hot, so I took a sip from my drink.

"Bet, I can easily do ten for twenty-two five." He gave me that sexy grin.

"Great, that's what I'm looking for. I'll have ten for you on Friday, and we'll see how it goes. Let's see if you're able to move them. Nothing beats a failure but a try, so let's go for it!" He nodded in agreement. "As long as you're trying, your ticket will be twenty-two five, and you can't beat that but don't ever try to beat me." I thought I'd throw that in for Scarface-type effects, although I knew P wasn't that type of guy.

P sat back in his chair. "So, it's all about Carmen now, huh? For years when we would talk on the phone, I wondered when you would come out. You know, Erik speaks very highly of you, and for you to set a price like that, you must have some pull. Shit, this is deep." He ran his hand across his face. "A female drug dealer. I'll give it a try."

Beep . . . beep.

"Is that me or you?" P asked, smiling, glancing at his pager.

"It's me." I looked at my pager and pretended to be rushed. Besides, Delano would be here any minute. "P, also, start saving your money so we can deal on a cash-up-front basis. This will keep the prices down and ensure you all that you're looking for. I'll contact you on Friday when it arrives. Just have your people in place because you'll only have until Sunday morning to get it all together." *I know he knows what that means.* "Also, I am having a party on Saturday, and you and all your boys are invited to attend. It is going to be a cookout to celebrate our success."

"C, you're so positive that this will be a success."

"Yes, I am. I do things by faith, and faith *is* the evidence of things not seen. The substance of things hoped for. Keep your faith at all times. Yes, we're doing wrong, but we still need to pray for each other as well as ourselves."

"True dat, true dat." He stood and began to walk away.

"The girls will be there looking for work, if ya know what I mean. Bring some swim gear, come and get your eat on. It'll be fun. I'll call with the details midweek."

"For you, C, anything." He paused for a moment. "Carmen?"

"Yes?"

"Are you married?"

"No."

"Are you with someone?"

"No, P, I'm alone. Just me and my son. If I had a man, I wouldn't be in the streets. Why do you ask?" Wouldn't a man know that if a woman had a man she wouldn't be in the streets, hustling, going for broke and risking her freedom? They called it "throwing bricks" at the penitentiary. Eventually, you built yourself behind a wall.

"Just curious how you got into this."

"It's deep. We'll talk one day. I know it is different dealing with me, but I'm here with quality and customer service. We about to become incorporated, a'ight?" I extended my hand, giving him a firm handshake. It is important for women to give men firm handshakes. It lets them know that a sister is right back at ya and ready to do business.

"A'ight."

"P, this is our summer. Look for me on your hip. My code is triple zeros."

He gave me that sexy smile and said, "So let's get it on!"

"Later." I watched him walk out the door to his emerald green Land Cruiser. Sipping on my drink, I waited for my next appointment.

I saw Delano walking up in there looking like Christopher Williams. This was a man I could marry, but not at that time.

"Why didn't you call me this weekend? I thought we were going out."

"Hi, Delano, and how are you today?" I asked sarcastically. "I can't get a hello, a hug, nothing but drama?" I opened my arms for an embrace, and he pulled in close and kissed me on the side of my face. Damn, he smelled so good. We returned to our seats, and he took a sip of my glass of tea. Yeah, look at them lips on that straw. I wished I was that straw. I began smiling at the thought, and he continued with his questions.

"My bad. How are you and lil' man?"

"We're fine, thank you. I intended on calling you, but I got tied up. I'm having a birthday party this weekend for a friend of mine, and I want you to come. You can bring some of your friends, if you like," I chimed.

"Sounds interesting. When and where?"

"I'm still working on some of the details, but I'll let you know once everything is set."

"Let me know if you need any help with anything," he said sincerely.

"Thanks for offering. Did you bring the money?"

"Money?" he said, responding as if he didn't know what I was talking about.

"Yes, T's money." *Don't get brand-new on me. I ain't in the mood.*

"Yes, and I don't like dealing with you on this level." He slid his chair away in order to look me directly in the face.

"Well, I'm sorry you feel that way, but we need to talk about this level and some other things. You're gonna have to deal with me because I'm going to be helping T out with his business." *He looks really disappointed with that, but the truth is, I'm not trying to date anyone at this time, especially not seriously. After my past experiences, I'm tired of men. My lil' heart is worn out.*

I gave him the new price of twenty-two five, and he was happy. Delano smiled and said, "I still don't want to work with you. I want to take you out to dinner."

"Delano, that won't be possible, and you know it. Let's try to be friends first, okay?"

"We can try that but you know you like me." *He is really pushy.* The more I resisted, the more he wanted me. We always want what we can't have. But I didn't trust him with my heart or my feelings. I wanted money. Nothing more, nothing less. Delano and I finished our meal and we talked about everything. Delano and I could have been the power couple, hustling together, making moves together, doing things together and—fuck it, it wouldn't work. No way.

—

"Stop playing. Yeah, bitch, we gon' play. I should have whooped your ass a long time ago. You kicked it with Erik with no fear. Straight larceny in your heart, like I wouldn't tap that ass for an infraction. Now you'll see. You'll see what I meant all those times I told niggas I'd be to see them. Pooh, baby, it's your turn to get to know your Chino. You wanna curse and talk like a man instead of a woman, now I'm gonna treat you like one." I tried to dart past him, but he snatched me by the hair, bringing me to my knees.

—

As soon as I got home, I made plans to send the baby to my mother's for the week. It was to be a week of moves and a week of faith. I needed to get to New York, talk to Erik and his connect, then I needed to arrange for some transportation and drivers. Then I could get this ball rolling. It was summer already and I wanted to be gone by the fall. In another state with a new home, with my son. Four months or fifty grand. Whichever came first. That was all I was giving myself, and I had to move fast.

The game was getting tight and competitive. Other knockoff escort services began to surface and attempted to match mine. And ballers from Gary, Indiana, also known as the GI Boys, had infiltrated Columbus with stickup moves, barbaric tactics and guerilla schemes, taking over blocks and small apartment complexes. One complex off 18th and Main they renamed the Carter after the one in the movie *New Jack City*. They slung rocks from that building's stoops and windows daring anyone, including the police, to stop them.

I didn't worry about what the next man was doing. I kept my eyes focused on my prize. I knew in the streets everyone got at least one chance, and I was determined to play my hand when my ace card was dealt. I didn't want *all* the money, just enough to reach my goal. I would do the best I could with what I had. Get mines while the getting was good.

I began to think of a way to put this together: there was Delano, who could do seven, and then G, who could do two. Then there was Paul, who could do ten. That was nineteen and I'd ask for twenty-five. This was my most risky gamble to date. I had to take the roll of this dice to make this a deal maker. Who could resist a sale for twenty-five kilos?

If I could convince this man in New York that I could move twenty-five kilos every weekend, then there was no way he would not work with me. I was uncertain of the average move in the street, but twenty-five of them thangs a week is a lot to someone new at the game. Not to forget the ounce of heroin that I needed. I could remember Chino doing two hundred of them a month, so I knew I could do half of what he did.

One time, Erik had told me that he could move more if he had vehicles with hidden compartments. He said he could lock Columbus down with sales. I'd almost met his supplier once. I was in New York, and I went with Erik to purchase some ganja to smoke. We drove to a corner store in Brooklyn, purchased some weed, rolled up a phat blunt and smoked it. Erik asked me if I wanted to come in and meet a friend of his, but I declined. Erik went inside, but I saw a Spanish guy wave at me. I knew it was *him*, but I had no interest in meeting him.

I was willing to bet that when I finally met the connect, it would be the same short Colombian or Dominican from the store. And one day I expected to meet him. *Dear God, please let me meet him*, I thought. I needed a plug.

I told T-Love of my meetings and my need for twenty-five kilos. He grabbed his head and screamed at me.

"C, are you out of your mind? I can't get twenty-five kilos."

"Can you get twenty?" I asked, ignoring his raised voice.

"C, I told you I have to talk to Erik. It's not as simple as you think. My relationship, my partnership, rides on my decisions."

"I can be in New York on Wednesday to talk with whomever. I've already put the shit in place. I spoke with P and Delano but I also got peeps who I deal with. The shit is already sold, quiet as it's kept. T, baby, I'm ready to ball." I jumped into the middle of the floor acting like a WWE wrestler and screamed, "Let's get ready to rumble! In the right corner, you got a thirsty single mom ready to campaign, never complain and get down for her crown! In the left corner, you got my partner, T-Love babay! Waitin' to tag-team Columbus, bring this bitch to its knees. Bow down!"

T really liked my ideas and the fact that I took the initiative to talk to Delano and P. Also, T didn't mind using me as the frontline man. He would put me out front so that it all would be on me. Well, I had been a frontliner before. I could handle it—I hoped.

T said he had been trying to get Erik's connect to work with him, using transportation and everything, but he kept putting him off. I told T he was not bringing him the correct figures, and that twenty kilos would spark his interest. T also revealed that the guy was already aware of me. He said he wanted to meet me on the strength that I opened a service, provided housing to the guys every weekend and supported them whenever they were in town. He recognized the fact that it took a community of people working together to make this drug trade happen. I was almost in. He knew my name already, so I was not a complete unknown. I had a chance.

"Look, T, please call me. When will you see him?" I pleaded.

"When I get in town, I'll talk with him. I'm telling you now, C, Erik will not go for it." He continued to fold a two-inch cuff into the bottom of yet another denim outfit. This one was green, with the Timbs to match.

"Just please try. Now, let's get you packed and on the road."

"C, I'll page you and let you know that I touched down safe."

"Don't forget because I do worry." The way to a man's heart is softness.

"I know you do, and I'll hit you on the hip, around three a.m."

"Here, give me a hug, and no matter what, thank you for trying. Bye," I said.

"Peace, I'm gone."

I called my mom, and she happily agreed to take the baby. I arranged a connecting flight to drop my son off and continue on to New York, all in one day. I made the arrangements for the party, and hired a DJ and caterer. I rented the pool house at the Lakeview Square Apartments in upscale Worthington and prepared the menu. I decided to serve nothing but light and nutritious foods, my New York chicken, shrimp kebabs, and vinaigrette-tossed salads. I would play premixed tapes for music. I had it all covered. All I could think of was that soon my come-up would be on. I could feel it.

Ten

I arrived at New York's LaGuardia Airport on Wednesday afternoon. T-Love had arranged for me to meet with his source. I had finally gotten his name.

I was anxious to get it over with. No turning back. This was what I wanted, right? I had learned a long time ago that everything happens in seasons. This was my season to reap my harvest. I was going to be blessed.

I noticed a man with a sign that read CARMEN. I knew I was dealing with some pros because they were on time: tardiness is a sure sign of an amateur. I made it to his Nissan Pathfinder. Inside, I found T-Love and two Latino men.

T introduced me to the driver, Victor, and the other passenger, who was named Capo. Capo sat silently, looking straight ahead. He didn't even acknowledge me when we were introduced. This gave me an uneasy feeling and made me think it was all a mistake. We drove swiftly through the city toward a restaurant in Queens. I was told I'd meet *him* there.

While I took in all the sights, it seemed like my nervousness went away and my appetite came back. I was starving. We went to an Italian spot, and I ordered pizza and a salad. As we waited for our order, three men entered the establishment. Two of them I didn't know, but the one who was slightly short and looked to be in his twenties was the same guy I remembered from the corner store in Brooklyn. The two men took the table next to me, and I shook the extended hand of the man who stood before me.

"My name is Dragos."

"My pleasure. My name is Carmen," I replied, releasing his hand and thinking of a way to stay calm. Dragos was a warm, toasted brown color with thin gold-rimmed glasses and a well-groomed goatee that he rubbed from time to time. As he spoke, he continued to stroke the hair on his face.

"I'm surprised, Carmen."

"Why?"

"I've heard a lot about you and I thought you would be more of a different type of lady." Dragos caught the change of expression on my face. "I thought you'd be more like a hip-hopper but you're a young lady. You look like a college student."

"Well, thank you." We gave each other a grin. Once my order arrived, he asked for a bottled water.

Taking a few sips of the water, he asked, "How do you like Queens?"

"I like it very much. I wouldn't mind living here."

"I have apartments all over, and you're welcome to stay at any one of them, anytime."

I wondered when T-Love would speak up. He just sat there stuffin' his mouth.

"Carmen, go ahead and eat. Later, we'll take a walk by the river and talk business."

"I'd like that." I could not stop smiling.

"So, tell me about yourself," Dragos quizzed.

"Well, I'm a single parent with a small son. I'm just trying to make it in this world for both of us."

"You don't have a husband?" he asked curiously. "You're very pretty and gentle."

"No. I had one, but he left me for another woman." *I figure, why start with lies?* "I've been struggling and just trying to put things together. I have a lot of goals."

"Please, tell me about your salon."

Deciding to put it all on the line, I opened my heart and gave an honest response. "Well, I, or we, had a salon, a very nice salon, and when my life went through some changes, I just let go and walked away from everything. But now I'm on my own, trying to be independent. I'm not looking for a man. So, Dragos, tell me about yourself." I had no idea what I was doing. The wrong question or answer could be a deal breaker, so I held my peace and paced myself as I attempted to get in where I fit in.

"Myself?" Dragos asked, obviously taken off guard. "No one has ever asked me this before." He held a look of peace on his face.

"I try to be personable," I politely responded.

"I can see that. Eat and we'll talk more."

"Thank you for taking time out for us to meet. I'm grateful."

"How do you know that you're grateful? The meeting has just begun."

"But I am. I'm grateful for things that you have no idea about."

"I must admit, I like this quality in you. You seem so optimistic. You're in the streets and still have faith."

"Yes, very much so. I know that God is up there watching me. I noticed your religious medallion. It's beautiful. You also believe in God."

"With God, all things are possible."

T was still stuffing his face, but he started speaking with his mouth full. "Yeah, yeah, I told you, Dragos, Carmen is mad deep. Hey, C, tell him about your service."

"Maybe later." I really didn't want to get into that right now. I turned to Dragos and continued speaking. "I'm having a small cookout in Columbus, and I was wondering if you would like to come?"

"Only if I can come as your friend," Dragos told me while patting my hand as a father does to reassure a child.

"I would be honored. I think you'll enjoy it. Perhaps I can show you around Columbus and you could even meet my son."

I knew I was making some wrong moves. In the streets, you try to keep everything a secret, but I wanted this man to see that not only was I a woman in a man's role, but I was a human being in this life and just trying to make it. Not as a baller or a gangsta, but more or less as a business-woman with big ideas who could be trusted. This approach worked so well for me so far that I wanted to try to make this family style, not mafioso style.

He continued smiling more and more, and I was comforted by this. I decided that when we took our walk, I was going to continue to be real with him and not be something that I was not.

Our drive led us to the riverfront in lower Manhattan. The weather was warm, but windy. It was just Dragos and me, all alone. Well, not really alone because his associates were several yards behind us. He had bodyguards that followed him everywhere.

"Dragos, I can't really believe that I've met you. People in the streets dream of meeting someone like you." So I've heard.

"Like I said before, I've heard a lot about you and wanted to see you for myself. What type of young girl does all that you have done and are trying to do?"

Trying to hide my defensive side, I put the ball back in his court with the same questions in an attempt to pick his brain. "What type of guy does all that you do and has all that you have? And look at you . . . you're young yourself." Dragos avoided responding to my inquiries but proceeded to ask me another question.

"How did you get into this"—he paused—"shall I say, line of work?"

I closed my eyes tightly, took a deep breath and let it out. "I was introduced to the streets by my son's father. When I met him, he was a small-time hustler of sorts, mostly stealing clothes. Then he went on to sell small quantities of cocaine and then on to the larger quantities. He did the majority of the hustling while I offered the support, but I learned a lot. We were happy, or I thought we were."

"What happened next?"

"The next thing I know, the money was coming in steadily, we started having problems, then he left, leaving me with nothing. I got into some jams out of desperation so I just made every attempt to work my hand at a variety of things. I don't like spreading myself thin because I have some financial goals I'd like to meet. I want to buy a house for me and my lil' man and move away from Columbus. Too many memories for me. I just want a new life. You know . . . start over. You ever wanted a new life?"

"*Sí, una vida nueva,* yes," he said, smiling.

"I know a life is something you must work at, not work for or wish for."

"So why coca?"

"Because I have some outlets, and I hope, now, a resource. Things happen for a reason, and in life, everyone deserves an opportunity. I think this is my opportunity . . . my opportunity for a new life."

"Do you think of your salon?" he asked.

"Yes, but that's over. That's in the past and I don't go backward. Dragos," I said, cutting to the chase, "I'm prepared to move twenty to twenty-five kilos a week. I just need a good ticket and for them to be delivered to Columbus. I think you're the man who can make that happen for me."

"You really think that?"

"Yes, I do." I looked right into his eyes. "As a matter of fact, I *know* you can."

"Erik and Timothy have been selling in Columbus for the last three years. Why do you think you can do better?"

"Because I'm a businesswoman and very good at it. I can make us a lot of money."

He looked at me, carefully searching my face for a motive and said, "Carmen, I have more money than I can spend in two lifetimes but you're offering me the opportunity to make even more with you?"

"Yes, I am."

"And I should take a chance on you?"

"Yes, you should, and I really think you should come to my party, too." With my perfectly lined strawberry lips, I gave him a confident smile.

He rubbed his hands, then his head, and looked me in the eyes. He took my hand and said, "Carmen, my family is the most important thing in this world to me. I don't ever want to leave them."

"And you won't have to." I gripped his hand harder.

"I'll give you a chance. I'll have fifteen kilos in Columbus for you by Friday afternoon, and *you* will be responsible for them. Not Erik, not Timothy. We all work together, but please know this weight is on your shoulders."

"I'll need to explain this to T and Erik. I don't want them to feel crossed, since they have been trying to work out this plan with you for a long time. Now that I'm on the verge of doing what they wanted to do, it's going to cause some ill feelings."

"Well, you must choose, because I deal with only one person at a time. You brought this idea to me, not them. Whatever financial arrangement you work out is between you three, but just know, these are my terms. Be careful what you ask for, Carmen, because you've just got it. The question is, do you really want it, and at what cost?"

Of course I want it. I'll look after T and Erik. We just want to be plugged. "Yes, I want it," I told him convincingly.

"Do you have any people in your corner? Any men with you? The streets can be rough."

"No, I'm alone, and I'd prefer it that way, but I'll consider getting someone in my corner if you suggest."

"*Bueno.* I'll come to Columbus this weekend as your 'brother' to attend your party, meet your son and bring your goods. Where are you staying tonight?"

"I'm not certain."

"You can stay at one of my apartments."

"Thanks for the offer. I normally stay with T-Love or Erik and his wife whenever I'm in the city. But I don't think tonight it would be right to stay with them, considering things have changed." I looked off into the water and admired the lights. He was still holding my hand. "Dragos, don't laugh, but I'd like to stay at a very nice hotel in a honeymoon suite. A honeymoon suite all by myself. Chino always promised me this, but his promises never came true. Now I can stay there, and can pay for it. That's what I want."

"No problem. I'll have my driver arrange it for you." Dragos let go of my hand, then kissed both of my cheeks.

"Leave all of your contact information with Victor, and he will give you mine. He'll also take you to the airport in the morning." With that, he began to walk off.

"Oh, Dragos. What's my ticket?" I asked, not really caring. I just wanted to be plugged.

"Carmen, your ticket is twenty." That ticket would put me in the position to stack thousands.

"*Muchas gracias*," I replied in my best Spanish accent.

"*Buenas noches*," Dragos said, impressed.

"*Buenas noches. Adiós*," I said, laying it on thick.

Eleven

"*Oooooh-Weeeee! Aaaaaaah!*" This place had it going on, and I was all up in the middle of it. I was here. I was in my very own honeymoon suite. All by myself. A complimentary bottle of Dom Pérignon sat on the black baby grand piano. There was a huge bouquet of beautiful yellow roses, two big, fluffy white Waldorf-Astoria embroidered bathrobes and a beautiful view of New York's skyline through floor-to-ceiling windows. There was a fully stocked wet bar, a huge garden-style bathtub, marble floors leading to a plush wine-colored carpet and a gigantic bed with silk linens of gold tones and goose feather pillows on which to rest my head.

"I need to call T," I said to myself. "Tell him it's on." I walked toward the phone, enjoying every step I took in the luxury of the suite. "Naw, I'll talk to him and Erik in Columbus." That was my best move because I didn't want to spoil this mood.

I decided to take a long bubble bath, but before then, I called the airlines to arrange my return flight to get my son back home. Then I called room service and ordered up some shit just because I could.

Afterward, I turned on some classical music. I walked to the bathroom as the melodic sound played throughout the suite. I smiled as I saw a phone near the tub, next to the toilet, so I punched 0 and waited until I received an answer.

"When my order is on the way, just tell them to come in and leave my food," I told the person who answered. "I'm chillin' so just bill the room." After hanging up, I stepped into the warm, bubbly water, allowing it to cover me as I sat down. I closed my eyes and submerged my body under the bubbles as far as I could without getting my hair wet, enjoying the serenity I was experiencing. *Heaven has got to be like this*, I thought.

A few minutes later, I opened my eyes and saw the bottle of champagne and two glasses that were on the side of the tub. I poured two glasses just for me. With one glass in each hand, I toasted.

"To me for getting the plug! I did it, I did it! I'm plugged!"

After my personal pampering, I called and checked on my son.

"Pammy, he's fine," my mother assured me. "Actually, he's playing with his cousins that he never has a chance to see." She cleared her throat, throwing the hint out there. Even a deaf man could have caught it.

"Well, Mom, I'm coming to get him tomorrow. I may stay overnight with you."

"That would be great. I miss seeing you. Actually, since you're not with Chino, you can come whenever you want . . . not when he says you can."

"Mom, please leave Chino out of this. Anyway, I'll see ya tomorrow, and I don't need a ride. I wanna take a cab. Put the baby on the phone please."

"Okay, here he goes. Come on, sweetie, it's your mama."

"Hi, boo. Hi, boo. It's Mommy," I said.

There were breathing and slobbering sounds. "Halo-halo, Mommy." The sound of my son's voice sent chills up my spine. *That's right, boo, I'm your Mommy, and one day, you will be proud of me.*

"Are you having fun, boo?"

More breathing and slobbering sounds. "Yes, fun, Mommy."

"I love you, and Mommy misses you."

"I wuv you. I wuv you." The phone dropped and I heard kids laughing in the background.

"Pammy, that boy is off and running." My mother chuckled. "He is in there with those kids having a good time. Did you have a nice talk?"

"Yes, Mom. Please be sure to watch him around the older kids. He doesn't like milk and be sure—"

"Pamela, I do not need your advice on raising a child. I raised you and you came out straight, as you kids say. Didn't you?"

"Yes, Mom. I just worry."

"You first-time moms are a total trip. You got a hip mama, and for your information, he does drink milk and eat everything you say he doesn't. He's not made of glass so he won't break, bend maybe, but not break." She laughed.

"Stop making fun of me." I pouted. "Just kiss the baby for me."

"When will he stop being a baby?"

"See, I got ya there. You always told me that I will always be your baby, and so my son will always be my baby."

"Ha, that's right. It's true, you will," said Mom.

"I gotta go. Kiss him for me, okay? And I'll see you soon. I love you."

"I will, and I love you, too. Bye."

"Bye, Mom." Hanging up the phone I remembered my childhood and what a wonderful mother I had. I really didn't have much in this life but my mom and my son, and for them, I was so grateful.

I wrapped up in my big bathrobe and finished one of the glasses of champagne. *Whew! This champagne is good*, I thought. I looked at the tray that had been delivered and tried everything. The strawberries were fabulous and the seafood I ordered tasted good, too. It had been such a long time since I did anything special for myself, and this felt good. I was on a honeymoon with myself and it was time to start loving me.

The room had a gorgeous window seat where I cuddled and picked over my food and drank more champagne. I stared out the window. The view was absolutely breathtaking. The more I drank, the more I gazed out the window. I had a serious buzz.

I went to change the dial on the radio because I was tired of classical music. Spanish music caught my ear and I decided to throw off my robe and do the salsa butt-booty-naked. Then I did the Macarena. Yes. La Macarena. I was pretty good at it, too. I swore there was a Spanish person in me waiting to come out. I loved paella, tapas and tortilla española—all sorts of Spanish food. I did a few more dance moves and then changed the dial again to the famous WBLS. They were pumpin' Shabba Ranks's remix of "Mr. Loverman," so I sang along. There must have been a Jamaican person in me waiting to come out, too, because I loved jerk chicken, beef patties, curry chicken, and goat meat, "mon." Then they started with the rap remixes. I felt the music, then felt a verse waiting to come out.

"Check it: this is the place where stars are born, and I'm the only one that can't be worn out by any place, any part of the world."

I finally figured out why I didn't have a rap career, 'cause my ass couldn't rap. Then they were slowin' it down with the slow jams. This was my shit!

I put my robe back on, grabbed a long-stemmed rose from the vase of flowers and sang into it. By this time, the bottle of champagne was almost empty but they were pumpin' my song by Teena Marie and Rick James, "Fire and Desire." I sang every note, off-key of course, but you couldn't tell me that. There must have been a black person in Teena Marie that came out. All I knew was if she and Rick ever hooked up again, it would be on and over for these other half-singing entertainers.

I started tearing the petals off the rose and throwing them over my bed. I poured me a drink from the wet bar, then I took my place on the fluffy window seat.

I sat and looked at the twinkling stars. It was lovely. The radio station pumped more slow jams, and that was how it all started. Me, booze and music. It was only a matter of time before the memories rushed in. They played that damn beggin' Keith Sweat, and he sang the same song Chino used to sing to me all the time. He would call the salon and sing it over the phone to me.

I could hear Chino's voice singing to me like it was yesterday and we were together, so I took another sip of the golden-colored liquid and reminisced. Once they played Marvin Gaye, it was over. I sang myself silly and the tears came, I hugged a pillow to my chest with my knees pulled up close and just started talking to my Chino:

Chino, I know you're not physically with me now, but I know that you can still hear me and feel me. I know this because I can still hear you and feel you. I never meant to hurt you. All I wanted was for you to be happy. To love you is all I wanted and for you to love me, forever. I gave you all my love, my time, my life, my faith and my dreams. I gave you my heart. I couldn't accept the thought of you not loving me anymore and wanting someone else. I know my friendship with Erik hurt you, but it really wasn't what you thought.

So many things went wrong. I accept our separation. We could never go back to the past again. We can't even talk on the phone without arguing, and we never used to argue. It's like we were never friends, like we can't even stand to hear each other's voice.

To add insult to injury, you told everyone that our son was not yours, even though you know I was always faithful to you.

You always told me that another woman would never come between us. You said this about a thousand times, and I believed you. And in the event that you didn't want me anymore, I always thought you would be decent. After all we had been through and after what I thought we meant to each other. But you left me for a girl who didn't even want your fat ass until your pockets got fat.

I struggled with you. I slept on the floor with you. I made twenty-five-dollar runs with you. I was the one you turned out to stealing clothes and pulling capers. Not her. Then you married her when I was eight months pregnant and acted like a straight-up bitch about everything. You held on so tight to material things. Why, Chino? Why couldn't you leave me and walk away with nothing, like how I found you? I stepped with nothing. You took our money, gave it to her, and then you took my car and gave it to her. But worst of all, you took your heart and gave it to her.

Yeah, I was jealous because I'm human, but I was hurt more because of your triple cross. That's the real reason for all the drama, and you know it. I never had a problem with your wife. You know this! But I never meant to hurt you, and you know this also. Our shit just went haywire. I could never really explain all that I feel but, Chino, I know that you know, and I also know that God knows.

God, if you're listening, and I believe that you are, then all I ask is that you protect and watch over my son. God, I love my son so much, and when I look at him, I see the best of your blessings. I also see the best of Chino and me. So I want to thank you for my son. And I want to thank you for the memories. I want you to bless Chino and his family. Watch over him and keep him safe from harm. And do the same for me. Please keep Chino happy. All I want is for both of us to be happy.

Please forgive me, Chino, for my wrongs, because I forgive you, Chino, for all the hurt and pain you caused.

Dear God, one day, it is my prayer, that I'll be able to tell Chino how I feel today and bless him like he has blessed me in my life, through the good times and the bad times. I want him to sit back and remember and feel special about himself. God, I just want to make it. I don't know the way, but please walk with me and keep me and show me the way to happiness. Damn, my glass is empty. Chino, wherever you are, may God bless you.

Twelve

The van, Dragos and the drivers arrived at the party like clockwork, and I had all the fellas lined up. I had on a designer crimson linen sundress that melted against my honey brown skin. Of course, my hair was looking *fierce*. I wanted everything to be perfect, and it was. Everyone was there, and the music was bumpin'. Dragos came looking all preppy in his crisp white Tommy Hilfiger short set. His drivers had on Tommy gear as well. Gabrielle was overjoyed, and China was working the room talking about, "Let that be the reason I make three grand tonight." I had no doubt that she would do just that. She looked great in the bikinis that I had gotten the girls. The boosters always came through.

I had taken care of my business the previous night, and it went well. I got rid of fifteen of them thangs, and the quality was all that, and the heroin was all that, too. I got $6,000 for one ounce. Hell, I only paid $2,500 for it.

T even brought his wife *and* his hoochie to the party. His wife had no idea about the hoochie. She assumed she was just another girl at the party.

T and his hoochie dipped into the jacuzzi together, and I swear it looked like she went down on him under the water! His wife just sat over to the side and acted unaware, like nothing was wrong. Maybe there wasn't anything wrong. Long gone are the days of the faithful-to-each-other couple, but everyone looked liked they were having fun.

I walked past China wiggling her ass with a plate of food in her hand, and she smelled like she was smokin' that stuff again, even though I told them *no drugs* at the party. For a crack addict, she had a fat ass that all the boys loved.

P and his crew arrived in freshly washed whips, lined in a row at the cul-de-sac entrance, rolling two and four deep to a vehicle. Delano strolled in late, taking the breath away from Spice as she made her move to approach him. The sound system was bumpin' house remixes, and the air was filled with joy as Gabrielle celebrated her birthday in style. Toy was flossing an aqua blue swimsuit with matching laced sandals and flirting with every guy there.

Erik showed up late, and after a dry hi he never said another word for the rest of the night. He was still mad that I had met Dragos, and even madder now that Dragos only dealt with me. I offered to split all the money three ways, but Erik had to put in some work, and he didn't like that.

It used to be that he was at home chillin' while T was putting in all the work, but now I had come along and changed the whole program, and he didn't like the new rules. Regardless of the fact that we had more money, Erik didn't want to do any work. I couldn't blame him, who likes to work? It wasn't an intentional double cross, but I'd be damned if they were gonna sit on they ass and still expect to collect free money from my hustle.

T agreed to become a driver and share the responsibility of getting the shipment. In the seat cushions of the vans were hidden compartments that opened with a combination. The compartments were airtight and lined with coffee grains to mask the scent from police dogs in the event of a search. Each van held fifteen kilos, and on the return trip, it held the money. Thus, in the likely event that the police did their racial profiling routine and bogus traffic stop, they would not be able to find drugs or money in the van. A driver with a clean driving record and no warrants was home free. I agreed to move the product in the streets and meet people and count the money, which I soon learned was a job in itself.

All Erik had to do was help move the product, deliver it and collect it. He didn't want that. So I offered to give him $30,000 for collecting only. That wasn't enough either—he also wanted a commission off each of them thangs. That shit was crazy. No way! So we couldn't agree, and Dragos refused to talk to him. Dragos said he was giving me a chance, and Erik was salty about this, so he elected to sip on his Heineken all night and stare at me with a hateful look on his face.

I decided to try talking one more time by bringing him another Heineken. I wrapped the beer in a white napkin and sashayed over to where he was standing. "Hi, Erik. How are you?"

Silence.

"Are you still mad at me? Are we gonna make up and work this out?"

"Yo, Star! T is my friend, not yours. You would not have known him if it weren't for me." He twisted his face into a grimace. You know, the one you give a hater on the streets for looking at you the wrong way.

He took another swig of his beer, and I continued my attempt to smooth things over. "Yes, Erik, this is true, but I thought after four years we were all friends. After all, I'm godmother to your nephew and I've stayed at your home. We've been through a lot."

"Still, I just feel like you overstepped your boundaries."

"Is it really that or do you feel like I crossed you?" I asked, already knowing how he really felt. I just wanted to hear him confess it.

"Not really, but why can't you get money from Chino? He used to take care of you."

"You said it: 'used to.' I was nothing more than a drug dealer's girlfriend, and that's all over now. He won't support me or my son so I want this for myself. Like you, I want more for my son. Perhaps I'll go back to school and go legit, but in the meantime, let's work together."

"No, I can't work with this. After we split this weekend, I'm out. You're out of your league, and soon enough you'll find out just how far out you are."

"Erik, I don't want you to be mad at me." I knew if Erik felt crossed, he might resort to something underhanded. He definitely had it in him to do some dirty shit, but I didn't think he would go there with me.

He took another swig of beer and continued. "Well, let's just say that all things have changed. Nothing is the same anymore. This is my last weekend. You know everyone. With your new prices, you'll have Columbus on lock. I can't do nothing here no more. Look at T-Love, he's about to get a divorce and don't even know it. Just watch yourself," he said in an odd tone.

"I will, and I won't be in this for very long. I promise."

He just looked real blank and stared off, drinking his beer. I walked away. *Is this the price I must pay? Our friendship?*

The birthday cake came and Renaye was singing with her beautiful voice. "Happy birthday to ya, happy birthday to ya, happy birthday." Underneath the singing, Carmen's voice told me Erik was sizing me up—but for what? I didn't know. He wouldn't hurt me. *God, please tell me, what is it? What am I doing wrong?*

Across the room I noticed a guy I had seen earlier in the evening. He looked very familiar to me. He was with Delano, and I assumed that they were partners, but he kept staring at me and watching my every move. *Where do I know him from? I just can't place him. Do I know him from Columbus or from someone? Who is he?* I decided not to approach him unless he approached me. Who was this dude in the jogging suit? Who was he?

Everyone I talked to said they were having fun, but G got an attitude because he got no attention. He kept running up in everyone's face trying to be all that he could be. I wasn't mad at him, but this was not the appropriate place.

These were ballers like himself, not customers. He had absolutely no polish. A rusty-brass-ass nigga, but he finally figured out the difference after he got dissed enough.

Delano was disappointed that I didn't spend time with him. I still didn't think he understood how deep in the game I was, but I couldn't discuss it with him because he wanted me to be a lady. It was like he had this golden image of me, and I didn't want to knock myself off the pedestal. I couldn't be real with him. How would he take the escort service? There were too many "what if's" when it came to Delano and I couldn't deal with them right then.

After the party, Erik, T and I decided to meet at the condo to discuss our business. We made $6,000 off each of the fifteen kilos, making us $90,000. Even though Erik refused to put in any work, I still split everything three ways as a sign of loyalty and good faith. I paid Dragos his $300,000. Three hundred thousand dollars! It was unreal. I was thrilled with my $30,000. I was now more than halfway to my goal, and in one more weekend, I would exceed it. My new life was closer to being a reality.

"You did it, C! You did this!" T exclaimed.

All Erik could do was be mad. He said, "I can't believe that Dragos worked with you. I had been asking him for years to do this."

Easing in between the two of them, I said, "Well, look at it this way, he finally did it. And *we* are a team. We made ninety thousand in a weekend. That should speak for something. This is about us. Now, are we homies for life or what?"

With a mouth full of food, T mumbled, "Yeah, Erik, she's got a good point. Carmen, you can be my homie and my boo. Come here and give me a kiss."

"T, you so silly, but today, I will give you that kiss." I kissed him right on them greasy lips.

Erik took another swig of his beer, stuffed his money in a bag and gave T a look that could kill. T-Love turned white as a sheet, stopped chewing and then responded, "I mean, I guess I think you did good."

Erik looked in my direction and said, "Pammy, you taking this Carmen shit to heart, huh? You really think you are Carmen, the baller." He shook his head and walked out the patio door.

I looked at T-Love with a perplexed expression on my face. "T, don't tell me he's jealous."

"I don't know what's up with that nigga. Fuck him." He gave me a high five and said, "I'm not stressing this shit! Where's your phone? I'm calling my hoochie. The wife is at the hotel."

"T-Love, she's one lucky hoochie, but what happens when you don't want her anymore?"

"Then she can look for another sponsor, and I can get me a new ho to lick my balls," T said.

"See, that's why I wanted my own. True, I want a man with money, but at the end of the day, it turns back into money. God bless the child who got *her* own."

Thirteen

On Friday, the vans came and went. Like the hands of a clock moving swiftly and surely, with equal certainty, the plan was executed. After three weekends, I had saved my prayed-for $50,000 and actually exceeded my goal. Erik no longer came, but I still sent him his third in an attempt at a peace offering. After sending him another $30,000, I decided I couldn't be a fool about it any longer so I would stop sending his third. I let go of any feelings of guilt I had. Shit! I was out there campaigning and trying to make it. Why couldn't he?

Dragos had increased my weekly supply to twenty-five kilos. I was now paying a fronted $18,500 for them and I was moving them no problem.

Two more weekends passed. There was still no Erik, so I sent no money back. Then one weekend he appeared out of nowhere and told me he wanted to put some work in. T-Love was with him, and he was real quiet. Normally, T was quiet, but only because he was eating something, and in that case, he would grunt once or twice. You could have heard a mouse piss on cotton before you heard a word come out of T-Love's mouth that day. Even the drivers, Capo and Ramón, thought that was odd. They heard the request and Capo pulled me to the side and spoke to me in a heavy Spanish accent.

"Carmen, do you think this is a good idea?"

"I'm sure," I told him confidently. "We go way back and he just had an issue with working for a woman."

"Okay, only if you're certain."

"It's good," I reassured him and walked back over to Erik and T.

Erik told me that he needed ten kilos. Wanting to be in agreement with him, I gave them to him in hopes it would squash any ill feelings. Once he received the ten kilos, neither Erik nor T looked me in the face. They just walked out the door and left. Normally, T stayed around the house or stuck up under his girl, or shall I say, his hoochie.

I realized that this life was taking its toll on me. It was getting to the point that if I drove down the street, I was paranoid of rival drug dealers, the police or stickup kids. It seemed as if the hoochies had all the fun.

I delivered the remaining ten kilos and did some window shopping at the mall to relax myself. I felt so uneasy about everything. I dismissed it as fatigue and needing a vacation. Sunday came around and still no sign of T-Love or Erik. I paged them, repeatedly and urgently using 911-911-911-911-911-000 to get their attention. When they didn't call back, I put my address 1104 and 911 to let them know to come to my home ASAP. I even put in T-Love's hoochie's code, which was 696969. Still, no answer. I decided to call Erik's home.

"Hello?" his mother answered with a Jamaican accent.

"Hi, Ms. Fournier. May I speak with Erik?"

"Hi, Pamela, how are you?"

"I'm well. Is Erik, Timothy or Diane home?"

"How is the baby? Him be fine?"

"Yes, him be fine," I said without thinking. *Damn, why won't she answer my fucking question?* "I was trying to catch Erik before I went out of town. Is he there?"

"Listen 'ere. Erik, Timothy and Diane have moved to Florida, but they don't want anyone to know. They asked me not to tell anyone. You never know what they do. Do you know what's going on?"

"No, ma'am. I don't." *I guess she doesn't know that I am the "anyone" she wasn't supposed to tell, huh?* "Please tell them I called and that I wish them well."

"Yes, I do that for you, and you take care of you and the baby."

"Ms. Fournier?"

"Yeah?"

"Thank you for the years of your hospitality. I love you."

"Pamela, you're welcome, and I love you, too."

"Bye!"

Because they had Jamaican and U.S. passports, they could be anywhere. I called the hoochie because I knew that T had told her everything. Pillow talk is deep.

"T-Love told me it was over last night and that I would never see him again. He gave me twenty-five grand, told me to take care of myself and that he really loved me but that he was moving to England. He also said, Carmen, you be talking shit about me and that they couldn't work with you. T said he got love for you, but Erik threatened to tell T's wife about me if he didn't go along with his setup. Carmen, T never wanted to hurt you, but he said you got it going on and that you would be all right." Then the bitch started crying and asking *me* if T really was gone.

"I believe he is," I told her, then I hung up the phone.

It was confirmed—I had gotten jacked for ten kilos. Robbed without a pistol. I just sat there in the middle of my kitchen floor and bawled until my eyes hurt and all the snot in my nose was on my shirt. I could believe it, but I was just fucked up behind the shit. Now I was really all by myself. Rule number two: don't trust nobody.

On top of it, I owed Dragos the money for the missing kilos. At my fronted $18,500, that meant I owed him $185,000—out of my pocket. I couldn't understand how they could place me in a position like this, to potentially place death upon my son and me. I didn't have the money, and I had no way of explaining it. Dragos's words rang in my ears: *"Carmen, you are responsible."*

As I sat on the floor, I realized I needed to make a decision. I stopped crying, then became angry. I went to my closet, pulled out my stash and counted my money. I had almost $80,000.

God . . . I know I said I would stop at fifty grand, but I was trying to do some things.

"Drop the act!" I said out loud. It was time to be honest and lose the excuses. "I'm just plain old greedy like most hustlers get in the streets. Just plain old greedy." Whew! I said it, and I felt better. I gathered all my money, except for $1,000. I figured it would get me through whatever it was I was about to go through.

I hit the streets, collected all the money, feeling numb. When I collected from Paul, he had a look on his face like he knew. Or maybe I was paranoid. It didn't matter because he had the money. G-Money was giving me the "I'm mad at you" silent treatment, so he gave me the money with no words. I didn't care. He could have thrown it on the floor, and I would have dove on it, picked it up and smiled. When I got to Delano, he wanted to talk. I refused to get out of my Jeep, so he just stood there talking to me.

"Carmen, you looking kinda rough, girl."

I continued to trace the outline of my car door along the rubber seal that keeps the moisture and air from getting into the car. I traced the door to keep from chewing it. Moving my hands up to grip the leather steering wheel, I said through gritted teeth and with dwindling patience, "Thanks a lot. Just give me the money."

"So, I gotta pay to talk to you?"

"No, I'm just in a rush."

"You're always in a rush. I'm gonna slow you down one day. I'll give you the money after I tell you something."

Shit, just what I need, a lecture. "What is it?" I asked, annoyed as fuck.

"Carmen, I'm here if you ever need me."

I won't ever need no man.

"I don't have much, and I may not be able to live like

you do, but I have my heart to give, and I want to be with you and your son. Give me a chance to make you happy."

These weak-ass lines.

"Let's go somewhere for a vacation—my expense—while your son is away."

Pamela was trying to break out, and I felt a tear forming, so I turned away to avoid eye contact.

"Chino, please stop playing. Let go of my hair. I'm sorry." He tightened his grip on my hair, and I felt the skin on my face pull back and my eyes widen. I was on my knees begging for him to end this game.

He leaned into my face, looking me dead in the eye and said, "Now say something, talk shit now. You always thought that you were better than me. Your mom always talking shit about me and how I feed my family. Thought you were too good for a nigga getting money. Look at you. Fuck you and your fake-ass family."

I grabbed his wrist in an attempt to loosen the grip he had on my hair as I felt long strands being ripped out in places. Pain tore through my skull, and I started seeing white dots every time I opened my eyes.

"Christonos, please, baby, don't do this. Let me go."

I had called him by the name only his mother used, hoping to bring back a memory and soften his heart. The look on his face did not change, and I realized using his real name had infuriated him more.

"How dare you call me that name? You ain't got it like that no more." He was seething mad and began foaming little slobber

bubbles on the sides of his mouth, spitting in my face as he con-
tinued to scream. Flinching at the flying spit, I had to make a
decision—continue to plead or begin to fight.

———

"No!" I said coldly. Here Delano was pouring his heart out,
showing his willingness to do anything for me and my son,
and I just didn't give a fuck.

"Carmen." Delano continued holding me up longer
than I wanted to be. For a tiny moment, I thought of running over what seemed like the good in my life with my
Jeep. I placed my car in gear, listening for a reason, and
said, "What?"

He stood up straight, shoulders back and said, "I love
you."

I snatched the bag from his hand and drove off. Who
needed that shit? Not me. I had all the money, but I was
short $75,000. I went to a pay phone, called Dragos and
asked if we could talk. I decided to be a grown woman
about things. I told him point-blank, "Dragos, I have some
problems with Erik and T-Love. They're out and not with
me anymore. I'm on my own. I'm a little short, but I want
to keep going. I'm willing to do what I gotta do. I can come
in person to talk more."

"Carmen, your sincerity always touches me. I understand about this life. Talk to my head driver. Good-bye."

I did as he suggested and talked to Ramón. I just wanted
to ensure that those vans kept coming and that I wouldn't
receive a Colombian necktie.

With renewed strength, I helped the guys get off to

New York. We packed the van with the money, and I briefly explained to them in my best Spanish what had happened. I was so grateful to have taken Spanish for three years in high school. This, combined with exposure to Latinos, really helped my conversational Spanish. We hardly spoke any English, because they didn't know much. But they did know how to say some things in English like, "money," "count money," "yes" and "no."

I sent them off and decided to go to a movie to calm my nerves. I wanted to think that Erik and T were playing a joke on me and that they would reappear, but I knew they wouldn't. They were gone, and it was up to me to repay their debt. "Our" debt. Besides, I was at point zero *again*. I had to bust my ass to pay Dragos and start saving all over again. I wasn't going out like that. Every thoroughbred takes a fall. This shit wasn't about money anymore. I had a point to prove and those who crossed me would eventually need me. I planned to get shit on lock and be the baddest bitch in the game.

Fourteen

Ring . . . ring.

"Hello, may I help you?"

"Hi, sweetheart." G always called me sweetheart before he asked for something.

"Hello, Gregory."

I listened to the hissing sound of him blowing smoke from his cigar before he continued.

"Meet me at the hotel. I'm here with Anthony and Marsha. They have something to show you. I think it'll be worth your time."

"Where you at?" I asked cautiously.

"The one on Morse Road."

"I'll be there in an hour."

"An hour?"

"Yes, G, or sooner."

"Please make it sooner."

"I'll try. Bye."

This muthafucka wants me to stop, drop and roll for his ass. I don't think so!

Ring . . . ring.

"Hello, may I help you?"

"Bitch!" *Click!*

Now who in the hell was that? Recently, I had become "bitch" to a lot of people, so I couldn't begin to narrow down who that was. I had other things on my mind. Just for today, I would be that bitch.

Finally, I would meet Marsha and Anthony. I had heard a lot about them—a boosting couple. I wondered what they were trying to sell. Maybe it was jewelry or perfume. Maybe shoes. Whatever it was, I would know soon!

I arrived at the hotel, clean as a whistle, wearing a Guess jean outfit with matching boots and purse, and smelling like gardenias, and G wanted me to buy some tools. Ain't that some shit? A bunch of tools, stolen from a hardware store. They were valuable, I was sure. But they weren't my style or concern.

"No, G. I don't want them." *These nickel-and-dime marks. I can't believe G called me here for this shit. I owe a king's ransom, and I'm out here looking at some Black and Decker.*

He continued to question me. "Why, C?"

"What can I do with these?"

"Sell them."

"To who?" I asked, actually expecting an answer from this clown.

"I don't know. You're resourceful."

"Tools?"

"Yes, it's a good price."

"A trunkful of tools." My mouth fell open. *Where in the hell is a microphone when you need one? I need to scream a Flavor Flav wake-up into the mic.*

"They've been waiting for over an hour for you. They expect to make this sale."

"How much?"

"Five hundred."

"Hell no!"

"How you gon' play me?" He threw his hands up in the air in frustration.

"I'm not playing you. You know I don't want tools. You need to talk to them. Let's go inside."

I parked my whip, and we walked into the hotel room.

"Anthony, Marsha, this is Carmen." G made the introductions.

"Hi, Carmen," they said in unison.

"First of all, how do you get all those clothes?"

Anthony answered, "Well as you see, I'm only four-eleven and my wife is four-nine, so, Carmen, the clothing racks are taller than we are. We just creep through them and nobody ever sees us. They only see the empty racks when we leave the store. People call us the Littles."

I shook my head no. "I really like the clothes, but these tools, I can't do it," I said, offering a polite rejection.

"G, you said she would do it!" Marsha screamed with an attitude.

"I just can't get rid of them," I explained.

"Give them to your husband," little Miss Marsha suggested.

Frustrated by now, I barked, "Look, I'll give you $250 for them, just because."

G blurted out, "No way! Carmen, you got the money."

No, this nigga didn't just call me out like this. "G, can we talk for a minute?" We walked out the door, just far enough away so they couldn't eavesdrop, and then I turned to him, got up in his face. "G, I'm out here trying to get money, and you call me out here to hustle backward. Yo, I don't hustle backward, and you had best not ever in this life, or the next, call me for some bullshit. You've played yourself, playa."

He tried to talk, and I continued. "I know I got money, nigga, but it ain't yours to spend. Understand?" I stood there until, like a kid, he nodded that he understood. I couldn't afford to go through this petty shit again.

I peeked my head into the hotel room and bid farewell. "Anthony, Marsha, I can't help you, but it was very nice meeting you." I turned to leave, and as I walked to my car, G kept complaining in my ear.

"G, what's up? I just can't use the tools, but I'll see if I can find someone who can."

"No, don't help me. I don't need your help." He started whining and rolling his eyes like a thirteen-year-old girl on the playground.

"G, it don't have to be this way. You catching feelings over some tools? What's really going on?"

"Nothing. You think you all that? You think you the shit?"

"All what?"

"All that, but you're not."

I paused for a moment, then spoke. "You know what, G, I am all that now, and my time is valuable . . . too valuable to be called away over some bullshit, but thanks for calling." As I walked to my Jeep, I realized this was once again jealousy, and it was getting old. I could expect it from a woman, but from a man, it's fucked up. Suddenly, G began to laugh like a maniac from a horror movie. I detected something in his laugh but I dismissed it. "Bye, Gregory."

He stood there and watched as I drove away.

I was cruising the streets with my eyes glued on my rearview mirror looking out for the po-po, a tail or a stickup kid on my trail. I thought about how much I had been using my phone lately and was wary of a phone tap. To relieve the stress, I decided to pamper myself. I went downtown to the City Center Mall and treated myself to a facial, manicure and pedicure. Inside the mall was a Caribbean bistro, so I splurged on lunch.

Afterward, I started window shopping, but I was ready to spend. Walking past Frederick's of Hollywood, I envisioned myself wearing the lingerie and silk and lace panty set on display in the window for someone special. I closed my eyes and I imagined a pair of strong arms embracing me, caressing me, making me feel like a desired, sensual woman, then a faint bump into me brought me back to reality. I looked to my left and observed a woman and a man who carried a small child in his arms walking past me. I realized I had no one. The things I really desired, money couldn't buy. But instead of wallowing in self-pity, I moved on.

Perfumania, my favorite perfume store, seemed to call my name as I neared. I couldn't resist the alluring mixture of fragrances, so I purchased perfumes and had them gift-wrapped for my mom and sister. Next, I purchased a beautiful red Armani suit for my sister because she had just started a new job.

Sure, I had money, but who knew what the future held? The future wouldn't catch up to the present and not let me spend the money I earned in the past. Be it death, the penitentiary or the grave, I was spending some of that money. Hell, Erik and T-Love were somewhere spending all the money I'd thrown bricks at the penitentiary to make, so I would, too.

I wanted to give Chino something, but what did you give a man who had everything? Then I knew—a toy. You gave a man who had everything a toy. Maybe one day I'd get Chino a motorcycle. I thought, *Whatever my Chino wants, he can have!*

And my son. What would I give my son? "Don't worry, baby. Mommy is out here getting down for her crown. You are gonna have more. I see that for you, and I'm gonna get it for you—by any means necessary."

Fifteen

Ring . . . ring.

"Hello, may I help you?

"Hello, Pammy?" It was my mom, and she never called me on my work line.

"What's up, Mom? Why are you calling my work line?"

"I was coming from the grocery store and noticed a car following me. Have you talked to Chino? Is he looking for you or something?"

"No, Mom, why do you think that you're being followed?"

"The other day I went to open the blinds in the dining room and noticed a car parked on the side of the house. A man was sitting inside, and I didn't really pay it too much attention, but when I was coming out of the grocery store parking lot, I saw the same man and car behind me as I pulled into traffic. Now, the last time you and Chino were feuding and you took his money and left, him and some other thug—"

"He's not a thug, Mama," I interrupted.

"Him and some other thug"—she pronounced every

word this time—"came up here looking for you. So what's going on?"

I had no idea, but I knew it wasn't Chino. I had only gone home once since I started hustling with the drugs, and I hoped to God no one was staking out my mom's house or putting a tail on her.

Immediately wanting to calm my mother's concerns, I said, "Mom, don't even worry. You know that you ain't did nothing wrong, and if someone is tailing you, it's because of your cooking. You probably have a stalker looking for your world-famous Star barbecue sauce. Don't stress it, and stop thinking the worst. Okay?"

"Okay, Pammy, I just wanted to talk to you and make sure you were okay."

"Mom, I'm fine, and since you called, I was wondering if you'd like to keep your grandson."

My mom happily agreed to keep the baby for me while I looked for a house and continued to get myself together. My mom had no idea that I was dealing drugs. I told her I was doing nails at home and was back in school. Nothing but lies. She didn't ask too many questions, probably because she didn't want to believe that I was in the streets. Many in my family assumed that Chino finally came through and was helping me out on the down low, so I didn't have to answer many questions. I just promised to hurry, get myself together and get back in contact with family.

As the weekend approached, I contacted the guys and told them of my new ticket. It was a high post as usual.

I decided to raise my tickets in an attempt to recoup my losses. I increased my tickets by $1,000. Even though there were gripes, everyone just rolled with it. I told them it was due to a drought in New York. What could they say? Droughts happen, prices vary, people get popped, people have falls and people take losses. Not to mention, the political aspect of drug importation. That was the way of the streets.

I figured that I would have Dragos paid in about three weeks of steady pumpin'. Plus, I was placing an extra thirty Gs on top of my payoff just on GP for being late to mend the relationship and to show some integrity. Shit, the bill collector gets interest if you're late, why not my supplier? I was like the United States Postal Service, rain, snow, sleet or shine, I was coming through. On top of it, the service was still bringing in about $2,000 a week, so I was happy about that.

I went to a Realtor I knew and I told her I wanted a house on a land contract, no questions asked. A nice home for me and my son. She dated a black guy who was in the game and instantly knew what time it was. He had been in the life, but with her being a white girl, she was able to get her foot in places that I could not get into. So I let her do all the legwork, for a discreet fee, of course.

I wanted the American Dream, though I wasn't sure if I would stay in Columbus. I still wanted to move, but I was keeping my options open in Columbus. Moving to New York was out of the question but a small town anywhere would work. All I knew was that wherever I ended up, my home would be mine.

All I could think was, Where is my Chino? If only he knew how much I needed him. I had been dreaming of him lately, and in my dreams, *he* needed me. He was calling out to me. I didn't know where he was or what he was doing, but I knew he was broke and in need of cash. I could feel it. He needed help, and like me, he needed to know he had someone he could depend on. Yeah, he needed me. My dreams never lied. I spoke right to his spirit.

"Chino, I don't have much, but what I have is yours, and I'm still here for you. Can you hear me?"

On the ground with my hair twisted in between Chino's fingers, I knew that I had to fight; not with my fists, but with a woman's mind. I looked up into his face with eyes full of tears and said, "Chino, baby, please don't hurt me. All I wanted, all I ever needed to know was that you loved me. I miss you and how you used to make love to me."

He began to loosen his grip, allowing me to assume a submissive position on my knees in front of him. I began to caress his legs up to his groin area as I continued to plead, "Chino, don't do this to us."

I began to bring my face near his knees and began to stroke and talk to his ego. "Chino, just hold me, baby. Make love to me." Knowing there was no better feeling than making up after a passionate fight, I tried to reach his desire. He loosened the grip on my hair but still held the back of my head and began to respond.

"Pooh, why you be trippin', acting crazy and shit." I began to unzip his pants and move my lips to his private area. Loosening his belt buckle, he placed the nine that was in his waistband on the chair cushion, which was hiding my .380 underneath.

When I felt his grip completely release from my hair, I made my move. As Chino relaxed and prepared to be sexed, I reared my fist back and punched him between his legs. The smack of his balls against the knuckles of my fist echoed in the room. He bellowed and doubled over in pain, holding his dick while falling to his knees. I stood over him, grabbed his gun from the chair and cocked the gun, placing one in the chamber. "Now, muthafucka, who's the bitch? Looks like you the bitch, Chino. If you only knew how to control your dick, we wouldn't be in this predicament in the first place. I wouldn't have bitches calling the shop, and we would be happy." Placing the nine to the back of his head, I screamed, "Now, muthafucka, what?"

I closed my eyes in an attempt to erase the memory. I felt tears escaping, but I wiped them away. I opened my eyes with an eerie feeling but that feeling was overcome by a tingling sensation in my right ear. As I began to rub frantically, I thought, *Damn, my ears are burning. Someone must be talking about me.*

Sixteen

"Chino, man, check it out! You will never believe what I found out. Okay. Remember I went to that party with Delano?" said Rock.

"Yeah."

"I went trying to mix it up and get us another hookup since Joe Bub Baby got knocked and we fell off."

"Right, right." Chino nodded.

"Well, Delano is still trying to tax me. Shit, we wholesale not retail. But I went anyway because he really started blowing up when he got his new hookup."

"How was it?"

"It was a small gathering, but it was real nice. It was at a party house up north for this girl named Gabrielle. Remember everyone was talking shit about this new *bitch* that's suppose to have it going on and serving up ballers with high-quality shit?"

"Yeah, real competition."

"Chino, if Joe Bub's ass wasn't so greedy and tried to cut a side deal, we would have never fell off, and he would not be in lockdown."

"So?"

"Well, I finally met that bitch, and she *is* as polished as we've heard."

"How do you know this?"

"Because I've worked with the best and that's you, and this bitch been schooled by the best. Problem is, she ain't really a bitch at all. She really is good people. Chino, it's Carmen."

"Who?"

"Carmen."

"I don't know a Carmen."

"Man, all the shit coming through stamped with TCP is from Carmen."

"TCP?"

"Nigga, you forgot the Triple Crown Posse?"

"I know about my Triple Crown Posse, but no one else's."

"Man, the bitch slangin' them thangs is none other than your Pooh. She is going by the name Carmen. She is a baller and got some people in her corner. There were several Spanish people at the party, and one she was introducing as her brother. But I know it ain't her brother. He's Colombian, and she was kickin' it all tight and shit with him. Remember, Pooh speaks Spanish also."

"You don't have to tell me about my Pooh. I remember everything about her. Are you sure? What did she say when she saw you?"

"I don't think she remembered me. I wasn't around her that much. I'm sportin' my dreads now. I wish the police would forget my face, but I remembered her. She was looking at me like I looked familiar. But I just kept moving out of her full sight. I didn't want to get my ass thrown out of there."

"Maybe it was her man she was with?" asked Chino.

"No, Chino, she's solo. He ain't her man. They just friends, business associates and pretending to be brother and sister. I watched her all night. Delano wants her, but she got him on hold. I noticed how he looked at her. Chino, Pooh was looking good, too. Just to see her laughing and holding her head up like she was—I was glad to see her like that."

"A'ight nigga, enough of that. What's happening with her? Was the baby there?"

"Why you want to know about her baby?"

"Fuck it, man. So what happened?" Chino reacted irritatedly.

"Oh, nothing you would want to know," Rock responded playfully.

"Don't make me drop you. Keep your info. I don't fuck with her. She is crazy anyway."

"Y'all both crazy as hell and really need to squash that old shit. Delano said her son is cute and a good baby."

"She be letting that sucka around my . . . the baby? When I see that mark, I will check him about that. Don't he got enough baby mamas of his own to fuck with?" Chino began to shift his weight back and forth from one foot to the other revealing his frustration.

"Look, I got a run to make. All I am saying is she got it on lockdown, and Delano ain't giving us no play."

"Was that sucka Erik there?"

"Yeah, but he was not with her, and to be honest, I don't think they were ever together like you thought they were."

"Who asked you that?"

"You know we boys, and I'm in your corner. But I ain't going into that shit. That's an old can of worms. I just try to look out and speak on what I see. But, it is like this: either we take the ticket Delano is offering us or you step to your Pooh, 'cause she got it going on, or we keep taking a beating like we have been. You know Pooh got love for you and would help you. She would help anyone out."

"Fuck that. I won't ask her for shit. We gon' be all right. We can make it."

"I can't keep starving. It's about business. I don't want to deal with Delano, but I can't hold out either. We've been in a slump for six months. I love being on your team, Chino, but I gotta eat, too. My pockets are hit."

"Right, right," Chino said blandly nodding his head up and down, understanding where his partner was coming from.

"I gotta bounce and make this run. Get back with me. Oh, also that escort service we use from time to time. The one that has Ashley and China. Well, that is Pammy's service also. Chino, Pammy done made a come-up. I like that about her because we all left her ass for dead. Go ahead and make that move. I'm with you until the end, and you know this."

"Yeah, Rock, I know this, and I'll talk to you later. Thanks for the info."

"Gone."

"Peace."

———

Shit! Here I am taking a beating and Pooh got it going on. Well, I guess it's not Pooh anymore, but Carmen. Where did she get that name from? I kept hearing about this girl slangin' them thangs, but it never crossed my mind that it could be Pooh.

Well, it did occur to me a little when I found out that she was doing good despite how I left her. Pooh got so much in her that I schooled her with, she can succeed at anything. I never told her that to her face, but it is true. I'm not surprised that she is still floatin'.

One night I was hanging out with her brother—her real brother, Young Ty. I named her brother Young Ty after my older brother. He was thirsty for knowledge, admired me and was handsome like my older brother. So I started calling him Young Ty. We all decided to get us some girls, and Ty called an escort service that he said he was cool with the owner of. So that was her escort service too that we used? She still didn't let on that it was her. I kinda missed her trying to get in touch with me. But she left my ass alone. I guess she was over me, which was good. She needed to go on with her life. I'm sure as hell trying to do so. I still think about her all the time. Problem is, I can't tell nobody about it. Everyone would think I am crazy to even be thinking about her. They would think I was soft.

After the drama, I couldn't turn back. I still can't believe my Pooh played her hand the way she did. I knew she had heart, but damn! I am not mad at her though. I deserved it and had it coming. Anytime you cross someone, there is a consequence.

My grandma kept telling me to be decent to her. She deserved that much. But for some reason, I just started torturing her, rubbing shit in her face and acting like I owed her nothing and she didn't help me with nothing. I drove her crazy.

All I wanted to do was let her ass know how I felt when I found her and that black-ass Jamaican Erik at that hotel that day. How the friendship that they developed in my absence affected me. She said they were friends, and he was someone she could talk to while I was away. It's a terrible feeling to think that the next man is taking your place or taking up slack in any area because you were in lockdown. I just thought that when I got out of jail, it would be all good.

When we first met, I had my concerns. You know, like if her love was true. But it was, and she was always there when I needed her the most, and here I am needing her again. No one ever knew how much Pooh did for me. Then I spread lies about the baby and about how the drama happened to further help myself. I mean, why would she help me? I let her starve. Why should she help me? Would she help me? Shit just got fucked up. Then I went and got married on her while she was pregnant. I ain't really shit. What women need to understand about me is that I don't sweat them. Yeah, I like pretty, but pretty is what pretty ain't. You can't take pretty to the bank.

I saw Pooh rolling in her Jeep on the streets, looking good with her head held high. I pulled up beside her and kept trying to catch her eye. Either she saw me and kept on movin', or she didn't recognize my new car. I told her brother about it, so I know that she knew I saw her, yet still no word from her. Pooh knew I was going to come around, and we was gonna work something out. But no, she couldn't wait. Hell, she had been waiting for me to come home from prison. Then I came home and wanted her to wait some more. I got carried away, and Pooh got tired. Now I'm with my wife, and I can't look out the window over a minute or stare off in space without my wife naggin' me and asking me, "You still thinking about that girl?" or "You still love Pammy, don't you?"

One day, I just told her point-blank, "Divorce me if you can't understand. You should be happy I'm here with you." My wife got what she wanted—me—and she still wasn't happy. She wasn't happy because she had me physically, and Pooh still had me emotionally. And the shit gave me a headache. Then I got me some more kids, two more boys. I love my kids, too. Problem is, how do I correct my wrongs with Pammy and still look like a man. I got enough on my mind, and I wished I could just talk to my Pooh, because when I talked to her, it was like my spirit was at peace, but I couldn't tell nobody this either. So many people looked up to me and depended on me. I had mouths to feed, people to see, places to go, moves to make.

I want to open another salon. But I don't have the money to do it. Every time I drive past our old salon, I get so mad, I could spit on someone. Pooh just walked away from the salon and said, "Fuck it!" But what else could she do? So I still ain't mad at her. She loved her salon, and I really wanted her to have it. Busted my ass so she could have it. But this ain't no memory lane, and I have got to get some money. So, God, you know I love my Pooh. I forgive her and I pray that she forgives me, too. Can you have her get in touch with me? Pooh, can you hear me? Remember, I always told you if you listen closely, that you could hear me in your mind. Pooh, I still need you. Can you hear me?

Seventeen

$\mathcal{I}$ ran into my baby brother, Young Ty. He was supposed to be in Ohio for school, but he ran the streets with his friends and Chino all the time. He had seen Chino at the Golden Eight Ball pool hall, where a lot of ballers hung out. They started kicking it after seeing each other there several times. Word got back to me about Chino. He was in the streets all night and used my escort service quite often. I was hurt for a minute because he could have gotten it from me, free of charge, but his money spent just like any other clients.

I heard his business was really fucked up. He was trying to get Young Ty to start selling kilos so they could work together—anything not to deal with me. Ty tried to pretend that the drugs he requested weren't for Chino, but I knew better, and Ty became fixed in the middle of our drama.

When Ty was fifteen, Chino and I became his legal guardians. Even though Chino and I were kids ourselves, we joined forces to save Ty from the streets, which was difficult because that was all he knew. He eventually got kicked out by our stepfather, making the streets his permanent home.

When Chino and I separated, we didn't know what to do with Ty. Ty would listen to my ranting about Chino, and when he was with Chino, he would listen to his ravings about me. Ty was unable to offer his sincere opinion due to his loyalty to both of us.

Chino was like a father to him, teaching him how to dress, what to do if he caught a sexually transmitted disease but, most of all, how to want more out of life. And I was his big sis, and he wanted the best for me. And the best for him was our home, a secure and familial atmosphere. Ty became the second displaced child in our breakup. I felt sorry for him, and responsible, because I could not pull our family back together.

I wanted to mend the fences for Ty and just give Chino some money. My family and friends would think that I was stupid for helping him. But no one knew what we were feeling or going through.

I still had a lot of old photos of Chino and the fellas from some of their cross-country trips. But I was ready to let go of that life. That was the past, and I had been making my own memories. I wanted to give him his old photos back. One day I hoped I would.

I decided not to work with Ty to sell drugs, but I sent my pager number to Chino through Ty. This would let Chino know that it was all good, and one day when he was ready, he would call.

Everything was going well for me. I repaid Dragos and strengthened our relationship, and I saved more than enough money to make a good life for my son and me.

Dragos was very pleased with the additional $30,000 I gave him as interest on the loss I had taken. Nevertheless, he made it clear that I shouldn't make coming up short a habit.

I had a nice stash stacked. I purchased a gorgeous new house in an expensive suburb of Columbus. It had four bedrooms, three and a half baths and a two-car garage. My son had a wonderful room and his own bath with all Mickey Mouse fixtures that he really loved.

My beautiful master bedroom featured a walk-in closet finished in light wood. It was so big, it could have been another bedroom. It had built-in closets and shoe racks. My closet was on full. I had been shopping like crazy, and the boosters had been very helpful as well.

I decorated my entire house all by myself. I purchased everything new and got rid of all my old items. I ordered one-of-a-kind furniture in breathtaking greens and ivories. I chose Italian fabrics and leather. I had plush carpet that cushioned my every step, and in my foyer and my formal dining area there were marble floors.

I finished off my great room with a large 100-inch TV that lowered from the ceiling with a laser disc player and surround sound. I went out and purchased everything I ever dreamed of and all that was ever promised to me. I went to a specialty store just for those items that added the finishing touch to a home like vases, rocks and black art. I put all these touches in every part of the house. It didn't take very long to exceed my prayer request. Not only had I reached my goal of fifty thousand, but I had well over a million dollars saved, a house and a new BMW. I was thinking of getting a sports car that went 180 mph in nine seconds, but I was afraid to crash. I purchased a flawless three-carat diamond ring and earrings to match. I even had a cleaning lady who did everything, including my laundry. I had it all.

The problem was, I still was not happy. I was happy with my accomplishments, but there was still something missing. The real high of hustling is the come-up. I had been working with various new shorties and had to admit, I was jealous because it was *their* come-up.

I met this one shorty as I was walking down the mall, shopping bags in hand. He walked up on me and offered me lunch. I was flattered, but declined.

"No, thank you." I decided to feel this stranger out to see if he was a gang member, store security or whatever. My main concern was that I didn't know him.

"Please. Lunch won't hurt you."

"Okay, I'll have lunch with you." I only said yes because he reminded me so much of myself when I approached Dragos. He offered to carry my bags as we walked toward the mall food court.

"We can eat at one of the mall restaurants or go somewhere else," he offered, pointing at the food court.

"The mall spot is cool." Does he think I would leave the mall with a perfect stranger so he could try to kill me? No way. I felt like a celebrity.

As we ate, he told me how he had heard about me and that he was looking to make it in this life.

"Carmen, I work for someone, and they taxin' me. I

don't even have a car or a place to live, but I've got heart. If you let me work for you, I promise to come up and do better. My folks live in the Windsor Terrace projects, and I want out."

"Right, right." I enjoyed listening to him because it's all about the desire to come up, because the money will follow. So I said, "I'll think about it."

He refused to let me get away.

"Ms. Carmen, what do I have to do? Kill somebody for you?"

I thought, *Fuck, this is 5-0!* Then I realized by the sincerity in his eyes, he wasn't. It was his heart, and he was going for broke. With that, he was in. I gave him the street name Cat because of his hazel-green eyes. He ended up being the best hustler I had ever worked with. Cat was married with a child on the way and stacking dollars in the process. I had no losses or problems with him at all.

I also had a new driver named Wade. I met him at a Philly nightclub. He was the thuggish, ruggish, bone type. Pitch-black in color with pearly whites that you never saw because he never smiled. He wore a poker face and corn-rows to the back, though he picked out his hair into a large fro sometimes to let it breathe. Every girl needs a real thug in her life, once or twice. She probably won't be planning her future with him, but she'll be having some fun. He was always rapping and rhyming as he aspired to be the next Jay-Z, always telling me, "Girl, you paid, spend that damn money. Smoke a blunt, have some fun."

He was a great driver, accurate and reliable. He was also

a great bedroom partner. Wade was a brother who could give the best mind-numbing head. Say-my-name head, make-you-scream head. Wade was a full-service thug: give back rubs, suck your toes, pamper you.

In the bedroom he always told me, "Lay down, baby, let me try something new on you. I'm going to do the slurp, suck and bubble blow move. Tell me if you like it, love."

If Wade had been charging, I'd have been paying. If he'd charged by the climax, he could've retired a billionaire. I called Wade whenever I was stressed and wanted to be sexed. He handled me like a champion.

My first encounter with him was incredible. We were driving, and he suggested a detour through Franklin Park. He directed me behind some trees, hidden from the view of cars passing by. I followed his lead and pulled in behind the bushes. He began to caress my neck and shoulders with his left hand. Placing the car in park, I closed my eyes and let out a deep breath, feeling instantly relaxed. It had been almost a year since a man touched me, and I was ready.

Wade continued, "Come in the back with daddy, baby."

I followed him to the rear of the van and watched him clear an area for me to lie down. Wade stood outside the door as I rested back on my elbows. He removed his shirt, revealing a six-pack midsection. Baby had the body of a Greek god. He licked his fingers, sticking his tongue in between them, and gave me a sexy grin. I thought, *Yeah, baby, let momma see what you got in them jeans.*

He started with my toes, sucking from the baby toe to the big toe. Next, he slowly removed my clothing with his teeth. Turning me over, he began to lick up and down my spine. His licks stopped at the crack of my ass, and I felt the warm saliva from the tip of his tongue. Wade continued, circling my asshole, lifting one leg over his shoulder and turning me over. He started giving me head as I squeezed the sides of his face, moaning with pleasure. His tongue felt so good that I didn't want him to stop—*ever*. As he slid his middle finger in and out of my vagina, I climaxed for what I believed to be the third time. It felt like ecstasy, and I forgot all about where we were and enjoyed the art of lovemaking.

I tugged at his belt buckle, anxious to feel him inside of me. I pulled down Wade's pants, and he was packing. Wade had no less than twelve inches of rock-hard 100 percent beef. Taking every inch was a task, but it was fun attempting to take it all as I felt his thickness between my legs.

He moaned when he fucked, so I knew he was into me. "Whose is it?"

All I could say was, "Yours, baby, it's yours." I moaned from pleasure and bit into my bottom lip with each climax.

Wade left me depleted of energy. I crawled into a fetal position beside him as he kissed my shoulder and covered me with the shirt he had been wearing. This man knew how to make love to a woman. He didn't ask dumb-ass questions like, "Was it good?" or "Did you cum?" When a man has to ask, he should know that the answer will be a lying "yes."

We got our sex thang on in between runs, but I still missed my Chino. He hadn't called yet. I knew he was just being stubborn. That's how he was. He once told me that love was stronger than pride, but so was the love of money, and he loved money more than anything, so I knew I would hear from him eventually.

Sittin' up in my luxurious room and thinkin' thoughts of my life, I began experimenting with drugs. I had gotten that miserable. The more I had, the more miserable I became. Wade would roll up his blunts and lace them with cocaine and one day I just decided to try it. I was slipping, then I let myself slip totally and began to snort cocaine. I preferred to snort by myself; this way I could listen to Marvin Gaye as loud as I wanted and allow my mind to drift wherever. Some nights I would sit up all night snortin', trippin', gettin' horny and snortin' some more.

During these times I wished Chino could see my home and see that I did well. He'd be proud that all he taught me really paid off. Noticing the stacks of $100 bills on my dresser, the white down comforter on my bed, the 500-thread-count sheets—I saw all I wanted, but I felt what I needed. "Damn, I miss Chino!"

Eighteen

Two weeks had passed since I had begun experimenting with drugs. And I decided to call it quits with the service and the boosters. It was just too much, and although they were my first loves in the life, I had to let them go. I told the girls face-to-face, and they were extremely upset with me. They were so faithful to the service that they laid big guilt trips on me. I vowed to get them all settled. I explained to them that it was over for me, and that they should want out, too. I was outgrowing this life. I gave each of the girls $1,000 as my last gift to them.

I also helped Gabrielle get her own one-bedroom apartment because she stuck with me through thick and thin. I offered the client list to Renaye because she had a great business mind. She was so excited and immediately took the reins and started her own service out of her home. I gave the other girls money and a farewell dinner, which was very emotional. We all ended it with China's line, "Let that be the reason we all do great things with our lives."

China didn't show up to the dinner, and no one had seen her for a while, so after dinner, I drove around some of the areas I thought she might be. Knowing her, she was out getting money. I cruised by the car wash, noticing all the hotties kicking it with the local ballers, admiring the cars as they rolled off the drying line. Sammy's Auto Clean was the spot in Columbus. If you wanted your car cleaned, you went there. If you wanted to meet some fine-ass brothers, you went there, too.

I pulled in and started kicking it with the fellas, asking about China. The owner had a thing for China and allowed her to hang around the place as she hustled the men for $20. I told her to stop that shit, but men gave China $20 just for a conversation.

I got my car washed and had to check one of the attendants about skimping on my shit. I wanted my shit Armor All'd down, fingerprints on the insides of the windows removed and inside doorjambs cleaned. Plus, cherry scent for the inside was a must.

Next, I cruised over to Expressions Hair & Nail Salon on Franksway Street to see if China was getting her nails done. She wasn't. Then I remembered hearing rumors that China had started with a pimp named Mark. He had a rep for being very hard on his girls. I heard he kept her full of coke and working straight 24/7. Something told me to try her grandmother's house because I knew she was the only family she kept up with.

I went to her grandmother's house, which was off of a main street in the heart of the inner city. When I pulled up, there were several cars parked out front. I had met her grandmother once when the girls and I brought China's daughter a birthday present, so I didn't think she would mind that I just showed up uninvited. I tapped on the door and a woman who resembled China answered and let me in. Her grandmother walked straight up to me, crying, and wrapped her arms around me. She turned to introduce me and said, "Everyone, this was China's friend Carmen. She tried to help her."

I was confused, and then stunned to realize I had arrived after China's funeral! China's look-alike younger sister, Gloria, led me to a back bedroom. She told me that they had found China in the alley. She had died of an overdose of crack cocaine and heroin. She had been beaten badly and the police were looking for Mark. I embraced Gloria as tears flowed down her face. She reached underneath the bed and handed me a newspaper article about China's death.

The article included a coroner's report of her autopsy that said, "Woman's cause of death was a combination of a toxic level of drugs and asphyxia. Subject was strangled, as imprints were apparent, in addition to ripped skin below the right ear. Blood vessels were broken in both eyes from the pressure of strangulation." I could not read any more as my tears joined Gloria's. No human being should have to die this way. China's daughter walked over to me and asked, "Can I go home with you tonight?" All I could say was "Yes." I got permission and sent her to pack.

My heart hurt for China. *Let that be the reason I get my ass out of these streets*, I thought. Starting that very night, I never picked up another drink or indulged in another drug.

China's daughter had so many questions about her mom and her lifestyle. Her innocent voice queried, "Is my mom in heaven?" I stroked her hair as I drove and replied, "Yes, your mom was the best, and she is in heaven with God, looking down on you."

"Will I ever see her again?"

"Of course, if you close your eyes you can see her. Plus you'll always carry her in your heart." I pointed to her chest to remind her that her mom was in there. She rubbed her heart and closed her eyes and said, "Carmen, I carry my mom in my heart. I want to die to be with her. Why did that man choke her?"

I wanted her to stop talking because with every word, I thought of my son, how the tables could turn and it could be my son with the questions. How would my absence be explained?

I pulled over and looked into her eyes and said, "Listen, you have to keep living and make your mommy proud. This is what she would want. She is watching over you. Your mom was a strong lady, and that same strength is in you. She loved you very much, and you have to always want to live." The tears fell down her little blushed cheeks, mixing with snot from her nose and slobber from her mouth. I wiped it all with my hands, not caring about the slimy goo. I just wanted to ease her pain.

I returned China's daughter to her grandma's the following night with the promise that I would visit. I gave China's grandmother some money and asked her if she wanted to move out of the projects, but she refused to give up on her neighborhood. The money, she told me, she would put away for China's little girl. I didn't have the answers. I only knew that I didn't want that to happen to me and my son. Most of all, I didn't want him to find out about me like that.

I told the other girls from the service and gave them all copies of China's obituary. That night I prayed! *God, thank you for your blessings and please, please bless China's family.*

———

Beep . . . beep . . . beep . . . beep.

Wiping the sleep from my eyes, I peered at the small screen of my pager but didn't recognize the number. Who was paging me this early in the morning? *This better be good.* 8322504228228. Who was this? 8322504228911911.

"Whose number is this?" I picked up my phone and dialed the number.

Ring . . . ring.

"Hello?" someone answered.

"Someone call a pager?" I asked.

"Pooh, it's me. You gave someone else my code 228?"

I was speechless.

He whispered, "Hey, how you doing? I got my white flag up. I surrender. I need you."

Without hesitation I responded, "Chino, where are you? I'm here for you."

Nineteen

$\mathcal{I}$ jumped out of bed so full of happiness that I felt like I was floating on air. *My Chino finally got in touch with me. Thank you, God! There really is a God after all. Now I can quit this business,* I thought. My mind was leaping forward to my new future: no more drug dealing, no more streets. I wanted to go back to school and get my degree. I was very intelligent, and I was ready to move on with my life.

I planned to meet with Chino and offer him his photos and some money for him and his new family. I felt whole. I was going to see my Chino and I could do something for him that he would know was from my heart. Not because he was a drug dealer or because he did things for me or because we were together or because he gave me anything. It would be a "just because" gift. We both knew he had never given our son anything, but I wanted him to know that there was someone he could depend on with no strings attached. This was not about a future relationship, that was over for us; this was about all we had been through.

I remember speaking to him on the phone after our separation, I was crying and accusing him of never loving me. He said, "Pooh, please stop. Let the past stay there. I'm calling now." And sure enough, he used to sneak and call me on the phone when others thought we never spoke. We tried to talk things out, but we couldn't because we were too busy blaming each other for all the wrongs in the relationship. Now I could finally close this chapter of my life. I would apologize and give him a gift that I prayed overwhelmed him like all the many things he had given me.

I thought, *Now . . . hmmmm, what will I wear? Because I must look fabulous.* I walked into my closet, scanned the shelves and racks of clothes and picked out a navy blue Armani suit.

"No, this won't work . . . too businesslike. How about a yellow linen short set? No, this won't work either . . . too casual. Or a dress with some gator sandals? Chino always liked soft and jazzy clothes. Wait, the perfect outfit! A Polo pullover with some jeans and loafers. Yeah, I'll meet him preppie-style." Every summer, we always purchased a Polo jersey and dressed alike. This outfit would be perfect, and to top it off, I would wear my old engagement ring he gave me. I always told him I threw it away, but I'd wear it now just to let him know that I still had it, even if I wore it on my right hand instead of my left. I'd wear the diamond ring that I purchased for myself on my left ring finger. Yes, I was married . . . to myself.

We were scheduled to meet at 7:00 p.m. at a seafood restaurant. That gave me just enough time to get my hair done, get my nails French manicured and run some errands. I was telling everyone that I was out of this life, and I would pass the scepter to Chino if he wanted. I knew Chino could handle my volume so maybe *he* could work with Dragos. Whatever Chino wanted, I wanted him to have it. Yes! I was on my way out of this lifestyle.

I paged G-Money and prayed he would return my call. He had a problem with me leaving the lifestyle. I saved my money, and the fellas spent theirs, because they figured they'd always be in the game. G was upset that I quit the escort business. Even after China's death, he still acted like he didn't understand why I wanted out. All G wanted was money and the streets, but I wasn't trying to hustle forever. I had a child, which meant I needed to be a responsible parent, and that involved more things than this life. Things that money couldn't buy. But here I was riding around in vans, sitting my ass on top of keys in hidden compartments and placing my life on the line. And for what? Mo' money. This was crazy.

The previous week, a baller named Nostradamus had gotten killed in a drug deal gone bad. Someone killed him over just two of them thangs. Then Paul got robbed by the same guys who supposedly killed Nostradamus. Next, one of Paul's boys, Clockin' (they called him that 'cause he stacked dollars), got knocked in a studio hotel.

The cleaning lady found a kilo of cocaine under his sink, and turned it in. When he got back to the hotel, he saw that his room had been cleaned, so he checked under the sink. His package was gone. He foolishly went to the front desk and asked for *his* package. Needless to say, they had him on lockdown. The game was getting whack!

To make matters worse, Dragos had sent me some weak

product, and I had major complaints and refund requests, and we all know ain't no refunds in the streets. So I had to work through that mess. I became suspicious of everything and everybody. I even suspected an elderly lady at the grocery store who I thought was following me was a tail. Once I even thought a kid's skateboard was a listening device.

I was tired. Hustlin' was definitely harder than working a job. It keeps ya on your toes, that's for sure, because as soon as you snooze, you lose.

I was relieved to be leaving. Hell, what if rivals tried to jack me and my no-pistol-carrying ass? I wanted out, and G would have to understand. People will play all types of guilt trips on you as if this was a real business, with benefits and a retirement plan, and I was responsible if they ate. In some ways it really was like that. Depends on your perspective.

When Chino went to jail, all the fellas in his crew fell off. Rock got evicted from his apartment. Ant became a house husband to some chick who was paying the rent while raising two kids, and their bills were soon overdue. They all fell like dominoes.

It was time for me to leave. I had my chance, now it was time for someone else to get theirs.

I pulled a T-Love move and called Wade over to the house for a booty call to relieve some stress. I showered, rubbed Bath & Body Works Warm Vanilla Sugar lotion on my body and waited. Wade never rang the doorbell; he always did this unique whistle when he got out of his lowrider that signaled his arrival. I opened the patio door wearing my birthday suit, he pulled a can of whipped cream from behind his back, smacked my ass and swooped me up into his arms.

Needless to say, I arrived to meet Chino a lil' late, and I could tell by the look on his face that he was pissed. After all, he never waited for anyone. People waited for him. But I smiled and we approached each other slowly. I knew he was wondering if I would hurt him again. I just walked toward him with open arms, and we embraced each other. It was a wonderful feeling.

"Pooh, step back, let me look at you." I did as he asked and turned around to give him a look from every angle. "You look good."

"So do you," I told him as I admired him from head to toe. "Shall we eat?"

"Yeah, I'm starvin' like—"

"Marvin, right?" I responded, completing his sentence.

"You know it!" His voice rang with a baritone sound.

"Two for dinner?" asked the maître d'.

"Yes."

"Smoking preference?"

Chino took the lead. "None."

We were led to our table and took our seats. "Your waitress will be with you in one moment," the maître d' told us as he placed menus in front of us. "Enjoy your meal," he said into the air as he left.

We placed our orders without saying a word to each other. Some young ballers were eating and passed our table. One recognized me and gave me his pager number and said, "Baby girl, give me a call. I'm trying to work out with you, yo." I could tell the attention made Chino uncomfortable.

"So, Pooh, you're a celebrity?" asked Chino while glancing at the tattered paper with the scribbled number written in blue.

"Nah, I'm just an entrepreneur—always for me, never for yours."

"Ha-ha, you got game in you."

I knew that would make him laugh.

Our food arrived and we both started slamming, just like old times when we went out for dinner. He even took a couple pieces of food off my plate. "Chino"—I smacked his hand playfully—"you always eating my food."

"And you know it."

We're breaking the ice. We both were chewing with our mouths stuffed, and at the same time, we looked at each other and said simultaneously, "I'm sorry." Then he winked.

"Chino, forgive your Pooh," I pleaded.

"Done. Pooh, forgive your Chino."

"Done. I never thought this day would come, did you?" I asked.

"I knew it would. It was just a matter of time. So what is this I hear about you in these streets? You know I never wanted that for you." He met my eyes dead center and I held his stare like a challenge. He broke the stare and looked away first, so I spoke the facts.

"Well, I had to do what I had to do."

"How is the baby?" he asked.

"He's fine. How have you been?" I attempted to make

eye contact as I tried to find out what was going on with him.

"Taking a real live beating," Chino confessed.

"Well, Chino, I'm here to help and give you what you need."

"Right, right."

"Chino, you can talk to me. You know this, man!" I said in a high octave, mimicking Chris Tucker's character Smokey in *Friday*. We both laughed. I was trying to keep the mood light because I knew his pride was wounded. He kept fidgeting.

"Pooh, I need some of them thangs."

Damn, is this what this meeting is all about? Kilos? "Chino, you don't need them, 'cause I have money saved up, and it's yours. How much you need?"

"I don't need you to give me anything. I can work for mine, and I don't want no handouts. I want to work and make my own money. I don't want you to be able to say that you gave me anything."

"Chino, I'm not like that, and you know it. Please don't do this. What's mine is yours. I can take care of you and your family just like you took care of me and mine."

He just stared off into space and said, "Pooh, that means more to me than you will ever know, but the man I am won't allow me to accept anything from you. I do want a good ticket since you *the* man now." When he said that, he still didn't look me in the eyes.

"I'm not a *man*, but I feel like one sometimes," I said sadly.

"Pooh, I just need some work. Some of them thangs. I gotta get down for my crown!"

I don't want to do this. Why won't he take the money? He will sell the drugs for the money, but won't take mine with no strings attached and no work involved. Damn, Chino . . . why?

"What ticket do you need?" I couldn't believe my ears as I responded purely out of habit.

"I need to get thirty kilos at a ticket of twenty each."

That's a low price for delivered and fronted kilos. Don't do it. Stay in control. You know how you are with him.

"No problem, Chino. I can have them for you in the morning. Is there anything else you need?"

Instantly, Chino's jaw tightened and he peered at me. "No!" he said through gritted teeth.

He mistook my willingness to help as arrogance and got insulted. This was not what I wanted.

"Chino, you know I got love for you, and I just wanna help." With that, I touched his hand.

"Pooh, I know. It's just fucked up that I gotta come to you." He jerked his hand away from mine.

"I understand. Maybe next time I'll come to you, but Chino, just this one time, because I'm about to retire."

"All I need is this one time."

"I have transportation, and you can use one of them." *Those vans are not yours—you're frontin'.* "This way you can be safe."

"That's straight, because I need to go to work in Cleveland."

"Ant still your driver?"

"Yeah, all the fellas still with me. They just waiting on work." Then I remembered the dude from the party.

"Chino, was one of your friends at a birthday party I gave?"

"Yeah, Rock was there with your friend Delano. I don't wanna talk about that party," Chino said bitterly.

"Neither do I." I just wanted to confirm my suspicions. "He looked familiar to me but we don't have to discuss it."

"You didn't invite me to your party to meet your new 'brother.'"

"You may meet him, one day."

"Pooh, you've got to be careful. You're putting a million-dollar hustle within reach of a lot of suckers. If they get knocked, they'll take you down, and that Colombian you fuckin' with won't like that shit. That may cost you your life."

"I know, that's why I want out. This will be my last run, Chino, and I'm only doing it because of you."

"Do you wanna ride to Cleveland with your Chino, just like old times?"

"Yes, I would like that. Thanks for asking because I need to do some shopping."

Chino laughed. "Need?" I reached for his hand. "I'm sure you don't need anything," he told me once he spotted the three-carat diamond that glistened on my left ring finger. I put my right hand on top of his hand, covering it completely and he saw the ring that he gave me. His eyebrows raised. "I need you, Chino." He couldn't respond. His pride was at its lowest and now he knew I never stopped loving him. "I do have one request."

"What?" Chino said suspiciously.

"That we'll stay at the Tower City hotel and you will let me take you shopping and buy you something just for you." I looked him in his eyes.

"You don't have to." He shook his head, resisting.

"I want to." I continued to make eye contact.

"Okay, Pooh, let's do it," Chino told me after an uncomfortable silence.

"Good, now let's order dessert." I smiled slyly.

Twenty

$\mathcal{I}$ was lying there next to my wife, but all I could think about was meeting Pooh earlier that day. It wasn't as hard as I thought it would be. It wasn't that hard. She was still the same ole Pooh, willing to give me her last. That was the Pooh that I knew and fell in love with. I only wished others knew her like I did.

I grew up in Cleveland, Ohio, in a family of hustlers. Those were some good times. I never saw my father work a job a day in my life. Rumor had it, he never worked a legit job, but he stayed paid. He had various hustles from the drug game to women. My pops is doing time right now, but I'll never know the truth of what really happened to my moms.

When I was twelve years old, I was sitting on our porch and waiting for my mother to come home and take me school shopping. Instead of seeing my mom, I saw the tears slide down my grandmother's face as she told me that my mother was found dead. They said she put up a good fight, but it wasn't enough to save her life.

My parents were a lot like me and my Pooh. They hustled together. They even caught a case together. That shit was real. My father took the time, and my mother took a deal. The deal my moms took landed us in the witness relocation program, which forced us to move away. No good-byes or nothing. Although my mother tried to make a new life for us on the run, she missed Cleveland and promised that one day we would be back. That one day came sooner than I thought. One day we were running, the next she moved us back to the city. Shortly afterward, my mother was found dead in an alley, beaten and shot.

My mother was my everything, and we were alike in so many ways. I often wondered why my dad had her in the streets. She had six kids that needed her. My grandmother took up the slack and raised us, but I still wonder what the hell was on his mind. That was my mom and the only woman I ever loved. She named me Christonos and was the only person allowed to call me that. My grandmother nicknamed me Chino when I was three, and that's what everyone else called me. No one outside my family knew my real name, with the exception of the one person I trusted: my Pooh.

I guess I am my father's son after all, 'cause I got Pooh out here in them streets, but she didn't know it yet. Yeah, Pops, I guess whatever the fuck was on your mind is the same thing that was on mine: money. Getting paid by any means necessary. Anyway, I can't cry over spilled milk. See, that was why people thought I was a cold person, 'cause I kept going no matter what happened. What else could I do?

Pooh said my supply would be available in the morning. I looked over at my wife, who was sleeping peacefully.

Damn, I wished I could but I couldn't. I ran my hand across my wife's thigh repeatedly, hoping to wake her. I gotta see my Pooh. I wondered if she would . . . yeah, she woke up. I turned on my back because my wife knew what time it was. She had that knockout head that would surely put me to sleep. *Oh shit, yes . . . yes!* She did that shit so well! I palmed the back of her head. I gotta do what I gotta do. *Thank you, God, for answering my prayers. Good night, Pooh, and thank you!*

Twenty-one

Well, I finally saw my Chino again, and it was nice. He looked really handsome, as always, with his honey brown skin. He had those full, deep-set eyes that my son inherited. Even in times of despair, he maintained those confident mannerisms that I fell in love with. The only problem was that I didn't want to sell drugs anymore, not even this one last time. I wanted out. A part of me was saying, "No more!" But another part was telling me, "For Chino, you must do this."

I called Dragos and asked him to add thirty more to my ticket. I listened eagerly as he replied, "For you, Carmen, no problem. There will be two."

I knew he had to send two vans to fill an order of fifty kilos.

"Will you please come see me, Dragos? I need to talk to you."

"I'll come this weekend." I would tell him it was over when I paid him for this shipment. I would also tell the fellas when I made my deliveries that it was my last run with them.

The next morning, I picked up Chino and his driver, Ant, who kept staring at me.

"Please drive and stop staring at me," I told him as I gawked back at him. "Yeah, it's Chino and Pooh in full effect. You know I got love for my Chino."

"I know you do," Ant replied. Ant knew that I would do anything and everything for Chino. We all go way back, but I knew all his boys were still mad at me over the past drama.

Chino and I sat in the back of the van and talked up a storm. We talked about old times and sang a few songs together, all off-key of course. But I could tell that he was still bitter that he had to come to me for help, but I hoped in time he would get over it.

When we got to the Tower City hotel in Cleveland, Ant walked to the front desk and got us checked into a suite. Chino and I had some time to kill, so we went shopping.

The hotel was attached to the mall, and I knew just the store I wanted to go to. It was a men's store that sold nothing but the best. I told Chino that he could have anything that he wanted, but all he picked out were two men's dress shirts. This was special for me because I was able to buy something for him without using his money. It was from my heart. We did a little more window shopping since he refused to allow me to buy him anything else, and then it was time for him and Ant to hit the streets and handle business moving that dope.

I only had to show him one time how to work the

compartments in the van. *Place the car in park, put your foot on the brake, turn the AC vent on, lift the rear window lever to open the front seat cushion, and the front window lever to open the rear seat cushion. To close, do the opposite.*

He remembered the combination instantly. Before he left, he leaned in, smacked me on my behind and said to me, "Be ready when I come back."

I knew exactly what he meant. "No, Chino," I told him seriously, "that's not for us. You have a wife."

"But you were my first wife."

"You're right, but you've moved on." With that I turned and walked away. This was supposed to be a happy time, and he had spoiled it by suggesting that I sleep with him. All I could think was that I wanted more and that I deserved more. Sure, I had let Wade do me with no commitments on several occasions, but those were horny, toe-curling, eat-me sex sessions. I cared too much for Chino to sleep with him. I didn't want seconds and I wouldn't be seconds.

I went back to my room and decided to call Delano. I was missing him and I wanted to hear his voice. Maybe it was because I found so much peace with him. When I told him that I was getting out of the business, all he had said was, "Good, because I want more for you." *Well, Delano, I want more for me, too.* I paged him and then ordered a steak and lobster dinner from room service. My room service arrived at the same time my phone rang.

"Hello?" I answered.

"Hi, Carmen."

"Hi, Delano, how are you?"

"I'm fine. What are you up to?"

"I'm just in Cleveland chillin'," I chimed, floating back into the fluffy pillows.

"I figured that was where this area code was from. So, you thinking about me, huh?"

"As you know, I'm trying to make some changes, and when I get back to the city, I would like to spend a lil' more time with you—that's only if you want to."

"I would like that very much."

I exhaled a breath of relief. "I want to get to know you better, Delano. I apologize for being so difficult to you and—"

"Shh, Carmen, there's no need to explain," he interrupted. "We'll work this out. Let's do something with our children. I want you to meet my sons."

He is a blessing. "My son is with my mom, but we can go pick him up."

"You sure you don't mind me meeting your mother?"

"I'm sure, Delano. These are the two most important people in my life, and I kinda like you." We both laughed. "Well, my food is here, so I'll talk to you later. I may page you again."

"I'll be waiting. Bye."

When I got off the phone, my message light was flashing. I dialed down to the lobby to check my messages.

"Guest Services."

"This is Suite thirteen-ten. I have messages?"

"Yes, from Chino. He said that he is thinking of you

and TCP for life. That's the only message. Is there anything else, miss?"

"No, thank you."

I ate my food and took a long, hot shower. Then I called to check on my son. As I lay alone in my bed, I thought about the message from Chino and a sense of euphoria washed over me. He never forgot.

My eyes began to get heavy. It was time to get a good night's sleep since we would return to Columbus early tomorrow. I planned to talk to Dragos in the morning and pay him. This would soon be over.

Chino arrived at the hotel late that night, knocked on my door and woke me up.

"Pooh, that yayo was excellent. I haven't seen that much dope in a long time. I was a lil' worried at first, but everyone liked that shit. The fellas that rocked it said it was just like butter. Can I get fifty next weekend?"

"Wait, Chino." I yawned. "You said just this one time and that was it!"

"I know, Pooh, but why let a hookup like this go?"

Not only was I tired but I was in total disbelief. "Chino, I'll turn you on to my source, and you can deal with him."

"No, I like it like this. I don't want to meet no one. Why should I when I have you in the mix?"

"Because I'm not your frontline man anymore. You can step to him yourself."

He began to pace back and forth.

"Okay, see, now you want me to look stupid in front of the fellas."

How could I tell him that, one, I was never supposed to give anyone that van combination; and, two, I really resented him wanting to keep me in this life for the sake of his own greed?

"Chino, I'll give you some money. If I get more drugs, more of my money will be tied up. Dragos already fronts me, but I had to pay up front with a deposit. Dragos has a two-million-dollar deposit of mine, which gives me an un-limited credit line with him. I just want to pay him, get my two million and get out of the dope game."

"Pooh, this could work for us. We can even work out something with the baby. Somehow this could all work out for all of us." *Now he is bringing the baby into this. My weakness.* My mouth wanted to say no, but my heart couldn't. This was always my problem.

"Come on, Pooh." He began to rub the sides of my face. This was not what I wanted, and he didn't want to let me out. I felt completely stuck and confused.

—

I looked down at my Chino kneeling before me as I pointed the nine at the back of his head and began to press the cold steel against his skull. He raised his eyes to look up at me. Not one trace of fear showed on his face, only pain. I lowered the gun from his head and stood there in front of him as shame swarmed my body like bees swarming a hive. That look took my mind back to the deepest secret Chino and I shared.

Three years ago when I was in our bedroom, I heard sobs coming from our living room. I came into the living room and found Chino on his knees covered in blood and praying. I ran to him and checked him for injury. His face was bruised from what looked like a pistol whipping. Chino told me how he had been abducted by some rival drug dealers who intended to rob and kill him. He told me how all he thought of was me and how badly he wanted to live. They stripped him naked and had him kneel before them as they pistol whipped him and bragged. He said he never felt so humiliated in his life.

Wanting to live and thinking of the life we were building, he acted like he was scared to death, fooling his abductors into a false sense of security and causing them to become too relaxed. He gained courage and snatched the pistol from the hand of one of his abductors. He killed all three of them with shots to the head, heart and stomach. Chino then jumped out the second-floor window naked and ran for help. He was assisted by an older white gentleman who drove by in a car. Only I knew what had really happened, and we shared the secret of those killings as we watched the news report of bodies being discovered in an abandoned house on Woodland Avenue.

Chino stressed how he never wanted to feel that way ever again in his life, and how if he were ever put in that predicament, he would fight instantly and choose death rather than to suffer degradation and humiliation. I was the one who cried with him and wiped the tears from his eyes. I placed my hurting baby in an Epsom salt bath and nursed his mind and body back to life. I whispered into his spirit that it gets greater later, that he was a king and that they had used drastic measures out of jealousy—building my baby back up. I was hurting with him and sad 'cause I couldn't erase the pain. It was no different than a man consoling his woman after she had been raped. He knows she has been violated in an unmentionable way, scarred for life, but there's nothing he can do.

Here I was, placing my Chino in that vulnerable position again, by my own hand. After that episode, Chino always went for death, and the only reason he showed me mercy was because of our past, the fact was, I was his Pooh. I dropped the gun and kneeled with him, holding him and saying my apologies, "Chino, I'm so sorry, baby, I remember that night. I wasn't going to hurt you. I promise." I lifted my hand to wipe away his tears and mine. He was shaking and not responding. I hugged him closely, but he did not hug me back. I continued to try to reach him. "Chino, baby, I'm here. Please, what's wrong with us?"

He abruptly pushed me back off him and backhanded me, splitting my lip. He snatched up his gun and rose to his feet. "How could you put me in that position after what happened to me? I killed those niggas that did that shit to me, and now it's your turn to get what they got. So now you a trick bitch, huh?"

We left Cleveland after breakfast the following morning and arrived back in Columbus. Everything went like clockwork.

Dragos was impressed with the work that I had put in. But when I told him I wanted out, he totally flipped on me with some story that I really didn't care to hear.

"Carmen, you can't do this. I need you to help me out now. On my end, I had some losses, and I need you. You're a big part of my team, and I need you to help move the product with me. How you Americans say, 'Don't bite the hand that feeds you.'"

Oh, now he a straight-up foreigner. I countered, "Dragos, that saying is good for anyone working together. How about this one: 'Do you know the difference between a workhorse and a racehorse?'" He looked confused, and even I didn't know what I was saying. So I continued to try to get out of this. "Or this one: 'Give a sister a break.'"

"I gave you a break," he snapped back in perfect English. "When you wanted to be on, I was loyal and only worked with you. What was that worth to you? Did you think it came without a cost? Now I want you to help me with my plans as I helped you with yours."

I listened in disbelief as this man stretched our relationship to keep me in the position of selling. Dragos knew damn well he could get someone else just like me to sell for him. Everybody was looking for a Colombian or Dominican plug to know. Now all of a sudden I was invaluable. Did he forget I had to beg up on this position, cut side deals and go for broke to work with him . . . *for* him? Now he wanted me to help him repay a loss on his end. I couldn't believe it. These muthafuckas didn't want me out because it was benefiting them. Dragos evidently had a new supplier. His previous supplier ran into some problems on the customs end of things.

The yayo was coming into the country in boxes of Dole pineapple cans. I received cases of canned pineapples, I opened them, took the yayo out and then had to repackage them. It was too much and too heavy.

Plus, I was tired of all the lying to my mom and my family, not to mention all the paranoia. I had a suspicion that the cops were closing in. How long could I expect a run in these streets to last? For every $1,000, eventually you paid the piper. Now Dragos didn't want to give me my deposit, nor did he want to let me retire. For every insinuation I made about ending my career, he had a response.

"Carmen, to end our relationship would make me very unhappy. This is a lifetime relationship, and now you want a divorce."

"No, I don't, but I need a break." My eyes welled up with tears.

"Get someone to help you."

I just wanted out, but talking to him was like talking to a wall. I had heard that these Colombians would get you to sell these drugs, then try to keep you selling, willingly or unwillingly. I was so tired but I decided then and there to make one last run and come up with enough money to bounce with no one's permission but my own.

"Okay, Dragos, I'll be in touch." He left, but he left two of his associates with me, like I was trying to escape or something. This made me nervous. Now I had chaperones? Ain't this some shit! I called Dragos and said, "I need to take two weeks for a vacation."

He responded by saying, "Absolutely, a vacation is good. Please come to my winter estate in the Dominican Republic."

Squirming out of the offer, I declined. "No, thanks, Dragos, I want to choose my own vacation spot and be alone with my son." This really made him mad. He said, "Carmen, why do you refuse me? I don't ask twice." Dragos had been raising his voice a lot lately, and this was normally a calm man. Our once calm relationship had the potential of turning volatile.

"Okay, Dragos, I won't mention it again."

"I see you've got deep pockets now," he told me. "You want to take your ball home and not play anymore. The game is not over until I say it is over. You think you don't need me because you have saved some money. Carmen, think again. I like working with you and I don't want to work with anyone else. Think about it."

What had I gotten myself into? I was going to have to plan an escape. In the meantime, I dealt only with Chino. I got him thirty kilos for the next two weeks and I left everyone else alone while I planned and plotted my next move.

My world began to crumble around me. When I stopped dealing with the fellas, they started to take a beatin' because none of them had saved their money. In the streets, no one teaches you how to budget your finances. Make a sell, buy some sneakers, make a sell, buy some gear, make a sell, buy some pussy. Saving was unheard of. There are no 401(k) plans for hustlers, no retirement plans, nothing.

They were all pressed, and Chino had his boys on the streets really taxin' everyone since I wasn't doing anything. G-Money got word that I was supplying Chino and he took it personally, like I would help Chino but not him. But truth of the matter was, no one would supply G. He was rumored to fuck up with money, and all his bragging about fuckin' crackheads had caught up with him. Chino told me that G-Money got fucked up his ass in the joint, so no one really messed with him, because who could really trust a booty boy? Jay-Jay was too happy to see his ass crawling back to him.

He started dating the same girl who did my nails at this salon on the east side of Columbus. He had her calling me, too. I got weak and returned his call trying to keep my enemies close and everyone on an even plane until I flipped and made my move. I agreed to see him one last time. My head was spinning around. I had so much going on inside of me.

Chino still had not done anything for the baby, and I resented myself for continuing to help him after I realized that he had not changed one bit. He was just out for the money, 'cause money was what was keeping his life together. All the substance had left him. He was a different person, and I was becoming a different person as well.

Then one night I had a dream. In this dream, God showed me that I was going to be arrested. I saw myself on the news, featured in a pyramid lineup of faces. At the top of the pyramid, I could clearly see my face, but the other faces were blurred. In the background, I could hear a newscaster speaking and talking about a big drug bust, the largest in Columbus history. I woke up in a cold sweat.

Twenty-two

$\mathcal{I}$t was 3:00 a.m., and I was wide awake, fighting insomnia.

It was time, I supposed, time to face that which I feared. I wanted to see my salon. It had been over two years since I'd been there. I heard there were changes: the wallpaper was different and the staff had changed. I wanted to see it and this time I was not afraid, ashamed or sad. Something in me wanted to let go.

I put on a sweatsuit and grabbed my car keys. I rode in silence, focusing on my destination. Since selling it I had refused to ever drive past it, always taking a detour rather than confront the memories. But that night, it was the only place I wanted to be.

As I pulled into the shopping plaza parking lot, I felt nostalgic, as if I were coming to work as usual. There was my parking space. There was the dry cleaners, the computer store and the pizza shop. Man, they had good pizza. There was the convenience store and the video store. It looked the same, but the feel was different. The magic was forever gone.

From my Jeep, I could see inside the salon. I was there in front of my salon. Sure, it carried a different name and had new owners, but it was still mine. Chino would come pick me up and pull his Blazer right up to the door. If I slouched down in my Jeep, I would look like he did in his Blazer.

I still had a lot of my salon memorabilia. The hair show competition tape where I won first place, the newspaper article about our opening, photos from various workshops. I even had a salon bag with L-O-QUENT HAIR SALON neatly scripted on both sides and a salon T-shirt. I didn't look at that stuff anymore. I closed my eyes really tight, and it felt like I was in the salon doing nails again. I heard the receptionist answering the phones, "L-O-Quent Hair Salon."

That day, I let go. I let go of it all. I felt the warm tears on my face and I started thinking about my son and how the money that I had set aside could pay for his college tuition. I hoped he would never have to go through what I had gone through. I tried to build a life filled with money and opportunity so that my son would not have to face the challenges of today's black man—gangs, the streets, prison and violence.

Am I a good mother? Is this the only way? I want my son to be proud when he looks at me. I want to provide food, shelter and clothing. I need to devise a plan to do this legally. I don't ever want to leave my baby.

I thought back to the good times at the salon. I heard my staff; we were laughing. There was Valerie at the first station. Val did great hair and was always there reassuring and supporting me. *Valerie, thanks for your friendship.* Then there was Lenaye, fresh out of beauty school, trying to be a better stylist. And Ms. Jewell. She had clients lined up and kept everyone laughing with her jokes. It was her fault the salon windows stayed fogged up. She was an outstanding manager with the will to survive. I learned so much from her. Next was Roger. He was a brother who did hair in a suit almost every day, and if it wasn't a suit, it was a silk shirt and dress pants. He never got dirty and turned out excellent hairstyles. Roger believed in the salon and stayed with me through the rough times. *Thanks, Roger.* There was Marcia (Chino's cousin). She did it all—hair, nails, eyebrows and makeup. My eyebrows have never been the same since she last did them.

There was Michael, who was from Detroit. He told the best grip and short stories you ever heard. He wore a Jheri curl in the 1990s but somehow he pulled it off—it looked that good. Then there was the salon's assistant, who we all called Baby. She was the salon's baby and kept everyone shampooed and prepared for service. She was a lifesaver on those busy, busy days. I could never forget my ever efficient receptionist/manicurist, Stacey. She kept my head on and the books in order.

I also had another part-time receptionist named Selima, and I still don't know how she got the job done. She only wanted free hairdos and nails. She was one of the models I used in the hair show who helped me win first place. She wore a black dress and my award-winning hairstyle. *Selima, we did that!* She was like a lil' sister but she was a horrible receptionist. We all loved her just the same.

Last but not least was Renardo. He was a grand diva. I still believe he was supposed to be a she no matter what the birth certificate said. Renardo and I went around and around over his ten-inch nails, but we got past that. I told him he could keep the makeup if he lost the nails. So we made it, and soon everyone grew.

There were others who came and went, but they were the ones who helped make the salon. They were the ones that believed in me and Chino.

To the staff, my L-O-Quent family, I never got the chance to say good-bye to you. I just walked away. Had I known better, I would have done better. I thank you, and I remember the fun. The salon is full. The lot is full, and our hard work is paying off. The clients are happy, and we are drinking daiquiris on a Saturday. They even have the flowers I arranged in that black vase. It is still on the receptionist desk. But all this is no more.

I sat in my Jeep crying, releasing that which I held on to from my past.

Let go! Pammy, it is time, just let go. I placed my hands to my lips and kissed them. Then I blew my salon a kiss good-bye. This attachment was over.

I drove off and never returned.

Twenty-three

Ring . . . ring.

"Hello?"

"What that *balla* life look like?"

"Hi, Chino."

"Pooh, I can't stop thinking of you—of us—and what happened."

———

I placed my head in my hands and cried, continuing to beg Chino to listen to me. He paced back and forth, cursing me and gaining momentum in his anger. Walking over to me, he kicked me in the side and continued taunting me, going back to how much in love with someone else he was. While he was waving his gun around in the air, I slid my hand underneath the pillow and felt the small .380-caliber gun. I flicked the safety latch off. Chino didn't detect anything; he was too engrossed in his ranting.

He began talking about the killings and how I was his weak link because I knew everything. How he ran with the gun, unable to wipe the prints off 'cause he was butt naked. When he got into the white man's car, he used the change of clothes given to him to remove his fingerprints from the gun. Chino and I buried the gun together, sealing our secret. Now he was talking about the location of the gun.

"Yeah, I went back and got that gun just in case you flipped on me. I can't even trust you no more. I have no more use for you. Pooh, your ass has gotta go. Have you said your prayers, love?"

—

"Did you ever think we would see each other again?"

"Yes, I knew we would. Pooh, what happened at the hotel?" Chino pressed.

"What do you mean?" I asked, playing dumb about his attempted booty call.

"You didn't want to be with me?"

"No, Chino, not that way. I don't want seconds."

"You had firsts and didn't act right. All I ever wanted was someone for me."

Relaxing into our conversation, I commented, "Me, too. I don't know where we went wrong."

—

Fearing the worst, I pointed the muzzle of my gun underneath the pillow at Chino and aimed. Tatt! He didn't know what hit him. Feathers from the ripped pillow floated surreally in the air between us. As the warm hollow point became heated, he asked, "Pooh, where did you get a gun?"

—

"It all went so fast. We stopped believing in each other."

"I know," I sadly replied.

"Pooh, I'm sorry," he whispered into the phone sincerely.

"Chino, I know, let's drop it. Everything I do, I think of you. I know we can't be together, but I still miss you."

"I miss you, too. We gotta do something to work this out, to make this right."

"What can we do?" I got excited at the possibility of a solution until I heard what he wanted.

"My wife wants me to take a paternity test."

I stopped breathing for a second. "On y'all's kids, right?" I questioned, knowing it wasn't the case.

"No, Pooh."

"You've got to be kidding! You constantly break my heart. We were together almost five years. The baby is yours, and you know it! Chino, anything that is mine or of me, you should accept. I would give you anything to help your kids and your wife."

"Pooh, calm down."

"No!" I yelled at him. "Like now, even though we hustle together, I still ask you for nothing off the top for my son—your son—and I know that you're getting money. This is crazy!"

"Shit! I just don't know how to correct this," Chino said with desperation.

"Correct what? Your lies? I will never agree to a paternity test. I want my son even if you don't."

He didn't say anything, so I continued, "Chino, here we go again. All I wanted to do was help you and thank you for the memories, but it's obvious we both have issues."

Finally, he said, "I don't know what to say, Pooh. I do miss you."

I shielded my face from retaliation as he dropped his gun and grabbed his stomach. "Pooh, don't shoot me again. Just drop the gun." I dropped the gun and ran to his arms. "Oh my God, I'm going to call 911."

Chino held me tightly. "No, calm down and call my boy Darren."

"I miss my Chino. I don't know who you are anymore." Fighting back the tears, I listened for a dream.

"I miss you, too, Pooh. Carmen is different," Chino said.

"Like Joe Bub Baby used to say all the time, I put the 'm' on actin' and made it mackin', it's just a role. How is Joe Bub Baby anyway?"

"You know I don't fuck with him after that triple-cross move he pulled," Chino said bitterly.

"Oh, I forgot about that. Where's his girlfriend, is she standing by him while he is doing his ten-piece extra-crispy prison term?"

I ran to the phone and did as instructed. Chino crept his way upstairs to the kitchen door leading to the garage. He raised the garage door with the remote from the kitchen.

"Chino, Darren said hold tight. He'll be here in five minutes." I became hysterical, asking him if he was okay.

He remained calm. "Don't worry, Pooh, it will be okay."

"Yeah, you know his girl Chazz Baby Love is in his corner. Chazz asked me about you. You should call her."

"Well, I'm glad she's standing by her man. I just pray he don't do her like I got done when he gets out." I said this hoping that Chino would get my meaning, then continued, "I should go see Joe Bub. We both should. He's doing ten years. Let the past be the past."

"Yeah, we should. I remember him being there for me when I got out of prison. Pooh, he used to ask about you all the time. He also knew you were getting money. Joe was for you, believe it or not."

"Chino, we could reminisce forever but I'm living for today and trying to get my life together so my son's life is better—"

He interrupted, "Despite what you think, I do care for the baby. I know with a mom like you, he'll be fine, so I don't worry about him. You've taken care of so many people; I know he is in good hands."

It seemed like an eternity before Darren's Jag screeched to a halt in our driveway. He ran inside and I fell into his arms, crying and talking about how I had shot Chino. He stepped back and looked at Chino for advice as to what to do.

Chino said, taking the lead, "Darren, I had a little accident, and I need you to take me to the hospital."

I screamed, "No, I'll take you!"

"You can't drive—you're hysterical. Besides, they'll arrest you for the shooting," Chino said while in obvious pain.

"He still needs a father. You had one."

"Maybe one day I can be that father. Just not now. But I

do know when he . . . one day . . . when he's a man and he talks to me, he will look in my eyes and see I got love for him and his mother."

"Love is what love does, Chino. Your love is doing nothing for him." Chino had no response to what I had just told him. " I gotta go."

"Where you goin'?"

"I have a date."

"A date? With who?"

"What?" I laughed, merely out of shock. "You gonna tell me you want a paternity test, you can't be a father to our son, but you can question me about who I go out with? You've *got* to be kidding me, right?"

"Pooh, I don't wanna hear all that now. Who is it?" Chino questioned again. "Is it that Jamaican Erik?"

"No."

"It's that sucka Delano, isn't it?"

"As a matter of fact, Chino, it is. He's good to me, and he cares for my son."

"Your son, huh?"

"You don't claim him."

"He can't replace me."

"I'm not trying to replace you. Replace means to substitute with the same."

———

"But I want to, please, I'm sorry," I sobbed.

Chino began to limp to the car, applying pressure to his stomach. Darren wrapped Chino's arm around his neck and helped carry him to the Jag. I put on my sneakers and jumped

*in the backseat against their wishes. Darren gunned it, racing
through red lights and headed toward Mount Carmel East Hospital's emergency entrance.*

"I don't want the same thing I had with you. I want more. I
deserve more, Chino."

"Yeah, you do. I know you do."

The phone filled with silence. Our moods were like a
pendulum.

"Pooh, you're growing up."

"Yes, I am, and I like it. I just want a family."

"Me, too."

"You've got one."

*Arriving at the hospital, Chino continued to warn me, "Pooh, if
you come into the hospital, don't say you shot me. Darren, take
her home."*

I continued to plead, "No, I want to stay with you."

*We ran to the entrance, gaining the staff's attention. They
ran to the car with a gurney and assisted Chino onto it. I kissed
the sides of his face and pleaded, announcing to everyone within
hearing distance that I shot him and how sorry I was and how
they had to help him. Inside the hospital, everyone was racing as
Chino began to lose consciousness.*

"How's your mom?" Chino said, changing the subject
abruptly.

"Fine, and your grandmother?" I replied, going along

with his game. I knew neither my mother nor his grandmother wanted us together.

"Lodie is fine, but I think your mother hates me."

"And you know this is true, brother. After all, you did leave her daughter for dead and with no support for her grandchild."

"I know, I know." Chino paused momentarily, then spoke again. "Uh . . . Pooh?"

"Yes, Chino."

"Let's go to a hotel, or let me come over."

"Have you not heard anything I've said? You're still the same. I want to be courted."

"Courted?"

"Yes, just like your wife was. You remember? You would take her to dinner, buy her presents, take trips behind my back."

"Here you go."

"It's the truth."

"We didn't have the money."

"Not at first, but when you made it, you gave it to another."

"I don't wanna argue."

"We're not arguing. I'm just stating the facts."

"Does Delano have any money?"

"Pooh, go home. Darren, take her home." Darren pulled me by the arm and pushed me out the door toward his car. He stuffed me into the front seat and drove off in silence. As we drove off,

the sirens of an approaching police car sped past us onto the campus of the hospital. It was sobering to watch the police car drive by.

"It's not about money. I know him, Chino. As a matter of fact, I know him better than I know you."

"Can we talk about this in person?"

"Sorry, no booty call here, buddy."

"Pooh—"

"Chino, I've gotta go, I'll talk to you soon."

As I slowly removed the receiver from my ear, I faintly heard him say, "Bye, Pooh, I love you."

Darren reached over, patted my leg and said, "You know Chino let you go free. That's love, baby girl. That's love."

Twenty-four

$\mathcal{I}$ had done what is known in the streets as "booking yourself." I had bit off more than I could chew and I didn't know what to do. Helping Chino come up against my wishes, wanting him to be a father to his child, being that woman in the streets and knowing right from wrong but doing the latter began to weigh heavily on me. I was in the middle of an internal battle with myself while pacing and waiting for Delano's phone call. He was a little late calling, so I prayed he didn't have an issue with one of his sons' mothers. We were going to go get my son from my mother's home in Michigan, and I was ready to see my baby. Luckily I didn't have to wait for his call for too long.

"Hello?"

"Hi, Carmen, are you ready?"

"Yes, I'm waiting for you."

"I had a little problem with one of my babies' mothers. She doesn't want my son to go with us. She said she doesn't know you."

I plopped down on the couch. *Why now?* I thought. "I was afraid of something like this happening. Delano, I don't need any unnecessary headaches. I won't hurt the child. Which one is it?"

"It's Karen, the youngest boy's mom. She usually has no drama."

"No drama?" I snapped. "Why is she trippin' then? Better yet, why did you tell her I was going?" I asked, somewhat confused.

"Because I don't keep secrets, and she needs to know that there's someone in my life. But we'll work this out. I think she still has feelings for me."

"Do you have feelings for her?" My heart pounded as I waited for the answer.

"Nothing more than friendship, but I'll talk to you about everything this weekend. I was calling to tell you to come over to my cousin's house and we'll leave from there, and check this . . . I'll drive."

"Uh . . . no, thanks, I'll drive. I don't think your car will make it to Michigan."

"I'll have you know that I have another car. The one you saw was my working car, and I'll drive safe." He laughed. "But for real, C, you live too far out, and I'm waiting for someone to stop over. Plus, I'm waiting for my older son to be dropped off so we can go. So go to my cousin's and leave your car there."

"Okay," I told him. "Um . . . Delano?"

"Yes?"

"Thanks for going with me to get my son."

"Carmen, it's my pleasure. You don't have to do everything alone. Remember that."

"I will. Bye."

"Bye."

Twenty minutes later, I pulled into the driveway of his cousin's house. It was stylish and had a shiny white luxury-series BMW in the driveway. Another car pulled in right behind me. It was a young woman and a boy about six years old. The little boy looked just like Delano. *This must be the baby and his mom. Here we go. Please don't let me get played. Here comes Delano out of the house with his bags. He's putting them in the BMW. Nice car.*

Delano approached me and leaned close to the window. "Carmen, get out of the car. No one will bite you."

"Hi, D, help me with my bags."

"No problem." The little boy ran to Delano.

"Daddy, Daddy, where are we going?"

"It's a surprise. A trip full of adventure. Do you know what 'adventure' means?"

"No. Can I have some ice cream?"

"Where is my hug at?"

A man not afraid of affection. He's good with his son.

Holding his son's hand, Delano led him to my Jeep.

"Carmen, I want you to meet my son. This is Lil' D, Delano Junior."

"Hi, Lil' D, or is it Delano?" I bent down to talk with his son.

"Everyone calls me Lil' D, but I'm a big boy."

"Yes, you are. So what can I call you?"

"Mmmm . . . . call me Big Lil' D." He looked toward his father for approval.

"I sure will, Big Lil' D." I gave him a high five. Lil D's mama moved timidly toward us.

"And, Carmen, this is Sheila, Lil' D's mom." We both held out our hands to greet each other with a handshake. Sheila was the prettiest deep-dark-chocolate sister I had ever seen in my life. Instantly, I wondered what happened between them.

"Hi, nice to meet you," I said politely.

"It's nice to meet you, too. I've heard a lot about you."

"Good things I hope." I looked over at D.

"Too good actually, but I trust D's judgment, and I hope you all have a good time," said Sheila in a less-than-sincere tone. "Come here, Lil' D, give Mama some sugar." Delano moved closer and placed a reassuring arm around my waist, touching the small of my back.

"Sheila, we have to get going. I'll call you tonight with all the contact information. Page me if you need me or want to talk to Lil' D," said Delano.

"I will. Talk to ya later. Bye, Carmen."

"Bye."

And we were off in the BMW headed to Michigan. I couldn't believe how smoothly everything went.

"Delano, that wasn't as hard as I thought it would be."

"No, Sheila is cool. Karen will be hard."

"We can work with it," I told him.

"We? I like it when you say 'we.'" He held my hand as he drove. I looked in the back at Big Lil' D. He was asleep as soon as we hit traffic.

We arrived in Michigan right on time. My mom was so happy to see me. She was even happier to see me with a man. My son was so glad to see his mommy, and I just hugged and squeezed him so tight he couldn't breathe, smelling his scent, the one that only a mother knows of her child.

"I missed you so much." I smothered him with kisses. "I love you."

"I wuv you." Lifting him in my arms, I turned to my mother and said, "Mom, he looks heavier."

"And he is. I feed that boy things that will make him expel a turd. Not junk food, not canned food, not Mickey D's or Taco Bell, but home-fried chicken and fresh greens from my garden. Need I continue? And who is this handsome young man?"

"Mom, this is Delano."

"Hi, Miss—"

"No 'Miss' here. Everyone calls me Mom or Star. This has to be your son. He looks just like you."

"Yes, ma'am—oops. Yes, Mom, this is my son, Lil' Delano."

"He likes to be called Big Lil' D because he is a big boy," I added.

"Yes, he is a big boy. Big Lil' D, how about some of Mama Star's homemade ice cream?"

His little face lit up. "Daddy, can I?"

"After you eat dinner, yes, you may."

"Mom, we're going to stay the entire weekend. I want to show Delano around."

"Sounds perfect to me. The guest room is all ready, and you all are welcome. They have some sort of jazz concert downtown off the riverfront, and I know you like jazz. Get some tickets and go. I'll watch the children. Your sisters are coming over with their kids, so there will be plenty to do for me and the kids."

"Sounds good, Mom."

"Now, let's get you settled."

We got settled in, and I was surprised when my mom put the boys in the same room, and me and Delano's things in the guest room. She's old-fashioned, but not naive. But I wasn't sleeping with Delano. I was too uncomfortable. I would let his son sleep with him, and I would sleep with mine.

"Carmen, your mom put our bags in the same room."

"I noticed that."

"We can't disrespect her like that. Hey, I got it."

"What?"

"How about if we all sleep together?"

"All of us?" I asked, surprised.

"Yes, me, you, my son and your son. It's a big bed, and that way I can still be next to you and my son." *Thank you, God.*

"Delano, I like that idea very much. Can I give you a hug?" I asked innocently.

"Of course, but why now?"

"Just because you make me happy."

"Can we throw a kiss in there because you make me happy, too?" Delano joked, giving me a sly grin.

"Maybe we can," I told him. And with that, he grabbed me and gave me a big hug and kissed me on the forehead and gazed into my eyes.

"Carmen, I want to marry you." I eased away from his embrace. These were the words a girl dreams of hearing, but I was confused. My hands became clammy, and I felt panicky. Was this my chance to be normal? I didn't know what to say, so I changed the subject.

"I want to go to the concert my mom mentioned tonight."

"That's fine. We can check out the concert, but did you hear what I told you?"

"Yes, Delano. Please be patient with me."

He gave me a hug. "Okay." Then he kissed me on the forehead again. "But first things first, let's eat whatever it is that's smelling so good."

"Yeah, my mom can really burn in the kitchen."

Delano and I had a marvelous weekend. We talked a lot but I still didn't tell him everything about me. He mostly talked about himself and his plans and told me he would be honored to be in my son's life. That really blew my mind. I didn't know what to say. Then my mom gave Delano the thumbs-up.

"Pammy, I see the way he looks at you. I like him. Let's keep him."

Delano never asked about my mom calling me Pammy. She only did it the once, and I didn't even think he noticed it. What would he have said if he realized Carmen wasn't even my real name?

I started thinking, *Can I tell him the truth? Can I tell him everything about me? Can I tell him that I dated men for money and all about the drama with Chino? That I'm a drug dealer and that I sold stolen clothes and that I'm confused and have gone through hell? He thinks my association to the life is just from hangin' with my boys. He would flip if he knew how deep in the game I am. Can I tell him this? Can I trust him? Can I tell him about Dragos? Can I tell him and show him who I am without losing him? Would he still want me? Finally, I'm sitting on a pedestal. I like it up here. I'm afraid. I like how he thinks of me, and I don't want that to end.*

God, when or how do I tell him all about me? How do I share myself with him? Please help me.

Twenty-five

Dragos requested that I come to New York. He didn't say why but assured me there were no problems. When I arrived at JFK Airport, his driver, Victor, was there like clockwork.

"*Hola, Victor.*"

"*Hola, Carmen. ¿Cómo estás?*" (Hello, Carmen. How are you?)

"*Bien. ¿Y tú?*" (Good. And you?)

"*Bien.*" (Good.)

"*¿Dónde está Dragos?*" (Where is Dragos?)

"*Está en Queens. Tú lo verás allí.*" (He is in Queens. You will see him there.)

"*¿Me puedes conducir, por favor?*" (Can you drive me, please?)

"*No, tomarás el metro.*" (No, you will take the subway.)

"*¿El subway?*" (The subway?)

"*Sí, Dragos te envía su amor.*" (Yes, Dragos sends his love to you.)

Victor dropped me off in front of Madison Square Garden. Standing before the arena, I felt as if I were entering a new phase of my life. I raised my head and noticed the marquee announcing a sporting event and imagined my name in lights. Carmen got plugged on this day! Returning to reality, I skipped down the stairs to the subway and was off, headed for Queens.

The New York subway was an adventure. People singing, dancing, loitering and, of course, rushing. I got off the subway in Queens and skipped up the stairs leading from the stop. Dragos was there waiting for me. We drove to an area with a large garage. We pulled into the garage, and I couldn't believe my eyes. There were over ten vans sitting chevron-style of various makes and colors. Above, there was a platform where men walked with guns, surveying the floor below.

As we pulled into the garage, the door closed automatically. I was so nervous and I kept asking myself, *You paid him, right?* My nervousness was obvious because Dragos grabbed my hand and reassuringly said, "Carmen, relax. It will be all right. I want you to meet my brother. Actually, he wants to meet you."

My eyes began darting from side to side, and I asked, "Why?"

"He's curious about you."

Shaking my head I said, "I don't want to meet him."

"Too late, here he comes." Up walked a very handsome man, somewhere in his fifties. The car door was opened, and I was led out.

"*Hola, Carmen. Por fin nos conocemos.*" (Hi, Carmen. Finally we meet.)

"*Hola.*"

"*¿Tú hablas español?*" (Do you speak Spanish?)

"*Si, pero yo prefiero el inglés.*" (Yes, but I prefer English.)

"*¿Por qué?*" (Why?)

"*Simplemente porque.*" (I just do.)

"*No seas nerviosa. Yo tengo una sopresa para ti.*" (Don't be nervous. I have a surprise for you.)

"*Un momento. ¿Como se llama?*" (One moment. What is your name?)

"Adrian."

"*Gracias.*"

Dragos began pulling me through the crowd. Workers were stuffing vans with bundled cocaine like an assembly line. Adrian stopped in front of a new Toyota van and said, "Carmen, this is your surprise. A new van just for you. Do you like it?"

"*¿Para trabajar o para divertirme?*" (For work or for pleasure?)

"*Trabajo.*" (Work.) "*¿Necesitas un automóvil?*" (Do you need a car?)

"No, just trying to understand the surprise. I mean, I have a Jeep, but I'm not sure why you're giving me a van."

"This will hold twice the amount of one of the other vans. Plus, it's fully loaded. It has two car phones—one is hands free."

"Really?" It was hard not to be excited with so much bling blinging in my face.

"Really, check it out. The combination is easy to remember. We can get you any color you want."

"Really?"

"Yes. I also have some cell phones for your use. Communication is essential. They have no phone bills and will last for at least three months."

"Three months of unlimited use?"

"Yes, a burnout, so what color do you want your van, because I can paint it if you don't like this color."

"No, champagne is a nice color, but I'm not certain if I'll need it."

"Why?" he asked curiously.

"I'm slowing down. Dragos knows this."

"No, don't slow down! Now is the time to move, to expand," said Adrian with a hint of panic in his voice.

Before I could tell him the same things I'd been telling Dragos, Dragos spoke to him, "Adrian, she'll be fine. Carmen, I can even work on your ticket." *Oh, so now he can work on my ticket.*

My hands were sweaty, and I couldn't move my mouth.

"I don't feel so well." I rubbed my face and closed my eyes.

"We've overwhelmed her, Adrian. Come, let's go eat and enjoy the city."

"Carmen." Adrian placed his hand on my back.

"Yes, Adrian?"

"We're here to help with anything you need. We're behind you all the way."

All I could think was, *Why now?* This is what I wanted all along, but it came too late. I remember Dragos telling me to be careful about what I ask for because I just might get it. But this time, I didn't want it. Hell, I couldn't even give it away.

Dragos, Adrian and I went to Long Island City and devoured seafood at a local restaurant. I didn't want to talk about the new opportunity or the van.

"Carmen, I know this game, and if you follow my lead, you will make millions every month," Dragos told me, getting back to the point at hand. "I'm dropping your ticket again by three grand, so now off each kilo you can make an extra three grand."

I decided to pick his brain since he was putting a harness on my back in order to work the shit out of me. I quizzed, "How did you get into the life? Is this an inheritance or what?"

He started laughing and responded, "You have been watching too many gangster movies. Not all persons of Hispanic descent are groomed for a life of crime. I have a sister who is a doctor. She graduated from Yale, and I have an uncle who is an attorney. He gives me a lot of advice."

I was impressed and felt a little embarrassed that I stereotyped him. "I feel you. People stereotype African Americans all the time. Is your wife Latina?"

"Yes, she is. Her name is Daya and she's from Brazil, but she looks like a white American. She has blue eyes and light hair, but once she speaks, you would know that she is Latina."

I continued, "So, what made you get your hustle on?"

"I met the right person at the wrong time in my life. I was laid off from my job as an auditor. I had been married for about three months with my first child on the way and was the sole provider for my family. A childhood friend saw me at a bar having a drink and thinking about my problems. He was in the life and had built a reputation for selling a lot of coca. To make a long story short, he offered me an opportunity to make money. Like you, I wanted to do it just until I could find another job or get on my feet, but we became close, and he took me to make a buy with him. During that buy, the deal went bad, and he was killed. After his death, I was passed the scepter of his business, and now I am in too deep to turn around. "On this level, Carmen, out is death or the penitentiary. Can you understand this? It is not a hustle but a way of life."

I sipped on my lemonade and wanted nothing but to return to Ohio and be Pammy again.

My pager went off, startling me.

"Dragos, let me use your phone. Paul is paging me from Ohio, 911."

"No problem," he said wearily, removing the phone from his hip.

"Is this a burnout also?"

"Yes, yours will be just like it."

I called the number from my pager.

"U Next Barber Shop," an unfamiliar voice bellowed.

Damn, he's at that slow-ass barber shop.

"Speak to P."

"Who dis?"

"Who dis?" I repeated disgustedly. "This is Carmen."

"Hold on . . . yo, P! You got a phone call."

"C?"

"Yes."

"Carmen, I got a problem."

"Are you okay?"

"Yeah."

"What kind of problem, P?"

"I need some time. I took a loss, but it's all good. I'm ready to work out. I mean, really work out. Just tell me it's on."

"Yes, it's on. We'll work out. I'm out of town, but I'll be back in the morning. I'll call you then."

"Thanks, C."

"Bye, Paul."

"Peace."

"Carmen, is everything straight?" Dragos asked curiously as I ended the call.

"Yes, it is." I sighed. "And I think I'll need that van."

"*¡Bueno!*" (Good!)

I handed him back his phone, and he just sat there smiling.

—

I was so glad to be back in Columbus that I could have done a cartwheel.

When I got off the plane, Delano was there at my gate with two dozen beautiful yellow roses. He bent down and kissed me on the cheek.

"D, you're getting taller."

He laughed. "Am I really, or are you shrinking? Do you have any luggage?"

"No, just this carry-on bag."

"Here, I'll take that." He placed my bag on his shoulder.

"Thank you."

"Do you have plans tonight?"

"No, not really. Maybe rest. I'm a little tired."

"Good," he said, disregarding my statement. "I've made plans for us."

"What type of plans?"

"Carmen, just relax and leave the evening to me."

Delano drove like a different person in the BMW versus the hooptie and I was just glad I didn't have to fear for my life. We left the airport parking lot listening to jazz. When I noticed he was taking a detour, I got a little apprehensive. "Where are we going?" I asked.

"How was your trip?"

"Interesting."

"Interesting good or interesting, you're still trying to digest it?"

"It means I don't know. D, I really don't want to talk about my trip."

"Whenever and whatever you want to talk about, Carmen, my ear is always here for you."

"I know, D. So where are we going?"

"You'll see, Carmen, just relax."

We pulled into the parking lot of a very nice restaurant. We used valet parking and were escorted in. We both had on Karl Kani jean outfits with 40 Belows (Timbs), which was not suitable attire.

"Delano, we're underdressed."

"No, we're kicking it. I come here all the time. Relax."

The maître d' seated us in a secluded corner. Delano had made a reservation. All eyes were on us, but my eyes were on him. The room was dimly lit, and candles illuminated our table.

"D, I'm so uncomfortable."

"Carmen, I've tried to tell you that I accept you just the way you are." He reached out to hold my hand.

"I love my roses."

"Good, I would have purchased more, but I couldn't carry them . . . too heavy."

"I have always wanted someone to bring me flowers."

"Here I am. Anything else?"

Ignoring his question and changing the subject, I turned my attention to the menu. "How's the food here?"

"It's excellent. The chicken cacciatore is great. I know you like Italian food. The spaghetti is very good, too."

"I've been searching for some good Italian food," I said optimistically.

"I believe you found what you've been looking for."

"D, I think so, and I'm starting to believe I've found more than just food."

He came close to me, embraced and kissed me right there in the restaurant. I felt as if we were the only people there. His kiss was very succulent.

"Excuse me," said the waiter, interrupting our moment.

"What's up, Charles? This is my girl I told you about. I got her to check out our spot. We're hungry so let's start with some champagne. Give me some Cristal."

"This is a celebration?" the waiter asked.

"Yes! She's just agreed to marry me."

"Congratulations!" The waiter rushed off.

"Delano, we are not getting married," I replied curtly, rather put off by his remark.

"Why not? Come here," he told me. "There's something on your cheek." I leaned in and then he kissed me again. "Do you like my kisses?"

Blushing, I answered, "Yes, but let's just eat."

"Fine with me, but you will be my wife."

The waiter returned, and we shared a toast. We ate delicious appetizers, and then we ordered the spaghetti with Greek salads. It was simply delicious. We shared an ablaze bananas Foster for dessert. We conversed and playfully fed each other. Our dinner came to an end, but not the evening.

We left the restaurant for the downtown Hyatt Regency. In the lobby sat a baby grand piano. As he checked into the hotel, I wandered over to the piano. Enchanted by its appearance, I took a seat, and I positioned my long, slender fingers over the keys as I had been taught from years of piano lessons. Something came over me, and I began to quietly play the melody from Stevie Wonder's "Ribbon in the Sky," which I had learned when I was nine.

My parents wanted so much more for me. They invested in opportunities that would make me well-rounded so that I could become something in life. First and foremost, I was to be a law-abiding young lady.

Delano stood behind me, moving my swing bob hairstyle to one side and kissing the nape of my neck. He then led me outside for a horse-drawn carriage ride around downtown.

When we returned to the hotel room, he had a gift for me—a leather jacket. Matching leather jackets, his and hers. I loved it. We settled into a plush sofa to watch movies and cuddle. It was so simple, but it was the most special night of my life. This man made me feel safe.

As we eased into the bedroom, Delano began to undress me, one layer of clothing at a time, until I stood before him with only a black thong on. He positioned himself comfortably on the bed and glanced up and down my body. As girls do, I got a little uncomfortable with the pouch of my midsection and did the suck-in-your-abs routine. Placing his hands around my waist, he pulled his face into my midsection and kissed above my navel. I placed my hands on his head and held him there.

Slowly he kissed my stomach, the sides of my waist and then my breasts, circling my nipples with his tongue. Chills covered my body as my nipples became erect and his tongue danced over them. Grabbing me tightly, he held my body, thrust me onto the bed and began kissing my mouth with full kisses. The taste of his tongue caused me to soak my thong. As he kissed my neck, his hands roamed my butt and removed the thong. He began playing with my pussy while fingering me inside and out. I moaned with pleasure and wanted to taste him.

I rolled on top of him, removed his shirt and revealed a chest with smooth hair. I began to kiss his neck, his nipples, and then I lowered my head to his pants to give him head. As I began to unzip his pants, he said, "Wait, baby, I want to take care of you first. Come up here and sit on my face. I want to taste you and watch you as I make you cum."

Those words were music to my ears. I assumed the

position over his face with the inside of my thighs near his ears and felt his tongue between my legs. As he sucked on my clit with soft, even licks, I began to pulse with sensation. Playing with my own nipples while he sucked my clit, I threw my head back and forth and began a slow wind with the rhythm of his tongue as he gripped my ass. Reaching climax number one, I moaned his name over and over.

Turning around to a 69 position, I opened his pants and was pleasantly pleased to see that his dick was long and thick. My mouth watered as I imagined how he would taste. I took in his length expertly, with slow even strokes. He felt like silk in my mouth. Once I tasted the precum, I was unable to wait any longer. I straddled his manhood and worked my hips like a hula hoop. Delano's eyes rolled into the back of his head in pleasure as he attempted to speak, but the only words that came out were, "Ooh, baby, shit . . . work that pussy . . . yeah . . . just like that."

When he could take no more, D placed me on my back and pumped up and down with strong, steady strokes, working my pussy to the fullest. Yes, I was getting fucked, and right, and didn't want this moment to end. We kissed each other deeply with the intensity of young love.

Delano's strokes became more intense, aiming for his intended target. A tingling feeling took over my pussy and the buildup of an orgasm was released. Just as I came, Delano came inside of me as well.

"Baby," he told me, "don't move. Carmen, wait . . . ooh shit!"

I was totally spent, overcome by ecstacy and pleasure.

Delano felt around and grabbed the edge of the sheet and covered both of us. The room smelled like good sex and we dozed off into a comatose sleep. Hours later, I woke up in his arms. Remembering his unselfishness in making love to me, I moved my head underneath the covers to find his dick slightly erect and began bringing it to full attention with soft kisses. Delano woke up with a deep moan as my mouth made love to his dick. Sucking on his erection excited me so much that another orgasm burst from between my legs.

Never before had I cum this way with a man. I knew there was something special about Delano. He began humming my name as I continued to deep-throat him. *How many licks does it take to get to the prize inside of my Tootsie Pop?* I thought. Twisting, squirming, moaning, he pulled my hair back from my face and pushed his dick deeper into my throat. The release of his slightly salty cum was the prize I had been waiting for. Tasting every drop of his cum was like savoring nectar. When I emerged from beneath the covers, he pulled me up to kiss him as we embraced each other tightly. Moments later, he began snoring softly and fell into a deep sleep.

Now, how do I tell Delano the truth about me? How do I tell him about the escort service, my real role in this drug trade . . . my past? I mean, what will he do and say when he realizes who I am? Who am I? I haven't even told him my real name. I know it's selfish of me, and he'll think I've been deceitful, but I don't want this to end. Can I keep this fairy tale for just a little while longer?

I just closed my eyes, inhaled the scent of his cologne, snuggled in close under his arm and drifted back to sleep.

Twenty-six

$\mathcal{I}$ woke up early on Friday morning, kissed my son good-bye and dropped him off at day care. No matter what, this was my last run. After my perfect night with Delano, I wanted to be truthful with him—to be my best self. I decided it was time for me to leave this life alone.

Dragos's boys were still following me but I didn't care. I was still going to get out. I stopped by an apartment that I used to hold the heroin. I needed the extra apartment because heroin needs lots of refrigeration, also this apartment was used as a dummy address. I also entertained a few people there as if it were my actual home. In the streets, I never let people know where I rested my head, but when they *thought* they were there, they become more comfortable, and it strengthened my superficial trust in the streets. I picked up the heroin, and then I met with G-Money. I gave him two kilos, and he gave me a bag of money. Later, I met with Chino and gave him his kilos. Then I went to a travel agency in the mall to arrange a trip out of the city.

I was in the process of arranging a vacation for Delano and me. I would reveal everything at that time. I felt a huge weight being lifted off my shoulders because I had a reason for my happiness. Someone to share what I had built but also someone who was with me because they loved me, not because of what I could do for them. Delano was real and for the first time in my life, I didn't feel alone. With Delano by my side, I could conquer the world.

The itinerary had us leaving on Sunday afternoon and I couldn't wait. I walked back to my car, anticipating being with Delano thousands of miles away. After leaving the mall I got into my car, where I had packed all my money in a multicolored duffel bag, and for good measure I stuck two tennis rackets on the sides of the bag, so to any casual observer, it appeared to be filled with tennis gear. I was getting ready to make a power move out of the city. A sharp pain struck me in the forehead, a precursor to the headaches I had been getting lately. I rubbed my eyes vigorously, then started the car. I wanted to just go home and lie low. I didn't plan on taking anyone's calls with the exception of Delano's.

Pulling out of the shopping plaza listening to an R. Kelly CD, I noticed in my peripheral vision a swarm of cars. I looked to my right and two cars screeched to a stop. I quickly looked to my left—two more cars skidded up and blocked me in.

Oh shit, a jack!

I blinked repeatedly and two more cars were in front of me and one in back. The one in back tapped my bumper. This shit was straight up out of some gangsta movie.

My first instinct was to try to memorize the drivers' faces. Shit! Where were Dragos's goons when I needed them? I thought they were following me. Bystanders came over to the scene for a better view.

I recognized one of the drivers from yesterday's breakfast at Bob Evans restaurant. *If only my car could go into jet mode, I would be safe.*

My mind darted quickly to the possibilities. The raised guns indicated that any attempt to flee was sure suicide. My next thought gave me some relief—I didn't have any drugs with me. Unfortunately, I still had more than half a million dollars in the trunk of the car, but without a search warrant, what could they do? It looked like I was about to catch a case, but what type?

It wasn't a jack. It was the feds—the federallies—an army of FBI agents with big-ass guns.

"Slowly get out of the car with your hands behind your head and lay down on the ground!" An agent screamed in the bullhorn. It was over. "You are under arrest!" I was on my way to jail, and all I could think of was my son. The agent continued, "You have the right to remain silent . . ."

My beautiful lil' baby. Mommy is so sorry.

The Feds rushed me and handcuffed my hands behind my back. "Anything you say can and will be used against you in a court of law." An agent jerked me up to my feet and began pushing me toward the car for transport.

Mom, I didn't mean to hurt you. I'm sorry for lying to you.

"You have the right to an attorney."

God, help me, I don't want to be away from my baby. Father, please forgive me.

"If you cannot afford legal counsel, one will be provided for you."

Who will take care of my son? Please, God, give me one more chance.

"Have you understood your rights as they have been explained?" He didn't wait for a response, he just shoved me head-first into the backseat of the car. They immediately went toward my trunk and they found the duffel bag with the cash in it. Right then, I realized I had been set up. That bitch-ass G set me up!

I later found out that G's story was that he had been set up for a kilo by Jay-Jay, who rolled on him because he had gotten caught selling to an undercover policewoman. One of Jay's workers set him up, so Jay-Jay was going to set someone up. That someone happened to be G, but Jay gave him a way out. In order to save his own ass, G needed to bring me down and the trail of setups ends with me—on lockdown and with no phone calls.

Once I arrived at the police station, I saw Chino, Rock, my brother Ty and Ramón. Turns out the feds had us all under surveillance. I'd had two sets of people following me, one set was with Dragos, and the other was the feds. I looked over at Chino, and he mouthed, "Don't worry, Pooh. It will be all right." Then he gave me a wink. All I could think of was my son.

The feds picked my son up from day care immediately after my arrest and placed him in protective custody.

We were all booked at the downtown Columbus police station. I later found out that my driver was stopped on the highway headed back to the house, and that he had drugs in the van. My brother was arrested on a humbug because I stopped by his apartment to make phone calls, and because of the lies that G told on him. The feds go on words, not evidence.

Chino was arrested because they followed him to Rock's house, where the feds found a kilo in a cereal box along with a gun and some money. Rock was just at the wrong place at the wrong time. They had me for a direct sale to a confidential informant, which was G's punk ass. I couldn't even get mad. Yeah, I felt betrayed, but G had lived up to his fullest potential—a lame-ass bitch nigga, snitch nigga.

They booked us, and because I was the only female, I was sent to the county jail in Franklin County. The feds confiscated all of my personal property. They didn't leave me with shit. They took it all, removing all the jewels from my fingers, neck and wrists, and placing my items in a Ziploc bag marked with my name for storage. I was told to strip butt naked, squat, cough and remove my hair tie. I was ordered to shower in a filthy community stall and change into some jail greens. For three hours, I was stuck in a holding cell that smelled like a piss and shit combo.

Finally, I was allowed my one phone call. I called my sister Lori in Michigan. I gave her a brief summary of what happened, but I wanted her to look into getting my son back. My sister assured me she would get me an attorney and that I would see her in court. I asked her not to tell our mother until we knew more and she agreed.

I was sent to a dorm and had the unfortunate opportunity

of seeing my dream become a harsh reality. There on the TV, headlining the evening news telecast, was me. All my business in the streets was broadcast; it was a complete loss of privacy. I was on another journey, this time instead of being on a come-up, I was being raped—public humiliation at its best.

My new home, a two-room dorm, was designed to house fifteen ladies. There were no less than forty of us packed in there, with one toilet and one shower. There were bunks in every square inch of space. Some of the bunks were in direct contact with the toilet.

The percentage of women incarcerated and charged with prostitution is extremely high. I, who was once an escort service owner, was now appalled at the thought of sharing a toilet utilized by someone who sold her body for a living. If you wanted to piss, there was no option but to share a toilet with women infected with HIV, hepatitis and other STDs.

The only available sink was used by all the women to brush their teeth, wash their hands, drink water, wash out soiled undergarments and what not. The sink was a vector for a hybrid of contaminants. I found myself an available spot in a corner and began attempting to fluff out what the prison system considered a mattress. It was full of lumps, even though it was only an inch thick. There were gaping holes where cotton spilled out along the sides. I curled into the fetal position, placed my tattered sheet over my head, used my wool blanket for a pillow and tried to fall asleep.

That night I was called out of the cell by a few federal investigators, and they asked me whether or not I wanted to talk to them. I said, "*No!* I will only talk to my attorney." I was living a balla's nightmare: *on lockdown*.

Twenty-seven

$\mathcal{B}$ecause the state authorities arrested G, that bitch nigga, snitch nigga G, we were all taken before a state judge Saturday morning for our bond hearing. There we stood, all five of us in a row: Chino, Young Ty, Ramón, Rock and me. It's not uncommon for the feds to snatch entire households, families and friends. My sister Lori was there along with Delano. They sat as spectators in the rows of the courtroom, looking at us anxiously as we awaited the judge's decision on our fate. My sister was surprised to see me standing by Chino's side and handcuffed. Chino's grandmother and his wife looked even more surprised by the sight of the two of us together than by the fact that we were busted. Just like I had told my family nothing of Chino, I was certain he had told his family nothing of me.

My sister got me an attorney, and I stood before the judge awaiting the bond amount. I was called forward first. The judge went into a huddle with the prosecutor, and then she looked up and spoke.

"Ms. Pamela Xavier, also known as Pammy Xavier, also known as Carmen, your bond is two million dollars cash." I almost fainted. I vaguely heard more words, but they resonated in my ears as a deep baritone voice, speaking in slow motion. "Ms. Xavier, you are a menace to society, and you have raped the city of Columbus."

"My son," I cried. "My sweet beautiful baby!" My cries drowned out everything else. The bitch just told me I wasn't getting out and would not see my son.

She continued to speak. "Ms. Xavier, it is of the court's belief that you are a flight risk. Your passport is revoked, and you are to remain in custody."

I hung my head in shame as I was escorted out of the courtroom and returned to the county jail. Not long after my arrival, my attorney came to visit me and said, "Pammy, you'll go for another bond hearing before a federal magistrate because your case is going to be turned over to the federal government, so we'll have another chance at bond. Now, about money. Your sister gave me twenty-five thousand dollars, but I think I'll need more to defend you properly. You're in a lot of trouble."

"How much trouble?"

"You could get life. Do you have any more money?"

Lawyers are fucking crooks. They're the ones who really get paid in the dope game. Plus they get to keep drug money. Isn't that some shit?

"Look, check this out, I'll get back with you." Nah, he wouldn't work. He was in this to get paid, buy a new Jag or something. Nobody was going to make a come-up off of me, especially not while I was in jail. Money laundering is often a charge given to drug dealers, but isn't the attorney the one who charges five to six figures to defend a case for an unemployed defendant guilty of laundering drug money? This guy wasn't trying to be in it to win it and I didn't need his type. What I did need was an experienced Jewish attorney. Everyone knows that the legal system is managed by Jewish attorneys, prosecutors and judges.

On the evening news, I learned that Chino and Rock made bond of $3,500. I couldn't believe it. How could they have received such a low bond? I was happy for them, though, because I knew how bad I wanted to raise up out of there.

They denied bond for my brother and for the driver. Our bonds were all two million in cash. Rumors flew everywhere that Chino was telling on people and that this was how he got out on bond. He had a prior record, and I was a first-time offender. This contributed a lot to the suspicion, but I knew my Chino would do the right thing. He would never flip on anyone. I knew I was the target. The feds wanted me, but I didn't understand them keeping the others.

I fired my first attorney and I acquired another attorney who came highly recommended because he had defended some other drug dealers and gotten them good sentences, plus he was Jewish. So I went with my new hired gun, Myer Levin, and his price was also $25,000. Problem was the other attorney had my first twenty-five Gs, so I was out of ready cash. I had a lot of money in the streets and at my home, not to mention the money that they caught me with, more than half a million cash, but it wasn't like I could ask the feds to give it back. When I met with Mr. Levin, I assured him that I would get the fee together.

"Don't worry, I'll get the money to you."

"Good. I'll work with you, but we have a lot of work to do. I've spoken with the prosecutor on your case. I've worked with him before, and he's the no-nonsense type. You need to take a deal. They want to give you life, and with these new drug laws, it's possible."

Whatever happened to "Are you guilty?" or "Did you do it?" Where's my due process?

"They want to take your son from you and are prepared to play whatever game you want. They don't want to let you out," said Mr. Levin.

"Will you still try to get me a bond?"

"Yes, I'll try, but it's doubtful." He saw the faint glimmer of hope disappear from my face. "I'm always going to be up front with you."

"Please do. I like to shoot straight from the hip. No games and no tricks. Are you a prosecutor in defense-attorney clothing? Will you sell me out?"

"I'm insulted," he told me as he gathered his paperwork and placed it into his briefcase. "I always do my very best."

"I'll see you in court on Monday. Go do your homework."

"Pamela, I'll do my best to represent you. Stay positive."

"I will. Someone will be in touch. Bye." He left the pro booth, and I waited to be escorted back to my dorm.

—

My absentee father came out of the woodwork and offered his house and his retirement fund for my bond. My parents had been beefing for years. They got divorced when I was seven and couldn't stand to be in the same room with each other.

My mom offered all she had, too, and I was scraping together all I could. It was tough collecting from behind bars. I was limited to collect calls only, and no one in the streets wanted to talk to me because when someone gets knocked on a drug case, she's hotter than a VCR in a crack house. I was soon learning how things went down once you're inside, behind the walls. Not to mention the standard inconveniences of horrible food, terrible living conditions, stealing, bulldogging and the incredible noise level.

I could barely hear on the phone, and if I requested that someone lower her voice, that was a provocation for a fight. I was in another world full of its own drama, and everybody was just trying to survive, missing their families and trying to get out, wanting to be free.

Twenty-eight

My attorney told me that my codefendants had approached the prosecutor for deals against me, and that was how they got out so soon. Still, I refused to believe that Chino would leave me for dead—again. I had given Chino ten kilos, and he was caught with only one, so I knew he had nine kilos out there, which meant he had money for me. So I had Renaye, one of my former girls, try to page him. I gave her several ways to get in touch with him. Chino never called her back. Renaye went and told his sister that I really needed to speak to him, and yep—the muthafucka played me. I needed money to pay my attorney, and Chino had it. He didn't give me nothin'. He didn't even try to get in touch with me.

"Renaye, are you serious?"

"Carmen, yes, I am. His sister was snotty as hell and didn't want to take my number. She finally did, but I got a feeling he won't call. I'm sorry. Is there anything I can do for you? I have a couple thousand and it's all yours."

"No, honey. I'm just thankful for you taking my phone calls."

"Carmen, I'm here for you, girl. Ain't nothing changed. My service is doing well, thanks to all you taught me. If you need me or anything, I'm here. Actually, we're all here for you. Gabrielle and I want to come see you. Can we?"

"No, not yet. I'm not feeling up to any visits yet."

Renaye paused for a moment. She was hurt. "Well, keep calling me, and if you need me to bring you anything, let me know."

"Thanks, Renaye. Bye."

Chino had done it to me *again*. I just knew he would contact me somehow, through somebody. I knew he would use one of our secret codes or something. That bitch got out and didn't have any intentions on looking back.

The following Monday, we all went again for a bond hearing before the federal magistrate, and as I stood before him, Chino refused to even look at me. My attorney did his best representing my family and the reasons for allowing me out on bond. We tried it all from reporting bond to ankle monitoring to homes to cash to property to retirement funds, yet the magistrate (Mr. Bitch at this point) said, "Ms. Xavier, you will remain in the custody of the U.S. Marshals Service. This is the prosecution's request, and you will remain until sentencing."

I leaned over to speak with my attorney, asking him, "What does that mean?"

"It means they won't give you a bond—you're not getting out. You're going from here to the county, and from the county to prison."

The words echoed in my ears as my heart fluttered rapidly. "Now we just need to work on for how long, and that's where I come in. Let me do my job."

As they led me out of court handcuffed with a waist chain and leg irons, I felt an emotion that I still can't find the words to describe. It was like my life flashed before my eyes. All the lessons. All the warnings. All the mistakes. All the regrets. All the betrayals and the wrongs that I had committed. All I wanted was for my son to have a father, for us to be happy and maybe with a lil' flavor, a lil' bling bling.

In the holding cell, thoughts floated through my mind. I remembered meeting Chino one day with the vans. I had decided to surprise him and take our son with me. I gave him a bath and tried to dress him so he'd be extra handsome. I brushed his hair and put lotion on his lil' face and just tried to make him look his best. I did all this hoping that if he looked nice, then maybe, finally, Chino would want him. My son was already beautiful, but I had run out of ways to try to get his father to love him. I thought maybe a new outfit would help in some way. Chino was happy to see the baby, but it still didn't make a difference—he had no love for me and none for our son.

Twenty-nine

$\mathcal{M}$y brother and Ramón were held without bond. Chino and Rock were allowed to remain on bond without any monitoring. They had reporting bonds. Now, one can call it skill or call it lawyer expertise, because he had a thoroughbred lawyer, but all I can call it is bullshit because he utterly abandoned me. I was glad he was out, though. I still had days where I operated under the delusion that he would tie up business for me. Maybe he could help me like I helped him. I even thought that now he would spend time with the baby and get custody of his son. Well, I was wrong.

Chino got his federal prints done as I waited in the cell. I glanced at him, but he still refused to look at me. Then he turned around and bounced up out of there, temporarily a free man. That was the last time I saw him or heard anything from him.

My attorney later told me things that Chino's attorney told him, about our past together. Chino told his attorney about how I'd shot him and that the baby wasn't his. He went on about how jealous I was of his wife. Weak-ass bullshit like that.

Then his family accused me of setting him up. What kind of setup would put me in jail and him out on the streets, free and with over $200,000 of my money in his pocket? Street bullshit at its finest. Money can't stop the drama, and money can't buy you love.

I returned to the county jail, and my attorney came to see me that night.

"Xavier, pro visit!" a correctional officer yelled.

"Coming." I was directed to the pro visit booth.

"Hi, Pamela, I have some bad news for you. The feds have seized all of your property." He shuffled through some papers, then continued, "They have a black BMW 525, a green Jeep, a white Jeep, a condo and a home in the Muir-field suburb. Sounds like a very nice home. You'll get copies of all this. I'll always give you copies of everything."

"Great, but I can't really keep paperwork in here. No lockers."

"I'll try to get you something to keep them in. It's a lot of paperwork, but we'll go over it all during our visits. I have a lot of questions for you, but first I need to tell you what you are facing. They have new federal guidelines that start at a mandatory minimum of ten years to life. Your drug sale puts you in the minimum, and they want to convert the money they found on you into drugs. When we get the motion of discovery in a couple of weeks, we'll know more. But as it stands, you're at a guideline level of thirty-four, and based on this, you're facing 151 to 188 months in prison, which is eleven to fifteen years, give or take."

I felt nauseous.

"I'll keep giving you information as I get it. I'll be meeting with the prosecutor soon to see what he wants to do with you."

"So, I'm screwed?"

"That you are, but don't give up hope."

I put my head on the table and lay there in response.

"There is still a light at the end of the tunnel. I doubt you'll get life, and they are very interested in talking to you. In fact, they've been calling my office. My last client got twenty years, and that was with a deal. I have got another client who pleaded to six years with the witness relocation program. You may want to consider a deal to help yourself before the others keep rolling on you and you end up with no chance."

These are encouraging words?

"Your name has come up with the kid who got caught at the hotel with some kids from the North Side gang, as well as with this kid who's in for murdering and robbing some drug dealer with a strange name. I forget it. Also, a guy named Joseph 'Joe Bob' Jamieson, who got a case a couple years ago, mentioned your name and Chino's in relation to his case. So they've got a file on you and your son's father. Chino's name has been downtown for several years, and this is the same prosecutor who prosecuted him on his state case. He's very familiar with Chino, and basically, they have someone to directly set you up. The feds always hear things—they're the feds—and now they got you. So just think about it, and I'll be in touch. You've got my home number. Don't hesitate to use it whenever you want."

I couldn't believe my ears. I began feeling panicked, so I blurted out, "How long will this process take? How long will I have to stay in this county jail?"

"Mmm? Let's just say for about fifteen months, give or take a few. My last client stayed for nineteen months."

"*What! Fuck that!* Just send me to prison. Why wait?"

"Don't worry. That's where they're sending you, all right, but it's a process, so be patient."

"No contact visits for fifteen months? I have a baby."

"Pammy, it's a squeeze. They know you have a baby, and they know you want to see and touch him. But this is how they do things. I don't make the rules. Anything else?"

"*No!* Keep me posted." *Fuck it! I want my mommy.*

Thirty

$\mathcal{I}$ was escorted back to the cell. Then I called my mom to update her on everything that had just transpired. I even tried to explain all that I had been doing to get into this trouble, but she just stopped me from talking and said, "Pamela, I am your mother. I'm not your friend. I don't care about the past because that is just what it is. We have to focus on today and tomorrow. We can't cry over spilled milk. I don't care if you did what they are saying you did or not. You're my baby, and you can't do any wrong. I will always be here for you. We will work through this. You are not alone."

I started to cry at this point.

"That's right, let it out. Momma will be there to see you and get my grandbaby. They're trying to take me to court over the baby, but Pammy, I will get him and bring him home. Don't even worry. I'll be there tomorrow. Your sister is coming, too. After we hang up, I want you to call her. She has something to tell you that I think you'll like. The God I know is a God of second chances and third chances. Your life is not over, and you won't be doing all the time they're saying you will. Don't listen to them. Get on them knees and pray."

"I am praying all the time, Mom. I feel all alone."

"You are never alone. Remember that God is always with you, and I am with you. You'll be fine. We will make it through this. Don't worry about your son. I will whip the Devil's ass before I let something happen to that baby."

The tears poured like endless drops of rain.

"You and your brother stick together. Start writing each other and do this together. It will work out. Just be strong, baby. Momma's here every step of the way. You can call me every day all day and talk to me. That is why I work. I can pay my phone bill. Don't let them pull you apart. I don't know much about the law, but I know about our government, and they ain't worth shit!"

"Mom, you don't curse."

"When my baby is hurting, I am hurting. I know you're not the criminal they're saying you are. Got you on the news and in the papers like you killed the president."

"It's nerve-racking."

"Stop watching TV. God will take care of punishing you for your wrong. Pammy, we must all pay for our offenses, but forgiving others and ourselves gives us hope for the future. I'm sending you a Bible, and it will be fine. Your family got your back."

"Mom, you always know what to say to me."

"That's 'cause I'm Moms. And that sorry-ass Chino, I told you he never meant you any good. He'll never change. It was always about what you could do for him in some form or fashion. But God will take care of you. I am on my knees every day praying for you, and don't make me get your grandma on her knees. It will all be over soon. You are protected. Come, let's thank Him. Say it! Thank God right now in the bad and the good because it could be worse. You could have lost your life. This looks bad, but the God I serve will turn it into good. You'll see."

"I know, Mom, and I thank Him for my life, my health and my strength. I feel Him with me because I have not fainted. I am still standing."

"Wipe them tears and hold your head up high. Cry if you have to, but don't feel sorry for yourself. You can make it."

"I know, and, Mommy, thank you so very much for everything. I love you."

"I love you, too. Do you need anything?"

"No, I'm fine."

"Well, I am coming to see for myself. You know all I got to do is look at you and then I'll be all right."

"I am glad you're coming."

"Now, don't pray for freedom because that will come when it's time. Pammy, pray for wisdom and strength to help you with this trial. Pray to see with your spirit eyes and hear what God wants you to hear. It will keep you grounded. Your spirit is free. Remember, no man can bind this. And your baby is in good hands. He is young. We will make it through this. Lori is there for you, and you two have always been really close. Call her as soon as we hang up."

"That's if I can get the phone. These phone lines are ridiculous."

"Do your best, but hold your ground."

"And you know I will. Okay then, I love you. I'll call in the morning."

"Pammy, I love you, and please keep your head up. You're not the first to be arrested, and you won't be the last. You can make it, baby."

"Bye, Mom"

"Bye, baby."

There was no way I could keep hogging the phone without a fight or a bribe, and commissary day was not until Thursday. I would call in the morning while everyone else was asleep. Using the phone in the evening was almost as hard as gettin' out of jail. I would take a shower and go to sleep. A good cry in the shower would do me some good. In county, I cried in the shower so no one else could see me.

—

"Xavier! Visit!"

"CO, Xavier ready!" Rubbing my hands on my clothes in an attempt to knock out some of the wrinkles, I wondered who was visiting me. I hoped it wasn't the girls, and my mom wasn't supposed to be there until the weekend. I approached the visiting room and noticed my sister.

"Lori! What are you doing here?"

"Well, you didn't call, so I got in my car, and here I am."

"I am so happy to see you. I was going to call today, but the phone situation is a mess in here. I was sleeping."

"Don't worry about it. You look good, even if it is in green." My eyes filled with tears. "Don't start crying 'cause you'll make me cry. Be strong. Now is the time for you to be stronger. We need to talk."

"About what? Please not this case," I said and began to rub my forehead.

"No, I just care about you. Your friend Delano is helping me find an apartment."

"Really?"

"Yes, he called Mom. He is really concerned and worried about you. I told him that you needed money."

"Why did you do that?"

"Lose the attitude. Because you do. Anyways, he gave me what you needed. I don't want to say it—this place may be bugged."

"He gave you all I needed? All of it?"

"Yes, girl, plus took me to lunch. He is downstairs with Kristen."

"Kris is here? Why is my niece in Columbus?"

"Because this is our new home. I found a nice two-bedroom apartment."

"What? Why? What are you talking about?"

"Your attorney said you'll be here over a year, and if there's a trial, it could be two years. I'm not leaving my baby sister in a county jail all by herself. No way! You need me."

"What about your job?"

"I'll get another one."

"I can't let you do this."

"Do I look like I am asking your permission? I'm like Nettie in *The Color Purple*. Nothing but death will keep me from you. I'm here until you get sentenced. And I'm going to get all the whites and clothing you can have and drop them off. I'll be at every court hearing and in that attorney's ass. I'll be at every visit. Mom won't let me keep the baby or I'd have him, too."

"You know how mom is about our children. Lori, I don't know what to say."

"You don't have to say anything. We are sisters until the end. I'll have a number for you soon. I am staying at a hotel right now. D is showing me around, but he's real busy. I'll be settled in about two weeks."

"I can't believe this."

"Well, you need to believe it because you are not alone. I am here with you."

"Please don't sing. You're making me laugh."

"Here, give me some." She placed her hand up to the glass. "I am your sister, and I love you, and you will make it through this. I promise."

"When we were kids, you never lied to me, and I still believe you." I placed my hand up to the glass, covering her smaller outline, and mouthed, "I love you, Lo-Lo."

"I love you, too, my lil' sissy."

"Xavier, visit's up," said the guard with an I-don't-give-a-fuck attitude.

"Lori, it's time for me to go."

"Don't worry, I'll be back. Don't forget, you are not alone, Pammy. These people better get used to me. Oh, I drove past your home earlier. The feds got it wrapped up like a Christmas present. We'll talk more later. Delano told me to tell you hi."

"Tell him I said hi, and give Kristen a kiss for me."

"I'll bring her up next time. I haven't explained to her why you are in here yet."

"*Xavier!* Visit is *up!* Move it!"

"I gotta go. Love you." I quickly got up, waved good-bye and was escorted back to my dorm.

Having my sister with me in Columbus was invaluable. She had become an important part of my legal team, and I looked forward to every visit. She tried to help me in any way she could.

I had lost contact with Dragos, but he stayed in touch with my mom and did favors for my son. I didn't want him to, but it was his way of sending me a message. "You look out for me, and I will look out for you."

When the fellas I dealt with found out I was being held without bond, they turned their backs on me. Hey, that was the way of the streets, right? On the outside, we are tight like glue. Once someone's knocked, all love is lost.

There was still no word from Chino. Rumor had him out spending all my money and having fun. Hell, if I were out, I would have fun, too, especially if I were on my way to jail. But I couldn't forget how he had abandoned his Pooh again. Sitting in a jail cell behind steel bars with no way out leaves a lot of time for reflection. I thought back to our unhealthy relationship. Keeping secrets, denying reality. I was stuck wondering what kind of bond we ever actually shared. What was our bond rooted in? I pulled out my yellow stationery pad and wrote a letter to the missing-in-action Chino.

To My Dearest Christonos,
Others call me crazy, stupid and dumb for helping you.
I, too, call myself these things. I could have gotten
out of the dope game, but I chose to stay. Partially, I
stayed out of greed, and partially because of my low
self-esteem. The dope game gave me power——power
over poverty. It, coca, gave me control. I was hustling
hard, climbing the dope ladder of success, all in an at-
tempt to make you proud. That was so important to
me. In the beginning, I wanted, no I needed, to take
care of my son. In the end, I just wanted to impress
you. When I'm asked why we are codefendants in
a federal drug case after our separation, I just don't
know how to respond. Then I think back to our bond.
It wasn't the baby's mama or baby's daddy drama,
because you don't even accept our son. It was the love
you professed to me every day we were together and
even when we were apart.

Perhaps our bond was rooted in the good times.
The gold, diamonds, jewelry and cars. Or was it the
bad times that brought us together? The times of need,
infidelity and harm. I shot you, but you forgave me.
I believed your forgiveness came out of your love for
me, and that we had beat the odds. In the dope game,
there are odds, too. What were the odds of each of us
stacking the dollars that we did? Was it just the money
that brought you back into my life? It sure seems like
that. And that really hurts me.

I hoped time would change you, so I made excuses

*for your behavior. I loved you so much. Chino,
you have failed me in love. You have failed me in
friendship. But I have failed myself by not loving myself
more than I loved you. Love, I have learned, is not
always required in relationships. Couples sometimes
love at the same time and with the same intensity.
Couples, at other times, love at different intervals.
We were unequaled and unbalanced. Though we both
sought wealth, I extended to you the greatest treasure,
unconditional love.*

 *I don't regret loving you. I do regret the choices
I made because of this love, and I am living with the
consequences. Consequences that now tax my son.
I realize now as I face my federal trial, I must love
myself first. I must love my son and be strong and
do what I gotta do for me. I did my very best, and I
know that you can still hear me inside. One day I will
understand. One day we both will.*

 Always,
 Pooh

I folded the letter and placed it with my legal mail next to my bunk. Maybe I would mail it to him, maybe I wouldn't, but there was a sense of closure simply in writing the letter.

—

I had a hard time adjusting to life in jail. The living conditions were unbearable. More than thirty women shared one exposed toilet and one unsanitary shower. The food was slimy, cold and often unrecognizable. Since when did bologna salad come with green chunks? But like my mom always said, if you're hungry, you'll eat it. After a while, the food didn't taste so bad. Ideally, at mealtime, the deputies were to bring trays of food to the inmates, who had to eat the meals in their dorm room. Then the deputies returned to pick up the empty trays. Many times the deputies ordered the inmates to pick up leftover food off their trays and eat it with their hands so the trays would stack better. That way, the staff didn't have to make two trips to pick up the cumbersome trays.

At first, I gave all my trays away. Later, I traded things for commissary. Still had me a hustle. I guess it's just in me. I had good days, and I had bad days. In the Franklin County Jail there was no light of day because the windows were covered with paint and there were no outside recreation privileges.

I spoke to my son on the phone often. I still hadn't seen him because there were no contact visits, and I didn't want to see him from behind glass. He wouldn't have understood why Mom couldn't touch him or hold him. The price for my crime, in addition to losing my freedom, included losing the chance to mother my son. I desperately wanted to get into prison so we could have a contact visit.

I took it one day at a time. No matter what I was going through, I had to keep pushing. I was a survivor, and I knew it got greater later. One day I would have a chance at a new life. Everyone gets a second chance. I could start over. I had done it before.

While in county, I saw the effects of drugs more vividly than I ever had in the streets. I watched women violently sick from heroin withdrawal and go into crack comas and come in with tracks all over their bodies. This was up close and personal. I couldn't believe I had a hand in contributing to this, putting this poison in people, especially my people. I was being educated on a whole new level, a spiritually conscious level. I was learning about myself and my life. They say your twenties are the learning years, and this was very true for me. I read a lot in there, and I wrote a lot. I started writing my story. After all, stories are sold, not told. Right?

———

"Xavier, visit."

"CO, is it a pro visit or personal visit?" I asked and got a nasty response. I felt like spitting on half these COs. They needed to sell baseball bats in the commissary.

She continued to snap at me. "No, it is a regular visit. Do you want it?"

"Yes, I do. Here I come."

"Hurry up."

I wondered who it could be. The girls had sent me some money and a card, but that was three months ago. At least they'd thought of me. I understood that they were doing their own things now. In fact, Toy came through county on a whore case. She was still out on the streets even after what happened to China. I talked to her for a brief moment at the county jail church.

I walked up to the glass and it was Delano. Let that be

the reason I always keep my faith! He was still looking very good, and I couldn't believe he was here to see me.

I was feeling slightly embarrassed by my appearance. My relaxed hair was gone, and I was wearing my shoulder-length hair straight to the back in French braids. I picked up the conference phone and sat down in the booth. He had his hand held to the window, so I placed mine up to the glass. My palm rested on the glass, dwarfed by his outline. I yearned to touch it and feel his warmth just one more time. I loved the way he had touched the side of my face and the nape of my neck and caressed me ever so gently down my spine. Remembering our night together, I closed my eyes and imagined his scent in my mind. His voice brought me back to reality.

"Carmen, just because I am in here and you are out there . . ."

"Wait, D, I am in here, you are out there."

"You know what I meant. But I miss you, and I think of you, and I want to be your friend."

"Delano, you know I'm hot. I can't believe you are here talking to me." I could feel my heart beating fast as I became more uncomfortable with my appearance, even while relishing the moment, this visit. His presence was so sudden, so strange and so needed.

"I'm not afraid. I want to be here for you. Do you need anything? I left some money on your books," Delano said.

"This is not wise. You shouldn't be here."

"I know you won't do anything against me. I'm not worried. You'll be all right. Just do what is best for you and your son. You know what I mean. You got a good lawyer, and I feel good about that. I saw Chino at the downtown mall with his crew, your codefendants. They're not thinking about you."

I began to cry, the evidence of being played once again spit in my face. I had to get past this and stay strong.

He continued, "Carmen, don't cry. You in jail, but you gotta think like you still in the streets. I was going up the escalator, and they were riding down, and it was a Wild Wild West starefest to see whose eyes moved first. It was obvious that they were strapped, but I was, too. I would love to run into Chino's ass alone, like at the car wash or somewhere. Where we could talk, ya know?"

"Yeah, I hear ya. Just leave it alone. I'm fine, thank you."

Delano became furious at my nonchalant attitude. "No, I don't care. I am gonna handle my business. Fuck that nigga! He left you for dead, and you still give a fuck about him?" He was frustrated and threw his hands in the air, wondering what was up with me.

"I don't care." I wiped a tear from my face.

He screamed into the receiver. "Well, I care! That motherfucker is going to get handled."

I pleaded, "Delano, if you love me, just leave it alone."

"Don't try that bullshit. I love you. That's why he's gotta be talked to, and when I see him, I am going to split his—"

I cut him off, preventing him from saying the unmentionable, "split his wig back." This meant murder in the streets, and who knew who was listening to us.

"Delano, watch yourself. Be careful. We on the phone, love."

"Carmen, I miss you." He continued to yell. "And if you think this is a fuckin' walk in the park, you're mistaken. They about to slam-dunk your ass, baby! The feds got a place for you." Tears welled up in his eyes, and I saw the pained expression on his face. A tear slowly inched down his face at a snail's pace. We sat holding the phones. He wasn't ashamed of my seeing him cry. I watched the tear descend and rest upon his trembling bottom lip.

Our eyes met and he continued, "You still got somebody out here that is for you. I got heart. Just say what you need done, and I got you." Immediately my mind went to what I needed the most, and that was to know if Chino actually moved the gun he had used in the killings.

"D, listen. I left something somewhere, and I need you to go and find it for me. I need to know if it's still there. Can you do that for me? Check to see if something is still there?"

I wanted to know if I still had a trump card in my back pocket. I would sit on what I knew and decide how to proceed from here. Play my hand and pull my information card or fold and do fifteen to the door. The cards I was dealt were not easy on the eye, but I knew that once I studied the game unfolding before me, I would get a chance to make a play.

The guard approached the booth, signaling the end of our visit. I maintained direct eye contact and kept smiling, wanting Delano to hear positive words in his head.

I whispered into the handset, "I miss you, too, Delano." I winked at him, carefully choosing the remaining words spoken. We sat for the remainder of the visit, tracing our fingers on the glass and giving each other a look that meant "handle your business by any means necessary."

He said, "Okay, you left something somewhere. Tell me where you want me to look."

All I could do was smile.

Carmen is awaiting her federal trial in the Franklin County Jail. Her sister Lori still comes to visit her faithfully every week, and her mother has custody of her son.

Acknowledgments

This book was not only the beginning of my new life but also a catalyst for the lives of so many others. This book started a company and an urban genre craze. Who would have thought, could have thought that God could take my tiny faith and propel my life into such greatness. My legacy, life, outlook—everything has in fact changed due to the inspiration to write this book. I shared my story to warn the others of the dangers of the drug game. It is a dead end.

I'd like to thank my Savior and Lord for being just one word: faithful. God is faithful to His children and to His promises. This book was written in the darkest prison cell in the United States. This novel has now been translated into two languages and associated with the birth of Triple Crown Publications. I thank you for reading, buying, sharing this work. I pray that my life is used as an example to encourage you to believe that even the biggest dream, God is able to do even bigger, exceedingly, abundantly above all you could ever ask and think.

God has given me a lifetime friend, Mychal Haggen. I love you, I respect you, and I'm so blessed to have you in my life.

Professionally I have to thank my editor, Malaika Adero, for always being open to trying new things. My lawyers, Robert Stein, Michael Gallagher, and Steve Barsotti, for keeping the vultures and wolves at bay. My original staff, whom I thought I'd never miss, but certainly appreciate your contributions to my success: Tammy, Mia, Benzo, Kevin, Steve, Victoria, Aaron, Rodney, Alicia. How do I tell this story and leave you out? When I think of us working with no money on those tiny desks above that animal hospital with two titles, your work established my firm (TCP) into the leader of urban fiction renaissance.

To my best friend, my mother, Eula "Star" Stringer-Thompson.

To my young son Victor and my dogs, Vegas and Roulette: Mommy loves you guys!

Fondly I'd like to acknowledge Teri Woods for her wisdom and just being so True to this Game with the time we shared. It's a very fond memory for me.

Last, I never knew that my life could change, that my life could be this way. I never knew that God loved me and that it would get greater later, but as they say: I made history and got the fairy-tale ending. This young girl from the East Side of Detroit made it out the hood. For this I am so thankful.

How great thou art!

VS